Swept Away

Books by Mary Connealy

From Bethany House Publishers

THE KINCAID BRIDES

Out of Control
In Too Deep
Over the Edge

TROUBLE IN TEXAS

Swept Away

Swept Away

WITHDRAWN

MARY CONNEALY

BETHANYHOUSE
a division of Baker Publishing Group
Minneapolis, Minnesota

© 2013 by Mary Connealy

Published by Bethany House Publishers
11400 Hampshire Avenue South
Bloomington, Minnesota 55438
www.bethanyhouse.com

Bethany House Publishers is a division of
Baker Publishing Group, Grand Rapids, Michigan

Printed in the United States of America

Library of Congress Cataloging-in-Publication Data
Connealy, Mary.
    Swept Away / Mary Connealy.
        pages cm. — (Trouble in Texas ; Book 1)
    ISBN 978-0-7642-0914-7 (pbk.)
    1. Texas—History—19th century—Fiction. 2. Christian fiction. 3. Love
stories. I. Title.
PS3603.O544S94 2013
813′.6—dc23   2012040430

Scripture quotations are from the King James Version of the Bible.

The internet addresses, email addresses, and phone numbers in this book are accurate
at the time of publication. They are provided as a resource. Baker Publishing Group
does not endorse them or vouch for their content or permanence.

Cover design by Dan Pitts
Cover photography by Mike Habermann Photography, LLC

Author is represented by Natasha Kern Literary Agency

13 14 15 16 17 18 19   7 6 5 4 3 2 1

I'm dedicating *Swept Away* to my daughter Shelly. Shelly is a gifted storyteller. She's animated and charming, with a smile that lights up a room and a talent for drawing people in and making them happy to be with her. She's also a natural athlete. I figured this out the first time she grabbed the edge of my kitchen doorframe and climbed it to the ceiling. She was about three at the time. I actually knew before then. She had this stunt when she was about a year old, involving . . . well, best not to go into details on that one.

Shelly would make a great storybook heroine, bright and beautiful and sweet. Also, she's a pretty good shot and she looks great in a Stetson, which makes her fit in my books even better.

Chapter 1

The sharp crack of a cocking pistol brought Lucas Stone's head around.

"I'll shoot if you so much as twitch." The deputy's badge gleamed in the dim lantern light of the stable, and his aim was true.

"What's the problem here?" Luke straightened away from his horse, his hands spread wide and raised slightly. He hoped this didn't count as twitching; he didn't want to give the deputy an excuse to flinch.

"Those your saddlebags?" The lawman looked at the bags Luke had just thrown onto his horse and used the gun to point at them. Not a careful man. He looked to be about twenty, and none too bright.

"They are. What's going on?"

"I got a tip I'd find money in those bags. Money from a stagecoach robbery that happened in these parts last week. Had a man killed."

A shiver went up Luke's spine. He'd noticed his saddlebags were moved. He'd left them here with his horse and, since there was nothing worth stealing in them, he hadn't

7

thought much of someone shoving them to the side, even going through them. Now he had a bad feeling that if he opened the bags, or let the deputy open them, there'd be something tying Luke to robbery and murder.

"You got a tip?" Luke tried to stall for time as he wondered who'd tried to frame him. Only one name came to mind. Flint Greer. A man who had good reason to not want Luke to make it home alive. "From who? I've only been in town a few hours. Just passin' through on my way home to Texas."

More honestly on his way to reclaim his home in Texas. "I just came in from far north. I have a bill of sale dated yesterday that proves I'm new to these parts." Luke reached for the breast pocket of his brown broadcloth shirt.

"Don't move!" The deputy's gun came up and his finger visibly trembled on the trigger.

"Easy." Luke wondered how the kid could believe there was a gun hidden in Luke's shirt pocket, but he slowly moved his hands away from his body. "You want to get the bill of sale yourself?"

Luke hoped he would come within grabbing distance.

Nodding, the lawman edged toward Luke.

Luke knew plenty about being tough, having grown up in north Texas, a land of stark rock canyons and roving bands of Comanche and Kiowa. That alone was enough, but he'd also spent years fighting in the War Between the States, and more time living off the land after the war. And he was boiling with anger as he made his way home to avenge his father's death. Those things combined to make him a careful, knowing man. A dangerous man.

This deputy was none of those.

Luke was close to home now, and Greer, the man who'd killed his father, knew he was coming because Luke had sent a letter, along with a legal document, telling Greer to get off Stone land. Greer didn't want Luke to make it home.

Luke knew a setup when he saw one. Which meant there was little or no chance he could talk his way out of this. Which left fighting his only way out. He braced himself, determined not to hurt a lawman—at least not too bad. But once a jailhouse door clanked shut, Lucas expected the only way out would be as he was led to the gallows.

The deputy reached for Luke's pocket.

Luke shoved the kid's gun upward, drove his fist into the kid's belly, then slugged him in the jaw. Luke jerked the pistol out of the deputy's hand, chopped him on the skull with the gun butt, and grabbed the front of his shirt to lower him, unconscious, to the stable floor.

Luke flipped open his saddlebags to find a cloth cash bag. Dragging it out, Luke looked at it for a few long seconds, tempted. Considering its weight, Luke knew it was gold.

It would come in handy. It'd buy him enough bullets to start a war, which was exactly what Luke had in mind to do.

With some regret, but no interest in turning thief, he dropped the money, then double-checked the saddlebags to make sure there wasn't more. Whoever had tried to frame him hadn't wanted to part with too much.

If this was Greer's work, the man was thorough. So if the deputy was here in the stable, where was the sheriff? Luke eyed the doorway and was sure if he walked out, he'd be facing a firing squad.

With grim silence Luke finished slapping leather on his horse and led it to the back door of the stable. A black horse on a black night, and Luke always dressed to move around undetected. No shining hatband. No silver trim on his boots or Colt. No jingling spurs.

Easing the door open, he saw a stretch of land leading into a copse of trees. Behind those trees, a bluff rose. He'd seen it earlier. But could Luke's gelding climb the bluff? Being afoot in Texas was a good way to end up dead.

His horse was game, so Luke set out, leading his mount, listening for every night sound, his hand on his six-gun as they paced off the distance to the shelter of the trees.

No one stopped him. If this was Greer's work, he'd be furious. He was a man who hired his shooting done and he expected his money's worth.

Luke reached the trees and decided to trust the black to find a way up. Mounting, he rode up the bluff and over the top. As soon as he was out of hearing distance, Luke slapped his horse's rump and they picked up the pace in moonlight almost as bright as day.

While he put space between himself and the posse that was bound to be coming, Luke wondered how much Greer had paid to kill Pa. Top dollar most likely, because the job had been done right.

Pa dead.

His S Bar S Ranch stolen.

Luke was headed home to set things right.

"Ruth, stop dawdling back there," Pa Reinhardt shouted. "I need you to take the reins."

Dawdling? It was all Ruthy MacNeil could do to keep from snorting with contempt. She'd been working since before sunup at twice the speed of any of the Reinhardts. But she knew better than to ask questions when Pa Reinhardt used that voice. Usually the back of his hand followed quickly if she didn't move fast enough.

She shoved the last box, containing the food and skillet, into the bed of the covered wagon and hurried around to swing up beside Ma.

"About time." Ma turned up her nose as if Ruthy smelled bad.

Ruthy didn't even comment on Ma being there, settled in, while Ruthy cleaned up the campsite. That was the way of things in this family she'd been dragged into.

Ma rested her aching back.

Pa yelled and doled out punishment.

Her dear brother, Virgil, leered.

Ruthy worked.

At the thought of Virgil, a chill drew Ruthy's eyes forward to the wagon ahead. Virgil was swaggering toward the second family wagon. He stopped before he climbed up on the high seat and looked back at her.

They'd be married when they reached California—Pa and Ma had declared it so. Virgil was willing. How Ruthy felt about it had never come up.

"You look dreadful, Ruthy. Virgil will despair of such a slovenly wife." Ma scowled, her usual expression. "Get that coat off. It will be blistering hot today."

Ruthy looked to the northeast, and the dark thunderclouds made her doubt Ma's forecast. Rain most likely. Ruthy felt a twinge of caution as she wondered if it was already raining upstream. How high was the river they planned to ford?

Virgil turned away and climbed up onto his wagon, so Ruthy didn't mind shedding the stifling coat that concealed her curves from Virgil's crude attention. She tossed it through the opening into the wagon box.

"Leave your hat on, for goodness' sake. Maybe you can keep that awful freckled skin from getting sunburned again.

You're peeling now from the last time you were so stupid as to leave it off. It covers that flyaway hair, too. Red marks you as Irish trash. You look a fright. You're lucky my son is willing to involve himself with such as you."

She didn't respond to Ma's comments on her appearance. Her long, loose-fitting coat, flat-brimmed hat pulled low over her eyes, and clunky boots suited her. Everything she owned except her skirt was a hand-me-down, mostly from Pa and Virgil since she'd grown taller than short, stout Ma just after her fourteenth birthday.

Yet it suited Ruthy to dress like this. She wasn't interested in drawing a man's attention, and that included most of all Virgil. She could only dream that he found her too ugly to be of interest. But his disgusting behavior, which she worked daily to avoid, indicated he found her red hair and freckles to his liking.

Which was nothing but the worst kind of dirty shame.

Ruthy had the reins in hand and sat waiting for the rest of the wagon drivers to get in place.

"Move out!" Finally the trail master hollered the order to the five wagons that remained in this once-long wagon train.

The lead wagon creaked as it began to roll and within a few paces dropped over the deeply cut riverbank. Another vanished, then another. Virgil was gone next—not forever unfortunately. Pa followed on foot between Virgil's wagon and the one Ruthy drove. He'd lead Ruthy's team across. With another glance at those thunderheads, she slapped the reins on her oxen's backs, feeling the need to get this crossing over with fast.

The Reinhardts' two wagons brought up the rear. They'd been with a much larger group when they set out from

Missouri, but the majority of the group had stopped to homestead in Kansas.

This group was headed for California along the south path of the Sante Fe Trail. Ruthy had no intention of reaching that destination with them. But the Reinhardts didn't need to know that.

As she descended the trail, she could see the lead wagon halfway across the wide, fast-moving water. They'd forded countless streams and rivers. Ruthy had lost interest in where they were as the miles plodded along, day after day, on their journey westward.

She heard thunder and an unusual burst of nerves shook loose a warning. "Pa, maybe we shouldn't cross just yet. Rain could raise this river real fast."

"Those clouds are miles away, you little half-wit."

"But it's raining upriver."

Pa didn't even look at the water, though he did take a glance at the sky. "Shut up and do as you're told."

Shut up and do as you're told. That would be her life forever if she married into this family. She'd been looking for a chance to run away and beg for protection and hadn't found one. And she feared greatly what tactics Pa, Ma, and Virgil might use to force her to say, "I do." The only way to stop the marriage was to be gone from the family and never be found.

Her turn came to ford. She had a reaction so strong, Ruthy felt as if God himself had struck her with terror. If she'd had her druthers, she'd have hopped to the ground and run straight back up to the top of the bank. But Pa led the oxen forward, and Ruthy stayed on the seat.

Just as the last wheel left dry ground, her nigh ox took a slight turn downstream, dragging its partner along.

Pa caught at the halter and yelled at the plodding beast, shoving at it to keep it moving forward.

"Mind what you're doing, Ruth." Ma gave Ruthy's arm a stinging slap that almost knocked the reins out of her hands.

Ruthy fumbled but hung on to the leather and drove with a skill that wasn't proper for a woman. She did as many chores outside as inside for the Reinhardts and was handier than any of them.

Ahead of them, the lead wagon had reached the far bank and begun to climb. It was a long way up to the level prairie.

Her wheels slid and water slapped against the wagon's underbelly.

Ma caught at the seat with a faint cry of alarm as the wagon lifted until it was floating. "Can't you control this team?"

A deep-throated shout drew Ruthy's attention in time to see Virgil's rig begin to drift. That surprised Ruthy because the lead wagon had rolled across on solid ground. Was the water level rising? Virgil's oxen veered downstream, pushed by a current moving faster than even a few seconds ago.

A deep rumble turned Ruthy's attention to the north for a quick glimpse of the clouds, heavy with rain.

At least the rain wasn't falling here. This river didn't need another cup of water to make it rush along even faster.

"I've got to go help Virgil." Pa looked back at her. "I've got these boys back in line. Try and hold 'em steady this time." He knew well enough that Virgil wasn't as good with a team as she was. No one was going to admit that, but Pa still knew where he was most needed. Virgil's team was swimming now, which gave them no direction except to be pushed along with the current. Ruthy noticed the wagon ahead of Virgil was floating too, its oxen's backs underwater as the slow-moving beasts fought to make it across to dry land. She felt her own wheels leave the floor of the riverbed.

"Glad we're getting the ford done now," Ma said. Though she was clinging to her seat, she didn't seem to realize the peril they were in. "The whole train would be across by now if you hadn't slowed us down."

Knowing that to be a lie, Ruthy didn't bother to respond.

Suddenly the rumbling thunder seemed closer, louder. Pa had reached the back end of Virgil's wagon and was clinging to its side, pulling himself forward with his feet floating. How could he guide the oxen when the water was over his head?

Ruthy's heart sped up as her team began swimming. She saw Pa look up at the clouds. The man on the lead wagon, now halfway up the riverbank, shouted at his beasts and cracked his bullwhip to speed them along. A second wagon reached the shore. A horse tied to the back of the third wagon pulled frantically against its reins and snapped them. It charged past the other wagons for the shore. The horse was doing better than the rest of them. The train master, the only man riding horseback, kicked his mount trying to reach dry ground. His horse stumbled in the rising current and plunged to its knees. With a shout of fear, the train leader lost his seat and went underwater. The horse swam for the bank.

Her jaw tight as she fought futilely with the reins, Ruthy knew her wagon wasn't going to make it. None of them still in the water were going to make it.

Turning to study the sky, a noise drew her eyes lower. A slap of rushing water gushed around a curve upriver. Right after the slap, a wall of water blasted around the bend, reaching the top of the riverbank. It rushed at them with the force of a runaway train.

Ma turned to see what the noise was. Her scream cut through the roar of floodwaters.

Pa froze as he faced the oncoming water. Then he scrabbled at the canvas cover of his wagon and tried to pull himself up the side of it. Virgil cried out in terror.

"Ma! Get in the wagon!" Ruthy tried to catch Ma and shove her inside.

"Let go!" Ma clawed at Ruthy's grip and leapt off the wagon seat into the river.

Water raged straight for them. Not even the wagons that had reached land were high enough.

There was no time for Ruthy to do anything but twist and dive into the covered wagon. She hit the bed just as the water slammed the wagon onto its side.

Water gushed in through the tightly gathered ends on the front and back and closed over Ruthy's head. She banged into something hard. Stars exploded in her eyes.

Tumbling, sinking, then flying upward, Ruthy had no time to do anything and no strength to hang on to a world gone mad.

The water lifted her high just as the wagon cover was torn away. She dragged air into her lungs. She tried to see what had happened to everyone else in her moment above water. There was wreckage but no people. Pa was gone, the team too. The wagon. Ma. Everyone.

Another wagon, flipped on its belly, raced ahead of her. Ruthy heard the pathetic bawl of an ox and saw one emerge out of the depths, only to sink again.

A man's head popped out of the water, but before she could identify him or see if he was alive, she fell, plunging downward. The water smacked her into the side of the wagon box. Her shoulder caught on something, and each pitch of the water wrenched at her arm until it felt like it was being torn off.

Sucked down beneath the torrent, the world went silent. Dragging at her pinned arm, she fought for freedom, for life as she desperately held her breath. Her lungs blazed hot with pain.

Something crashed into the wagon and smashed it apart, but her arm remained trapped between a pair of wide planks. Everything erupted upward, dragging her along. She choked, sucking air into her lungs between coughing, terrified of how long she'd have before being dragged under again and not allowed another breath. A tree loomed only feet ahead. Crashing into the tree, chunks splintered off the planks she was riding. But the two boards pinning her held. She clung to the slender remains of her makeshift raft.

Before her, the river curved. The floodwaters blasted into a steep, stony bank. She saw Virgil just ahead, his limp body drove hard into the unforgiving rock. He took the terrible blow at full speed, his arms and legs flailing as he struck. She saw no sign of him fighting the water or being aware of the impact. Ruthy knew it would be impossible to survive. And she was racing straight for the same wall of stone.

A scream ripped from Ruthy's throat just as a fist of water punched her. She hit the granite bank. A hard crack stunned her and left her numb.

The floodwaters pulled her down into darkness.

CHAPTER 2

Leaned low over his gelding's neck, pounding out the miles, Luke put space between him and that rotten little cow town.

A posse had come, as he'd predicted, but with a good jump on them, there'd been time to leave a false trail. They followed it. Still, he pushed hard for hours, careful about tracks, keeping off any trails a normal man might use. Luke had learned to be sly in the woods and he used every bit of his skill. The posse would probably go home. But he wasn't about to get cocky. His horse needed a breather, but he wanted more miles between him and that lynch mob.

Trees ahead told him he was coming up on a river. He'd forded the Arkansas a while back, which made this the Cimarron. He was getting close to home. Slowing to find a way across, he made out a game trail so faint that only hard years surviving in the West told him it was there.

Urging his horse onward, he wended his way down the steep bluffs. If it was shallow, he'd wade for as long as he could, pick a stony spot where he wouldn't leave tracks and come out a long way from where he'd gone in.

If there was any pursuit left, that ought to end it.

The sides of the river were slick with mud. The game

trail was treacherous. The grass and brush were knocked flat. Floodwaters had recently rushed by, running so high they reached the top of the bluffs.

When he reached the bottom, Luke hesitated to head downstream. To be caught by another flash flood would mean certain death in these depths.

Which meant few men following would go this way.

A good enough reason for him to choose it.

The water was smooth and shallow. His horse stopped to take a long drink, then moved along in the cool October breeze, the running water gurgling and tumbling around his hooves. They made good time for several hours and, as Luke began to watch the banks for a way to climb out, he saw boards ahead. Frowning, he wondered if a rancher lived nearby and had lost a wagon in the flood.

Then he got closer and saw someone lying on the boards. *A woman!*

Rushing forward, he gained dry land and tied his gelding to a shrub.

He dropped to his knees beside her, knowing the chances of her being alive were slim. He tried to roll her onto her back and realized her arm was wedged into a knothole in one of the planks. She was warm—alive. Her chest rose and fell. Carefully he worked her loose from where she was caught.

He lifted her into his arms and carried her to the slim strip of sandy soil along the bank. Lowering her to the ground, he saw an ugly gash in her matted red hair. Judging by the condition of the battered-down grass, he estimated the floodwaters had passed through here at least a full day ago. She'd been a long time trapped on that plank.

"Miss?" He gently patted one of her pale, dirt-streaked

cheeks. She moaned but didn't wake up. Pretty little bit of a thing. Ash white skin with red splotches peeling as if she'd been in the sun too long. She'd had a hard time of it.

With a quick look he decided she had no injuries except that crack on the head—none on the outside anyway.

"Miss, can you hear me?" He had no idea how to make an unconscious woman wake up until she was good and ready. The presence of those varmints on his back trail goaded him. He couldn't leave her and he had to press on, so the only choice was to take her with him. He lifted her gently.

He couldn't make good time with a double load. But he was close enough to home that caution was more important than speed. His horse could take it slow. He covered up his tracks, mounted up, juggling the woman and his reins, and headed on for his north Texas ranch.

Unless a town had sprung up since he'd left Broken Wheel, there wasn't anywhere to leave her this side of home. And he had no intention of turning away from his course.

They headed downstream as Luke kicked around his choices. All he knew for sure was that he'd just picked up an unwilling passenger on his way to start a range war.

⌒∞⌒

Ruthy's eyes blinked open and the pain knocked them shut again.

"You awake, miss?"

The world was rocking. Her head throbbed, and only knowing how bad it would hurt to move kept her from being sick to her stomach.

The flood. Her hand fumbled at the front of her dress. She was too dry to still be floating.

"My head." She tried to reach for the pain and something . . . or someone . . . restrained her arms. That brought her eyes open again. She was ready for the pain this time and kept them open to focus on a man . . . rocking her? He was dark, his eyes a velvety shade of midnight brown. He had a deep dimple in his chin that drew her attention for too long. His hair was black as coal, his skin so tanned he almost looked like an Indian. But his perfect English, laden with a Texas drawl, said he wasn't.

"You've got a mean bump on your skull, miss. Best not to touch it."

Then she noticed the horse.

"Where are we? Who are you?" She remembered Ma and Pa Reinhardt and Virgil. What had become of them?

"I've got some questions too, miss. Name's Luke Stone. I found you run aground on a riverbank. Looked like you'd been riding the current a while. Where's home? Don't you worry, I'll help you get back to your people."

"I-I don't know exactly where we were. Our wagon train got caught in a flash flood." Her throat sounded ragged.

Luke reached for his canteen, and Ruthy was suddenly aware of a thirst so terrible it felt like its own wound.

"The whole train? Aren't they fifty or a hundred wagons long? How'd you lose all of them?" The man stopped lifting the canteen, and Ruthy was so desperate she almost reached for it to wrestle it away from him. Her arm hurt bad enough she decided not to start a fight with a man whose corded muscles looked to be more than up to besting her in a struggle.

"We were five wagons, split off from the main train. All five were hit. I think two of them were out of the river and headed up, but then the water came." She shuddered and buried her face against Luke's chest. "It was a wall of water. It came around a bend as high as the top of the bank. There was rain upstream."

"Should've had sense not to cross." The man adjusted his grip so her head was lifted a bit and she could see the world better. His strength was so great that he moved her to suit himself with only the slightest shift of his broad shoulders. He raised the water to her lips.

"I wasn't in charge or we'd have stayed on high ground until the sky cleared." When had Ruthy ever been in charge of her own life? She sipped the water and it seemed to soak into her mouth before it even reached her throat. She drank again.

"Don't drink too fast or you'll cast it up." He lifted the canteen away.

She wanted to grab at it, fight him for it.

"So what about the rest of your people?" It was almost as if he were offering her the water in exchange for answers to her questions. But no one would be that low-down, would they? Then Ruthy thought of the Reinhardts and decided nothing could surprise her.

"I don't know how anyone could survive that flood. I don't know how I did." She remembered her wagon tumbling. Oxen bawling. She'd seen Virgil's body. No sign of life. Ruthy clutched Luke's shirt, felt a terrible agony in her arm, but held on anyway. "I should go back. See if anyone made it." Ruthy lifted her eyes to Luke Stone. "Can you take me? Can we ride upstream and search?"

True, she had plans to escape her family. Ma slapped her and Pa was a lazy complainer and Virgil paid her disgusting attention. True, they'd never spoken a kind word to her while she toiled for long hours every day for years. True, they were none too smart and none too clean and none too honest. But that didn't mean she wanted them dead.

Much.

"No, we can't," Luke said.

His answer caused a wave of relief so strong she felt guilty. "Why not?"

She realized no matter what his reason, she was going to accept it.

"I'm headed south, and I'm in a hurry." His horse continued to wade relentlessly in a direction away from where she'd last seen the Reinhardts.

Ruthy hoped he remained strong in his refusal. A woman saved from a deadly situation couldn't exactly dictate where her savior was riding, now could she? This way, the choice to go back and spend days on a futile search was out of her hands. Why of course she'd have gone back and hunted for those dreadful Reinhardts. Except Luke was in a hurry. She had no choice in the matter; she had to go along in whatever direction he was heading.

Why did she feel as if she were making excuses to God?

It was because when her turn came to stand before the pearly gates, she needed to be ready when He asked her why she'd left her family to drown, that's why.

She debated, then decided there was no sense asking for forgiveness yet. She needed to quit sinning first. It was wrong to be so cheerful, and she did her best to suppress it.

"Why are we in the water?" She saw the steep banks and a cold curl of terror did plenty of cheer suppressing. "More water could come. We need to get to high ground."

"Nope. Not yet." Luke seemed unusually alert. Of course she was comparing him to Pa and Virgil, who looked on the edge of napping most of the time. Luke's focus moved left to right, behind him, overhead, always his eyes roving. The alertness went beyond just watching. He was listening, smelling, most of all thinking. Ruthy knew what that was like, because hiding in the woods when Virgil was hunting her had given her sharp skills of her own.

Even so, she felt like she was buried alive at the bottom of these high banks. Ruthy was tempted to shake the man for his terse answers. She decided to avoid questions he could answer with yes or no. That wouldn't be hard. That was mostly how she spoke to the half-wit Reinhardts.

"Tell me why we're riding in the water."

He looked down at her, his eyes shaded by a broad-brimmed western hat. She had the sense that he was making a decision, and she was afraid she wouldn't like it.

"Miss, I don't know you, and it ain't polite to go asking a lot of questions in the West. If I tell you my business, you may have cause to regret knowing it."

"Are you an outlaw?"

"Not in any honest court in the land, I'm not."

Which meant he was.

"I'll get you to the nearest town, and you'll have to make your way from there. Folks will help you find your family." He seemed hard and knowing about the land, but not a cruel man, at least not in his handling of her.

A small shudder was uncontrollable. "I had plans to leave my family when the opportunity arose. They aren't my family, more like I . . . I worked for them. It's a shame they probably all drowned, but I won't miss having them around. Maybe I can find a job in this town."

It would be wiser to get on a stage and travel far and fast before she settled down, but she had no money for a ticket. Her only possessions were the extremely filthy and battered clothes on her back. It wasn't going to be easy to put space between her and the Reinhardts. But if they survived, maybe they'd think she was dead. Yes, of course they'd assume she'd drowned. They wouldn't hunt her any more than she planned to hunt them. She could risk stopping for a while. Earn a bit of money.

"I know a man or two in Broken Wheel, the closest town. They might help you find work. Best to not let on you know me, though. I've got trouble to face and a bad hombre might decide to make you part of it."

So he was taking her to his home. She was tempted to blurt out her fear of Virgil finding her—although she was quite sure he was dead. But just in case, she'd like to ask Luke for his protection. Except if she did, it might annoy him to the point he'd turn around and find the Reinhardts and hand her over, the better to shed any responsibility for her.

Of course to do that, he'd have to veer from his course.

"Where are we?" She thought they'd been in Indian Territory when the flood hit, although they'd been riding for weeks and she admitted to being more than a bit lost.

"Texas. You've floated a fair piece, miss. Probably one river ran into another more than once while you were float-ing along. Doubt we could find your family if we tried."

Which suited Ruthy right down to the ground.

"Can I have some more water?" She wondered how long it'd been since she'd eaten.

He let her drink longer this time until her belly was full and her throat much soothed. The quenched thirst wed to her relief at being irretrievably lost made her aching head heavy. "Is it a long way to Broken Wheel?"

"I hoped to make it there by nightfall. Once I leave this streambed, I'll make better time."

"Well, wake me when we get there." Her eyes flickered shut.

❧

Luke was tempted to laugh. She was a trusting little thing to fall asleep in a stranger's arms. Not all that worried that he might not be an honorable protector, never mind that his arms would get mighty tired.

A pretty little thing, too. She was coated in long-dried muddy water. Her red hair was stiff, her sunburned skin peeling. So calling her pretty was saying a lot.

He wouldn't mind seeing her all cleaned up.

It looked as if he had little choice about carrying her while she napped, and so he did as he was told. The sun was at high noon and he rode along, not pushing his overly burdened horse, enjoying the shade of the towering trees lining the stream. The banks showed the ravages of the flood that had passed through, yet there was no sign of a storm upstream so he stayed down here, lengthening the stretch between entering and leaving the waterway, to make pursuit all the more difficult. He finally picked a rocky spot, rode up onto the plains and headed for home at a fast clip.

They'd covered a fair distance, and the land was taking on the broken look, with the layered red rocks that surrounded his ranch, when he spotted a rocky stretch, wooded, with a spring trickling from a stone. His horse could use a break, and his little saddle partner should probably have more water and something to eat. He'd've finagled a meal without stopping if not for her, but he couldn't show up in Broken Wheel before dark anyway.

Reining in his horse, he swung down with his arms full of sleeping woman.

Her eyes flickered open. They were so blue, so pretty that they seemed to glow out of her dirty face.

"You're strong." She spoke so softly he leaned close to catch every word. Those blue eyes blinked and fluttered and he had to think for a while before he figured out what she'd said.

"You're not a big parcel to carry around." The way she watched him, her words, woke something up inside him. He felt himself turn into her protector, a man who would fight wars to keep her safe. He looked at her pretty pink lips. They were all tidy despite what a mess she was everywhere else. He realized he was thinking of kissing those lips and it was like a cannon exploding.

Straightening, he laid her on the ground so fast it might've counted as dropping her. Stepping away to give her a bit of time to gather her wits—and maybe gather his own—he hitched his horse to a scrub mesquite and pulled beef jerky and hard tack out of his saddle. He kept real busy refilling his canteen with cool water, then settled in to rest his back against one of the countless flat slabs of stone that dotted these broken red rock canyons.

He managed all of that in the time it took her to push herself to a sitting position. She groaned with every move.

"Are you hurtin', miss?" He couldn't do much but sympathize, but he could offer her that.

"Hmmm." It wasn't exactly an answer, but he got that she was agreeing.

Then she lifted her hands to eye level and gasped. "I am filthy."

"Well, floodwater'll do that to a woman."

"So true." She flinched and rubbed high on her right arm. "I ache all over, but this shoulder—"

"Your arm was stuck in a knothole all the way to your shoulder. Being pinned to the boards you were floating on probably saved your life. It kept your head above water while you were unconscious."

Moving cautiously, she lifted the skirt on her calico dress, a badly faded brown, which was probably the mud. Luke had no idea what color it was supposed to be.

She put her hands in her hair and visibly shuddered. She was close enough to the spring, a spate of water gushing from a crack in the rock, that she just crawled over, stuck her hands in, and washed almost frantically. When she was satisfied, she filled her hands with water and drank deeply.

"Be careful, miss. Drink slow and don't overfill your belly right at first or you'll get the collywobbles." Luke wasn't sure a real thirsty person could keep from drinking to excess, but he saw her fight for control and win. She was a tough little thing. "What's your name?"

She threw him a nervous look over her shoulder. "I can't stand what my hair feels like. It's caked with mud." She stuck her head in the gushing water and let it drench her. The water ran brown as it rinsed her hair. He suspected the move had more to do with not answering his question than with a real need to wash her hair.

Speaking from under the water, she asked, "You don't by chance have a bar of soap with you?"

He did and he handed it over. "I intend to reach Broken Wheel around nightfall and make contact with my friends Dare and Vince. They'll be expecting me, and we've got a lot to do."

"I'll be quick." She rubbed the soap into her hair, which to Luke's way of thinking wasn't a quick choice.

"Could you please leave me a moment of privacy? I need to wash ... um ... more thoroughly."

It was no more than the absolute truth. "All right, but don't be all day about it." Luke moved into the woods and stayed facing away from her. "Call me when you're done."

But Luke remembered enough about his ma and little sister to be resigned. So he got comfortable and settled in for a nap.

CHAPTER 3

SEPTEMBER 1868—ONE MONTH EARLIER

The men standing high on the only trail to Luke Stone's ranch, now in the possession of Flint Greer, sent a chill up Dare Riker's spine.

The lookouts, one on each side of the red rock towers in this huge canyon Dare had heard called Palo Duro, had their rifles in hand and aimed straight at him. Each of them gave Dare a salute. It looked friendly enough, but Dare knew they were sending a message. They were watching every move he made.

The townsfolk said Greer had started staying close to home because of his wife, but Dare wondered if it had to do with word getting out that Luke Stone was coming home. He'd also heard the guards were new. Greer had only begun posting them in the last three months or so.

Dare was glad of this chance to ride out to the Greer place. He'd have a better picture of what Luke was up against.

Since he'd come to town a couple of months ago and set up shop as the town's only doctor, he'd never seen Flint Greer. He'd heard stories about Greer turning hermit since he'd gotten married and maybe that was it. But Dare figured it had to do with Luke.

Dare'd ridden out most of the way on a decent road. It had narrowed to a wide canyon with a stream cutting along the base of high bluffs on the west side. Then that canyon kept getting tighter, the strangely layered red bluffs higher, and closer to the road.

At some point the stream went underground and the canyon got so slim the wind blew through and made a quiet, mournful song. There were big rocks scattered all around, and the road twisted in a well-worn trail as if those rocks had been there for a generation. Dare looked up and saw more rocks clinging to the side of the bluffs—boulders and red granite slabs that looked like they only needed the slightest excuse to fall. Even without the gunmen training their muzzles on him, it wasn't a ride to make a man relax.

Luke had told plenty of stories of home when they'd been locked up in Andersonville, so Dare recognized this road into the place. Luke's pa had picked this spot because there was Indian unrest when he'd settled, and he'd been able to defend his ranch by putting sentinels on the bluffs along the trail.

Just like Greer had now.

Getting into this place was going to be a problem for Luke. Being called out to Greer's for doctoring was giving Dare a good chance at seeing the lay of the land with his own eyes. Almost as soon as the canyon widened, the ranch house appeared.

He rode up to the front door and swung down, tying his horse to the hitching post. Dare counted the men he saw around the place. A couple of them looked like loafers, but they had sharp eyes and wore their guns tied down. Dare wondered if they were really more guards than cowpokes. The story was that Greer had hired on some dangerous hands just lately. He was acting like a man getting ready to fight a war.

Dare reached the front door just as a blond boy stepped out. "Go on back to town. We don't welcome visitors."

"I'm Dr. Riker. I was sent out by someone who said your ma'd been hurt."

"My ma took a . . . a fall. But she's fine now. Whoever sent for you shouldn't've done it."

The boy was skinny, gangly. Boys could grow at real different ages, but Dare thought the kid might be fifteen. He was aiming toward tall, not there yet, but big feet and huge hands said he'd make it. His hair was golden and his bright blue eyes snapped with anger.

"Long as I'm here, I'll speak to your ma before I ride all the way back to Broken Wheel."

Annoyed at being called out for an unneeded errand, Dare figured he wouldn't let it bother him. In fact, it was good luck, a chance to see that well-guarded canyon and the layout of the ranch. The boy didn't move from the door as Dare walked up to it. Rather than talk more to a kid who wasn't old enough to make this decision anyway, Dare gently but firmly pushed past him into the house.

Two rooms opened off either side of the entry. Straight ahead was a stairway to the second floor. To his left, a woman sat in a worn-looking upholstered chair, frowning at him as if disgruntled that he'd come in. It had to be Mrs. Greer.

She was golden. Dare had never seen anyone quite so pretty. Her hair was a tawny gold color. Her skin was almost the same shade, except Dare's doctoring drew his attention to a grayish undertone that told him she was sick or in pain, or both. She blinked her eyes at him and they were like none he'd ever seen. They seemed to glow with a yellowy-gold light. It reminded him of a mountain lion he'd seen once, a beautiful critter.

"I'm a doctor, ma'am."

"I heard. And I heard my son tell you I'm fine." Glynna Greer's lioness eyes flashed with anger.

A snarling, beautiful critter.

"Go away and don't come back."

A snarling, beautiful critter who looked eager to bite his head off. This woman was more like that lion every minute.

A young girl of maybe eight years stood beside the chair, nudged up against her ma as if she were trying to hide from sight.

"The hired hand took it upon himself to send for you. I'd have stopped him if I'd known he was doing it. I insist you leave, now."

Dare walked toward her as she talked, figuring the closer he got, the more he could see. And what he saw was pain. There were furrows in her forehead that made her seem older than Dare had thought at first glance. The gold in her eyes was dimmed, and he saw tracks down her face that could have only been left by tears. He reached her side and crouched.

"I'm Dr. Riker. Dare Riker. As long as I'm here, tell me where you hurt."

The woman looked at him, then tilted her nose up. "It's a twisted ankle. I'll be fine. Be on your way."

"Let me see." Dare controlled his annoyance at the high-handed dismissal. He reached for her leg, and she raised her hands as if to ward him off, then gasped in pain and subsided in her chair.

And she hadn't moved her ankle one speck. So she had pain elsewhere.

Lifting her bare foot, Dare noticed one lace-up boot and a white stocking on the floor beside her chair. Moving the swollen ankle gently, he felt her stifle another gasp.

"No sin in admitting you hurt, Mrs. Greer."

"I'm fine. You're wasting both our time."

The venom in her voice drew his attention. She looked at him as if his hands were unwashed, as if his touch disgusted her.

"Can you move your foot?" He was watching her face to catch any glimpse of pain because she was being so close-mouthed. As he knelt there at her feet, being treated like a lowly servant, he thought he saw a shadow on her cheek on the right side. Like an old bruise. But then she turned her head aside to look at her daughter and Dare wasn't sure.

"I can move it." She demonstrated so, which gave Dare the confidence her ankle wasn't broken. "It needs to be bound tight and you need crutches. Do you have any? I can bring some out from town."

"I'll get by fine. Don't bother with crutches. And I can wrap it myself."

Why in the world didn't the woman want a doctor's help? "I'm here. It won't take long. I'll do it."

Dare looked at the boy. "Are there any crutches in the house? If someone has trouble once, they often keep them around."

"I've never seen any," the boy said in a sullen tone. "I think there's a walking stick in the back room."

It wasn't good enough but it was something. Dare fought the urge to bark with his army major voice at the young'un. "Get it."

35

The boy ran off.

"I will pay you nothing for treating me." Mrs. Greer clenched her hands together on her lap. "My husband is one of the richest men in the area and I know only too well how men like you try and cheat him."

"Men like me?" Dare felt his brows lift nearly to his hairline. Rather than fight with the arrogant little snip, he gave her doctor's orders. "You must not put any weight on your ankle."

Thundering footsteps announced the boy's sprinting return as if he was terrified to leave his mother alone with Dare. He carried a cane, its top curved. It would help.

"We can get by with this, Dr. Riker." The boy leaned the cane against his ma's chair. "You need to leave."

"As soon as I've seen to your ma's ankle, I'll go." And he'd go with great pleasure. "After it's wrapped, I'll carry you to your bed. If you must get out of bed, ask your husband to carry you or use the walking stick or crawl if you have to, but keep the weight off your ankle or it won't heal properly."

"If you insist on wrapping the ankle, then do it. But you won't be carrying me anywhere. I don't want your hands on me."

Dare lifted her ankle and arched a brow. His hands were most definitely on her.

Mrs. Greer blushed. "Well, I've made it clear I don't like you tending my ankle, haven't I? That's the only . . . familiarity I'll allow. And be done with it quickly. I need to get on with making my husband's dinner."

"I just told you to stay off your feet. Your husband can make his own meals for a few days."

"No, he can't." She said it as if she were reciting from the Good Book.

"It won't bear any weight." Dare decided he was indeed wasting his time. "I guess you'll figure that out when you try and walk. What happened anyway?"

"I just stepped wrong and fell."

He remembered the motion she'd made when she wanted to stop him from coming close. "Do your ribs hurt? Are you banged up anywhere else?" He thought of the bruise on her face, but if there was one, it was old. He was dealing with a clumsy woman.

That little nose tilted up again. "I want you out of my house."

Dare turned to the boy, who glowered at him. "Get me some rags, son. I'll tear them into strips and get this wrapped quick so I can stop wasting your ma's precious time."

The boy looked at Dare resentfully. Dare got the feeling this was the boy's usual expression. Nothing personal. "Hurry up if you want me out of here so all-fired bad."

The boy looked to his ma, and Dare saw her nod.

She said, "Hurry. There are rags in the closet under the stairs."

The boy turned and ran. There was considerable warmth in the woman's tone for her son. Dare was thankful for that.

Looking back at the pretty, ill-tempered woman, Dare noticed the little girl standing silent through all of this. "What's your name?"

The girl seemed to withdraw even more, edged closer to her ma.

"Her name is Janet. She's shy of strangers. Don't pester her." Mrs. Greer's voice was so frigid it made Dare want to start a fire.

The boy was back in seconds with the rags. Dare tore long strips and bound Mrs. Greer's swollen leg tightly.

Though she did her best to cover the noise, a few moans of pain got past her clenched jaw. Dare knew her ribs were hurt too, but he wasn't fool enough to think the woman would disrobe so he could bind them.

Truth was, Dare had never done such a thing for a woman. Well, once he'd delivered a baby, but only once. And now he had one pregnant woman in his care, and it was scaring him to death. He'd been reading everything he could find about childbirth. Beyond that he'd never treated a woman. He mostly stayed to places inhabited by men. He treated men's wounds and illnesses. If he was to ask a woman to disrobe, it certainly wouldn't be against her will, as he was sure it would be with Mrs. Greer.

As he finished, he was torn between riding away fast and staying to do his duty as a doctor. "If your ribs are hurt, they need to be wrapped."

"They're not."

"But if they were—"

"I told you I'm fine."

Dare spoke overtop of her protests. "It will ease the pain considerably if they're bound very tight. You can do it yourself."

Their eyes met, and for just a second the haughtiness faded and her snooty nose lowered a bit. "If . . . if my ribs ever do hurt," she said, pressing a hand against her chest in a motion Dare didn't think she was aware of, but it told him the truth, "I'll remember your advice. Now go. Get out of my house."

Her words stung like the lash of a scorpion's tail, and Dare left, glad to be shut of the woman. *Men like you try and cheat him.* As if he'd come out there for the money. His jaw clenched when he thought of her sneering.

He rode down that canyon again, seeing the men, mad enough to tell them he didn't like being under their guns.

He'd give Luke the details of what he'd seen, and when it came time to toss Greer off this ranch, Dare would take pleasure in seeing that snide missus—no matter how pretty she was—lose her home, too.

Luke had never carried a wet woman before. Honesty forced him to admit he'd never carried any woman. But why did he have to start with a soaking wet one?

She hadn't exactly asked permission to wash her clothes. He'd fallen asleep instead of riding herd over her, so he deserved what happened.

When he woke up and called out to her, she asked for just a few more minutes. In the few minutes he slept, she washed her dress. And when he called out to her, she redressed in her wrung-out-but-still-drenched clothes. When she told him he could come back, her hair was hanging loose and she was barefoot.

She asked if he had room in his pack for her soggy shoes and stockings and a few other bits of female clothing he couldn't recognize in their tightly wadded condition. Truth be told, he might not've recognized them if he'd been able to see them clearly. Women were a mystery to him. He stowed her things away, and as they rode along, she dried. Some.

He did too. Some.

She asked him for a comb, but he hadn't owned a comb in years. He ran his fingers through his hair every morning and slapped on his hat and was done. Why did women have to make everything complicated?

As they rode along in the wild, rugged country, the rocks that looked like red layer cake grew up. The grass became increasingly sparse, growing in rounded clumps. There were junipers and cottonwoods, with mesquite trees that sometimes reached a good height but were more often stunted, growing out of stone instead of dirt. Luke startled a white-tailed deer. Under normal conditions he'd have shot it and dressed it. He was running low on grub. There'd probably be time, as he was getting to town before sunset. But the need to be quiet, and knowing Broken Wheel was close enough a gunshot might draw attention, had him letting the deer go.

He might live to regret not taking the shot. Ruthy had eaten a good share of his jerky. She'd taken a drink every few minutes, as if her stomach couldn't bear a heavy gulp but the thirst kept gnawing at her and driving her back to the canteen.

Eventually, probably once her clothes weren't so miserably wet, she fell asleep. Her hair had dried in the Texas breeze and it had gone wild, springing into silky red curls that were far brighter than he'd guessed when he'd seen her in her mud-soaked condition.

The curls danced in the wind in a way so happy that Luke felt his spirits lifting. And considering he was going to face down the man who'd killed his pa and stolen Luke's S Bar S Ranch, that wasn't something that came easy.

Since she was asleep and wouldn't know, Luke rubbed one of the little corkscrew curls between his fingers and enjoyed the silk of it. He'd never thought much about a woman's hair. Now he found himself fascinated. He wanted to sink his hands deep into it, let the silk run over his calluses.

She smelled like his bar of plain old lye soap, but somehow on her it smelled way better. It made breathing deep a pure pleasure.

As the sun dropped over the rim of the bluffs near Broken Wheel and dusk settled in, the little woman stirred. Luke had left the main trail. Though he'd seen no sign of travel on the road he'd followed, caution had him threading around the jagged rocks in the wide canyon his pa had called Palo Duro, Mex words that meant hard wood. It wasn't an easy life but it had suited Luke, and guilt ate at him that he'd left Pa to hold down the ranch alone.

He spotted the first lights in Broken Wheel and found a heavy stand of cottonwoods, fronted by a thicket of mesquite and grama grass that ran along the west side of town. It took him only seconds to find the house with two lanterns burning in one window, the sign Dare had told him to watch for. Dropping back, he found a place to picket his horse. He dismounted, woman in hand.

She opened her eyes. "Where are—?"

"Hush!" Voices carried a long way on the night air. They were a ways off from town and being in the woods helped mute the sound, but Luke had learned caution in a hard school. "Can you stand?"

She nodded. He lowered her feet to the ground, and she just kept sinking. Luke picked her up again and moved her away from his horse's iron-shod hooves and eased her onto the soft leaf-covered ground to wake up at her own pace. He tied his horse, pulled a packet out of his saddlebags—more than a little surprised to see any jerky left—and snagged his canteen.

He scooped her back into his arms and carried her to the cottonwood stand near Dare's house. Getting close enough to whisper was no hardship. "We need to wait until full dark before I try and go in to talk to my friend. I'll ask him if there's a place you can stay."

The woman nodded.

"You ready yet to tell me your name?"

Her eyes got round with fear. It looked like the little woman wasn't kidding when she said she didn't want to go back to her family—in the event any of them had survived, which Luke doubted.

"Don't tell me, then." He looked at the springing mass of her curls and said, "I'll just call you Rosie. Between your red hair and your sunburned skin, it suits you. You want some more to eat?"

She nodded with far too much enthusiasm. He handed her a long skinny strip of dried venison, and she put her attention to chewing it up like she was starved half to death. Considering how much she'd already eaten got him to wondering just how long she'd been floating downstream.

He helped himself to the scrap of meat he had left, and they passed the canteen back and forth. When she finally stopped tucking all his food down her gullet, he said, "We need to wait until the town's gone to sleep, then we'll slip in quiet-like. That's my friend Dare's house, right there in front of us. Dare will go fetch Vince and Jonas if they've gotten to town. They're friends, too. Vince sent me a letter and some legal documents and told me he was setting out for Texas. I had them all signed and witnessed back in Denver and I got my will in order."

"A will?" She whispered nicely, which meant she was awake enough to be thinking.

"Yep. I found my sister in Colorado. I was at Dare's house when a letter arrived from my Pa. It told me where my sister had gotten to. She has herself a tough husband, and he's from a tough family. They can hold this land if need be. I named Callie in my will, in case anything happens to me. The letter from Pa included the deed for my ranch. Pa signed it over to me before he died and got it in the mail."

"Your father is dead?" In the dusk, Luke saw her sympathy and it warmed him. With all the mess surrounding his father's death and his ranch being stolen, he realized he hadn't taken much time to grieve.

"It happened while I was on the trail. He's been gone a few years now. I can't just ride into town and stake the claim to my ranch. I need to have everything in order. Then I'm going to go out to my ranch and throw that murdering coyote off my place."

He said it with confidence, but he knew it wasn't going to be easy.

"The man living there claims to have bought my pa's ranch, but he couldn't have. Pa didn't own it to sell. He'd already signed the S Bar S deed over to me, had it all legally witnessed, and mailed it to me in care of the one friend I'd mentioned that Pa could find."

"Why do you need to ride in at night?"

"Because the man who took it over has been trying to kill me since I sent word I was coming home."

Rosie gasped. "Trying to kill you?"

"Yep. I was running from a posse on trumped-up charges when I found you. Twice before, I had a near miss with a stray bullet, only I don't think it was so stray. I sent Flint Greer a letter, all legal and proper, throwing him off my land. Now I've got to show up and make a lawless murderer obey a signed document. I expect there to be gunplay involved."

"And that's why you're going in at night?" She shook her head again as if she thought maybe she wasn't awake at all.

"I might not make it down Main Street if I rode in during the day. I expect he's got a lot more friends in this town than I do. I've done a lot of listening since I headed for home, and I've heard Broken Wheel has fallen on hard times since Greer cornered all the ranch land in the area not held by Indians. I think if I can just live long enough to make sure everyone knows I'm the true legal owner of the S Bar S and I've named my heirs, I can win this fight without much shooting trouble."

"Much?"

"Life hasn't been such that I look on the sunny side of things, and Broken Wheel is a wide-open town. Bullets fly on occasion."

"And you think I'll b-be able to find a j-job in such a town?"

Luke shrugged a shoulder. "They hadn't oughta hurt a woman, Rosie."

"My name is Ruthy." She must have decided it was safe to tell, but he'd already kinda gotten to like the sound of Rosie.

He decided not to change. "I've got a lawman who knows I'm on my way, and friends in town who have come to fight by my side. If they've all gotten here, we can claim my property. I need to go in and make sure things are set, but no one needs to see me until we're ready to make our move. I'll wait till the lights go out, and then we'll slip in and talk to Dare."

"He's one of your friends? And you're sure you can trust him?"

"If I can't trust Darius Riker, then I *want* someone to

shoot me." He said it, but he hadn't seen Dare since about a year ago when he drifted through Dare's home in Indiana. And Luke had no wish to catch a bullet in the back for trusting the wrong man. But Dare was one of them. A Regulator. In Andersonville Prison, they'd done the dirty work everyone wanted done but no one wanted to do. It was a friendship woven with blood and honor.

Yes, he'd trust Dare Riker with his life. For the hundredth time.

His jaw clenched as he watched the lights in town wink out one by one.

The quiet eased his tension and he realized Rosie had fallen asleep where she sat. The woman had lived through a few long, hard days, no doubt about it. And what was he going to do with her in this wild town?

In the cool night, the sound of a tinny piano echoed out of the one building still lit up. Occasional outbursts of laughter were carried along with the music. Duffy's Tavern was still in business.

There was one other lit-up place on this side of town—Dare's house. Two lanterns burning in a first-floor window. The house was on the edge of town, far enough away from the saloon that Luke didn't need to wait for that rowdy mob to quiet down. But there might be men out and about on their way to and from the saloon, so he kept his eyes and ears open.

Looking down at Rosie, Luke felt a moment's regret at waking her. But it was time to go, and she'd be safer inside Dare's house anyway. He hoped.

Crouching, he gently shook her shoulder, rocking her awake.

She moaned in her sleep, and he quickly covered her

mouth with his hand. Her eyes shot open and she struggled, but when her eyes focused on him, the fear drained out of her on a sigh. He lifted his hand, conscious of the warmth of her breath, then gently touched her slender shoulders, mindful of the one she'd hurt. "Sorry."

She nodded in silent acknowledgment of his apology. She looked fragile beyond belief. Her red hair looked black in the moonlight. It contrasted with her pale, sunburned skin scattered with freckles. Her eyes had a ghostly gray tone, though they were light blue in the daylight.

"It's time to go in. I didn't like waking you, but I can't leave you out here."

She rubbed her eyes and ran both hands through her hair. It was so snarled her fingers got tangled up, and he thought she might need help retrieving them.

He eased her to her feet. She was a skinny little thing. But few people had the time or money to get fat in the West.

Luke caught her when her knees gave out. She probably ought to be taken to a doctor, considering all she'd been through. And in this town, that was Dare, and that's where he was taking her. Most likely, if she got some sleep and food, she'd get well on her own.

His arm felt real good around her waist, and he didn't let go as soon as a man might have.

She looked up while he was still hanging on and their gazes locked. A breeze fluttered her hair, and Luke felt the curls brush his face. For one second he forgot where he was and the trouble he'd brought with him. All he knew was he was alone with the prettiest woman he'd ever seen. Watching her, her watching back. Silence stretched. The world receded until he felt as if they were the only two people on earth.

A sharp hoot of an owl swooping nearby penetrated the silence and broke up whatever madness had come over him. He turned her to face the town. "See that—" He sounded hoarse, so he stopped talking and cleared his throat. Twice. "See those twin lantern lights nearest us?"

"The ones in the window?" She sounded steady enough.

It irritated Luke that what had been a confusing moment for him had apparently not bothered her much. She was still letting his arm support her, though. So maybe she was still sleep-addled.

"Yep. We move quick and quiet to those lights. Can you walk or do you need me to carry you?"

By way of answering she straightened away from him, wobbled for a few seconds, then steadied herself and lifted her chin. "I can walk."

She might be skinny and pale, but she had a solid spine. He admired that. If he'd've had her in his regiment, she'd've been one of the quiet ones who carried her weight and stuck with the troop on a long forced march.

"Let's go." With his hand resting on her lower back, they left their cover and walked straight to Dare's back door. Luke was surprised at how much he was looking forward to seeing his old buddy. When he reached the back door, he tapped with one knuckle four times. He waited to a count of five, then rapped three times, then waited and rapped four again.

Luke waited only seconds before the door was jerked open. Dare's eyes went from watchful to flashing with pleasure.

"Get in here." Dare looked past Luke's shoulder into the darkness, checking for trouble, then grabbed his arm and dragged him forward.

Luke went in, and only when he stepped forward, guiding Rosie, did Dare notice her. He must've been looking for taller trouble.

With an arched brow, he asked, "We got to bring a date? No one told me."

"Yeah, like you can get a woman."

With a chuckle as deep and raspy as his voice, Dare slapped Luke on the back, and that turned into the closest thing a man wanted to a hug.

"Darius Riker, this is Rosie. Dare's the town doctor. Rosie was floating down a river, unconscious. I had to either bring her or leave her to some two-legged wolves I had on my tail."

"Pleased to meet you, Rosie."

"It's Ruthy."

Dare smiled but it didn't reach his eyes. "I hope you're not walking into bigger trouble than what brought you to that river, Ruthy. Go straight ahead, kitchen's on the right. Coffee's on. Stew pot's hanging in the fireplace. I'll go for Vince and Jonas. No light."

Dare dodged around Luke and went out, shutting the back door silently. Luke felt a twinge of annoyance. *No light?* It was an insult to warn Luke of the obvious. Dare thought Luke had gotten soft or he'd've never said that.

In the murky light of the hallway, Luke said to his little woman, "You want some stew?"

Her smile was warmer than Texas in July.

CHAPTER 4

Ruthy did her best not to run toward the kitchen and food. The only light in the kitchen was cast by the glowing red of the burning wood inside the stove. This must've been the room the lanterns were in, but they'd been extinguished. Moonlight helped a bit, coming through the kitchen windows.

"I wonder how long I was floating? I feel like I haven't eaten in days, even with the jerky you gave me." The stew smelled like heaven. Warm and meaty, layered with the aroma of onions and potatoes and carrots.

"Looked like the water had gone through a day ago, not much more than that. But you could've been riding that current for days. You've got a cut on your head so you were probably unconscious for most of it. There are a lot of branches off several good-sized rivers that lead into this area, so who knows where you started out."

The stew was pushed to the back of the stove to keep it from scorching. Plates sat in a short stack beside the stove, and a ladle hung overhead. She scooped up two plates while Luke sawed away at a loaf of bread right beside her. They were sitting down to the savory meal in under a minute.

"Eat quick. Dare won't tarry, and we have work to do when he gets back."

The first bite almost brought tears to her eyes. She savored it for just a few seconds before her appetite roared to life and made her tuck into the meal. Even knowing she had the manners of a wolf, she barely chewed before she swallowed. Before she was half done with her plate, she was suddenly so full she could barely get the bite she'd already taken into her belly.

Laying her fork down, she said, "That was delicious but I can't eat any more."

"It's like that when a body goes without food. Your belly shrinks to nothing and your brain is used to starving." Luke's midnight brown eyes took on a distant look.

"How do you know what it's like to starve?" Ruthy's hand clenched on her fork.

"I spent a while in Andersonville during the war."

Ruthy gasped. "You were in Andersonville Prison? I've heard of all the death and deprivation."

"Yep." Luke set his fork aside, his plate empty.

Ruthy shoved her plate across the table to him. "No sense letting this go to waste."

Luke started in on it with enthusiasm. "A man learns how to survive on nothing or he dies."

"From what I heard, anyone who got out alive was lucky."

A laugh that held no humor drew her attention to his bleak expression. "Lucky. Never much figured any luck involved in that purgatory. And almost worse than starving was when—"

The back door opened on a whisper. Luke gulped down the last of the food. His expression had been so grim, so full of foreboding she was almost glad he didn't say whatever he'd planned to say.

Dare came into the kitchen. "I found Vince." Right behind him strode another man. Ruthy couldn't see details, but he wore a black vest and a white shirt, open at the collar.

Luke stood from the table and shook the newcomer's hand, slapping him on the back. "Invincible Vince, how are you?"

The three of them smiled. Vince was the tallest and dressed up almost like a city slicker. Dare had the look of a western man. Luke was shorter than either of them, although still over six feet, darker, his hair and eyes a flashing black. He had broad shoulders that had been wonderful to rest against. She might have come around in that stream, gotten out, found food. But it would have taken every ounce of her strength, the miraculous hand of God, and a whole lot of luck besides. The way she saw it, she owed Luke her life, and she had yet to tell him thank you.

Why hadn't she? There'd been time. She remembered the moment they'd shared, the long look. He was the most attractive man she'd ever seen, and she knew all too well a plain little redhead like her didn't attract men.

Virgil didn't count.

"I'm good." Vince's smile was white in the darkness as he greeted Luke. "I just got into town a few weeks back. Just barely got my practice set up."

"Practice?" Ruthy said it, then wished she hadn't as all three men turned toward her.

"Vince is a lawyer, and Dare a doctor." Luke smirked, which made no sense. What was funny about that?

"A doctor and a lawyer? Luke, you're among educated men."

51

There was a pause and then all three men broke into laughter.

Vince said, "What've we got? Maybe twelve years of education?"

"Surely you have to go beyond that to be a doctor or lawyer," Ruthy said.

"I mean twelve years between the three of us." Luke smiled. "And I bring the average down because I never went at all. There wasn't a school in Broken Wheel. Ma taught me reading and ciphering at home."

"I have the most schooling of this rabble," Vince said. "I went clear through the eighth grade."

"And I learned doctoring during the war," Dare added. "I got assigned as a medic in Andersonville and I learned because I had no choice."

"Dare claims to have gone four years, but I see no evidence of education."

"I'm self-educated and mighty proud of it." Dare shoved his hands in his pockets and bounced on his heels as if he couldn't stand still.

Luke said, "Vince became a lawyer since the war ended. He got stuck one winter in a cabin in the Rockies with Blackstone."

"Blackstone?" Ruthy asked. "Who is he?"

"Not a he, an it." Vince gave her another flashing smile. "Or I should say a *they*. Blackstone's *Commentaries on the Laws of England*. There were several volumes. And all the food I could eat, thanks to a well-stocked cellar. Best winter of my life."

"Of course, you've had a miserable life," Dare interjected.

"That's the plain truth." Vince grinned, then the grin faded. "And the misery ain't over yet."

Dare looked out the kitchen window. "Let's go in my office. I've got heavy curtains in there. And if my lantern is on, people will just think I've got a patient."

Luke swept the plates from the table.

"Just leave them in the sink." Dare gestured toward the door to get them moving.

"I'd be glad to clean up in here." Ruthy frowned at the messy kitchen.

"Nope, not now, Miss Ruthy. We need to make some plans, and I think you're included in them whether you like it or not." Dare led the way into the hall and to a door just across from the kitchen. They went into the dark room, and Dare touched Ruthy's hand, startling a squeak out of her.

"Easy, miss. Just showing you the way to a chair."

"Did you find Jonas?" Luke came up beside Ruthy and guided her away from Dare and helped her find a seat. Speaking in her ear as she sat, Luke said, "Jonas Cahill is a parson. He's actually got a little bit of education."

"Jonas left a note. Old man Hingle is dying and Jonas is sitting with him and his brother. Jonas'll get over here if he can." Dare spoke from in front of her, and lower, as if he'd sat on the floor.

A match struck off to the side and Vince lit a lantern. She still hadn't gotten a good look at him. When the lantern flared to life, she realized he was as handsome as any man she'd ever seen—not counting Luke. But Vince's was a smooth kind of handsome, clean-shaven, lean, his clothes neat.

Dare struck a match, and she could see him better. He was kneeling just a few feet in front of her, at a fireplace. A crackle told her kindling had caught and the room brightened. Dare had a rough look about him. His blond hair was shaggy, and his mustache drooped.

Vince turned up the light on the lantern and leaned against the door, his back holding it shut as if he expected intruders.

Dare stood and walked away from the fire, then back, his movements as sleek and quiet as a pacing cougar, but moving, always moving. Ruthy wondered what ate at him that kept him from being still.

Vince was the opposite. A silent presence, like a predator. His eyes glinted in the flickering lantern light. The room brightened as the fire grew and Vince caught her eye and smiled. His teeth shining white. Ruthy looked away and saw the room for the first time. This was where Dare did his doctoring. A high bed that must be where he examined patients stood away from the wall so he could get on both sides. Cabinets lined the room nearest the head of the examination table. A desk to the right of the fire was covered with oddly shaped things that were most likely doctor's equipment. There was a door behind the desk, and any open space was filled with shelves crammed with books. Dr. Riker might not have much formal schooling, but he was a man who studied.

Luke sat in a wooden chair beside Ruthy and stretched out his legs toward the fire. Ruthy got the feeling he'd take a nap if he had one minute of silence.

Luke hadn't felt this safe for a long time. Years. Before the war, and that was a long time ago. And now he was starting another war. He had no business feeling relaxed. Especially when loyal friends might end up dead because they were backing him.

He hadn't asked for help. He'd just made the mistake of

talking about it with Dare when he'd wandered through Indiana, idle, rootless, missing home something fierce. He'd stayed long enough that a letter arrived with news of Callie. Pa had also enclosed the deed to the ranch.

Dare had written the others to come and help—before he'd told Luke he was doing it.

And while Luke rode out to Denver to talk with his sister and make sure she was all right, his friends had begun to filter in to Broken Wheel, or nearby, quietly, no mention of a connection to Luke Stone.

Dare had told Luke to watch for a general-delivery letter when he passed through a town near Broken Wheel. Neither of them were even sure what towns were in the area, so Dare would have to wait until he got to Texas to find out. Dare would send a general-delivery letter to John C. Riker, Dare's father, containing any information necessary. It couldn't have Luke's name on it in case word got to Greer that Dare was in contact with Luke.

Luke's friends were strong men ready to back a fellow Regulator, just as they had at Andersonville. Even Jonas, a man of God, also a man of justice. He might only fight with words, but Jonas's words carried power and truth. He was a solid man to have on your side.

Luke prayed his troubles could be solved without Jonas being dragged into a gunfight. Luke didn't want to have to shoot anyone either, and he'd worked hard to try and prevent that. He was white lightning with a pistol, deadly accurate with a Winchester, and the commanding officers had found that out and made sure he always had good weapons and plenty of bullets. He'd done his share of killing in the war. That killing had given him nightmares and left him with ugly memories that tormented him. That torment had fed the trouble between him and Pa until Luke had to leave the ranch. But Pa was dead now and the S Bar S Ranch stolen, his sister driven from their home. It couldn't be allowed to stand, not in the United States of America. Not in the land Luke had fought to preserve.

A twist in his gut that was pure guilt reminded Luke he'd abandoned his family. A lot of this disaster would have been prevented if Luke had stayed home. Or maybe Luke would be dead now, too.

Maybe if he'd stayed, his sister would have trusted in Luke's protection and, instead of running, she'd have been killed.

Every time Luke got to thinking about how staying would have made things different, juggling all the *what ifs*, he thought of good endings and bad, more ups and downs than the bluffs surrounding the Stone ranch. It was maddening and a waste of time since he couldn't change what he'd done, but that didn't stop his mind from circling and circling around his regrets.

"Let's get a few details straight." Vince spoke and it shut down the fretting going on in Luke's head. "Jonas already knows what we're planning. I've got the papers all in order that deny Greer's ownership of the ranch. I've already filed them with a judge."

"Here in town?" Rosie asked.

Luke thought it was nice of her to care enough to pay attention. The woman had to be worn clean out.

Dare stopped pacing. "One of the Regulators is a circuit judge for this area, Leonard Bird. Another, Big John Conroy, is a Texas Ranger and he's heading this way. We've got the law on our side." Dare went back to pacing.

"The Rangers will help, but they're not the law in Broken

Wheel," Vince said. "Greer's got the local sheriff on his side. We'll get no help from there. Greer owns the land in a circle all around Broken Wheel so there aren't other ranchers left to stand up to him. And most of the townsfolk are afraid of him. He's driven away those that won't knuckle under to his way of doing things."

"I've got the documents proving ownership and I'll deliver them to Greer." Luke was tempted to do some pacing himself. "The man has a mighty big ranch. I listened while I rode for home and heard his name. He's added thousands of acres since he stole my place. I want my land back, but that ain't enough. I want Greer to pay for killing my pa."

There went the twist in Luke's gut again. "I can't prove he pulled the trigger. But I can prove he forged the bill of sale of the S Bar S, because Pa didn't own it. He'd signed it over to me all right and legal and mailed me the deed. So Greer lied about Pa selling out, and my pa was dead and couldn't challenge Greer about it. I think a judge will put Greer behind bars for theft if a good lawyer"—Luke nodded at Vince—"like Vince here, makes the case."

Vince smiled. "At your service."

"But you don't think Greer will stand by quietly while you let the law get involved?" Rosie sank deeper into the chair as if trying to escape the coming storm.

"No." Luke was as sure as could be of that. "Judging by the three attempts on my life since I've headed home, it's safe to say Greer is going to fight me with everything he's got."

"Besides that," Dare said, "Greer's a hothead. Word around town is he's got a temper that blows once in a while. He's not quite sane when it happens."

"And throwing him off his land oughta set him off good."

Luke shook his head and took a quick look at Rosie. "So what are we going to do with you while I start a range war?"

Rosie sat up straighter. "Can I g-get a job maybe? Here in town?"

"Nope." Dare didn't elaborate.

"She should be able to find work sewing or working at the diner," Luke said.

"This is a mighty small town, and a stranger gets noticed." Vince crossed his arms, settling himself more solidly in the doorway. "A man might've come riding in with no need of explanations. But a woman—there aren't any of them little critters here."

"None?" Luke surged to his feet in surprise. "There aren't women? There were several families when I was a kid. Not a lot. Never enough to start a school. You said Greer had made it a bad town to live in but *none*?"

"Nope."

"What about Harvey Foster and his family?" Harvey's son Gil had been Luke's best friend as a child. The two of them had made friends with a few Kiowa children and even a Comanche boy once. They'd run wild in the rugged canyon. Gil had been a big part of why Luke had fought for the North. Harvey was an emancipated black man who owned a small ranch near the Stone ranch. When the war had come along, Luke couldn't see fighting for slavery. He'd argued with his pa about it before taking off to enlist in the Union Army.

"I've met no one by that name, and I'd say I've met everyone. And he surely isn't ranching in these parts, because no one is ranching except Greer. We're a long way off the main trail out here, and with restless Indians still around, it's not a welcoming place for a family," Vince said.

"I can't think of a way to explain Ruthy here to anyone. No woman has ever come riding in, for any reason in the weeks I've been here. If one did, she couldn't come in alone and expect to be treated right. So, Miss Ruthy, you'd need to come from somewhere. You'd need to have a reason to happen by here. We'd need to find someone to ride in with you and it can't be Luke, because he's a known man with trouble to face. And if you came in with him, then his trouble is yours. It isn't that easy to show up in a town this small. Dare or Jonas or I could ride out and stay away a few days, then come back with you. Or we could take you somewhere safer, get you to Fort Worth maybe. But we'd have to push hard to get you down there, then get back in time to help Luke. I doubt we could do it in a week, even if we pushed our horses until they near to dropped, it's that far south and east."

"Is there a stage in town? Could I somehow—?"

"No stage." Vince shook his head. "Freight wagons come once in a while. But there ain't no rhyme nor reason to their coming. I suppose we could ride out in four directions and watch the trail. When a wagon comes along, if we could get the driver to stop and wait while we fetch you from Dare's house and you get on their wagon with some story as to why you're coming into town, that might work. Except a freighter's always a man in a hurry and all kinds of men work as mule skinners. Not all decent. We'd have to get him to go along with a lie about how you came to be on his wagon. Then you'd need to—"

"Okay," Rosie said, cutting him off. "I get it. There's no way for me to be in town. So what do we do?"

Rosie stood from the chair and went to Dare's desk and started tidying. Luke couldn't decide if she just needed to move because she was nervous or because the untidy desk really bothered her.

"We hide you." Luke sat back down, bothered by the womanless town. What had happened to Gil and his family? Greer had a lot to answer for.

"Where?" Ruthy made tidy stacks of Dare's doctor supplies.

"Probably here," Dare said. He kept moving, circling the room.

Ruthy's hands stilled. "I can't stay in a house with a single man. That's not proper."

"And I suppose that plank you were floating on in the stream was proper?"

"I couldn't help that."

"You can't help this, either." Luke was done with this discussion. "Listen. We need to figure out how to get those papers to Greer without getting shot out of the saddle. I know the ranch well. I think if I—"

A loud rattle of wagon wheels clattered toward Dare's house. He shot out of the room and was back in seconds.

"Oh, good night. It's that crazy woman again, Lana Bullard. And her husband is just as much of a lunatic."

Chapter 5

"I thought you said there weren't any women in town."
Ruthy plunked her fists on her hips.

"Well, there's one. No, actually there are two," Dare
said. "Greer is a married man and has a couple of children."

"I don't remember Greer having a wife." Luke was on
his feet.

"She's a mail-order bride." Dare had a tone to his voice
when he mentioned Mrs. Greer that distracted Luke for a
second. "Someone said she's only been here about a year.
Has a couple of half-grown kids, one of 'em a girl, so if you
count the girl, there's a third woman in the area."

Ruthy raised her hand. "Four."

"Women everywhere you turn." Vince smiled at Ruthy.
Luke saw her blush at Vince's attention and he didn't like it.

"Mrs. Greer and her young'uns stay to themselves. I've
never once seen them in town, though I did ride out and
treat her for a sprained ankle. She's a snooty woman, not
a word of thanks nor a penny in payment, even though
Greer's a rich man."

"But Mrs. Bullard is in town from time to time. She's
expecting a baby," Vince said. "She's married to Simon
Bullard, the foreman out at Greer's place."

Dare shuddered. "I swear she just comes in so I can hold her hand. Every word I speak is like an oracle straight from God. And when she's not hanging on my every word, she's furious at Simon for her condition. I'll be up with her for hours. You've got to hide. All of you, quick. Come on." Dare shoved Vince toward the back of the house just as the front door slammed open.

Luke and Ruthy, only a pace behind, just ready to step out of Dare's office into the hallway, froze and looked at each other.

The frantic man shouted, "Come quick, Doc. We need help."

Dare stuck his head in the room and hissed, "Vince got out the back door. You two get in the storeroom."

He closed the door in Luke's face.

Luke caught Ruthy by the arm and dragged her to the only other door in the room. He yanked it open and shoved her in, hurrying in behind her. He closed the door only seconds before Simon came in, still hollering.

"She's in pain, Doc. What's happening?"

"Dr. Riker, you've got to help me!" His wife's screams echoed off the office walls.

Luke hadn't gotten more than a glimpse of this closet. There were shelves lining a space about four feet square, each loaded with unknown things that stuck out at random. He was afraid to move for fear he'd bump something and knock it to the floor and bring Simon Bullard, who probably had orders to shoot Luke on sight, right to their hiding place.

The chaos might've covered a few little sounds but not much.

"I think the baby's coming!" A woman screamed so loud, Luke felt sorry for Dare's ears.

"You have to relax, Lana." A sudden garbled sound made no sense to Luke and he tensed.

There was the sound of something being knocked to the floor and it rolled and bounced against the storeroom door.

"Simon," Dare said, his voice coming out strained, "help me here. Keep her arms off my neck."

Luke was all of a sudden glad he'd never made the medic detail at Andersonville. He whispered to Rosie, "Is she strangling him or hugging him?"

Luke felt Rosie shrug. All in all, he was glad to be in a tight little room with a pretty woman who, if she thought about it right, would have to admit he'd saved her life. A little gratitude might be in order on her part.

She swayed, and his arms came up to steady her. He knocked into something sticking out on a shelf and it toppled. Only pure luck made him grab it in time. It felt soft, like a bundle of rags. When he stopped its fall, it hit something solid that slid a few inches. The scratching sound was as loud as an explosion in the tiny room.

Ruthy inhaled sharply.

Lana shouted, "Simon, you get over here!"

Which covered the sounds from the storeroom nicely.

"Lana, honey, I'm right here."

"It's your fault I'm expecting this baby and—"

"Let's get you more comfortable, Mrs. Bullard." Dare's voice was loud.

Luke wasn't sure if Dare was speaking so loudly to reach into Lana's panicked mind or if he'd heard the noise from the storeroom and was trying to cover it.

Probably a bit of both.

The chaos continued in the other room until Luke started to relax and think about spending the night standing up.

At one point, during a particularly loud storm of wailing tears, Luke worked up the nerve to take a chance on getting comfortable.

"Rosie," Luke whispered, "did you see how big this room is?"

"I saw a little." She leaned close to answer, which Luke found almighty pleasant.

"Let's try and sit. We might be here all night."

"Mrs. Bullard, I need you to lie down." Dare sounded surprisingly calm for a man doctoring a screaming woman. It was demoralizing to think Dare had gotten used to it—most likely through hours of practice.

"Doc, you're my only hope. Simon Bullard, you get that bottle of whiskey over here and give me a drink. I need something to cut the pain."

"You probably shouldn't drink when you're expecting a baby, Mrs. Bullard. At least not often and not to excess."

Since Luke figured no one should drink often and to excess, it didn't mean Dare had any idea what he was talking about. Luke figured as soon as he got a chance, he'd advise Dare to take up ranching.

"You're right—it might be a while before we get out of here," Rosie whispered back. "If we're real careful, I think there's room to sit." Her hands rested on his forearms, and her quiet words were accompanied by the sweet warmth of her breath.

"Be mindful of the shelves." Luke had a lot of nerve giving advice, considering he was the only one who'd bumped into anything so far.

"You can't be in labor yet." Dare was using a comforting doctoring voice, only at a pretty high volume. Ruthy and Luke were being quiet, so Luke decided this was about trying to penetrate Lana Bullard's panic. "It's too early. But there can be some early pangs and those are real hard on a woman."

Even through a thick wooden door, Luke could tell Dare was being sarcastic.

Luke leaned real close to keep quiet, but also because he found he liked being close to Rosie. "If we're going to sit, it'd better be now. She's bound to tire out and quiet down. You go first. Let me hold your hands to keep you steady."

"I should have never married you, Simon Bullard. What was I thinking?"

"Well, Lana, honey, you was prob'ly thinkin' you was gettin' a mite old and fat to be workin' abovestairs at a run-down saloon, earnin' a livin' on your back."

A shout of pain cut off Simon's idiot slice of truth.

"Lana, I told you to relax." Dare was a brave man and no one could deny it. Luke would've made a poor doctor, because along about now he'd've pitched both of these fools out on the board-walk.

"Doctor, I'd be lost without you." Lana sounded almost worshipful, as if her very life hung on Dare's word.

"And, Simon, I've suggested before that you need to put Lana's past away and *not mention it again*." Dare was shouting toward the end of that.

"That's right." Lana talked over the top of Dare. "You stop throwing my past up at me. Now give me that whiskey."

"Lana, I told you not to be drinking—"

Clasping her hands, Luke helped Rosie sit without worrying too much about noise. She had tiny hands, but rough, with thick calluses. Luke's ma and sister were women who weren't afraid of hard work. And they were about the only women Luke had ever known, and his sister had been young still when Luke had left home. As a child, Luke had lived far from women—aside from his family. There was Gil's ma; she'd been a nice lady, but he'd mainly stayed outside playing and didn't really know her. And there were precious few women in a war. Then he'd been to the mountains trapping and spent some time with Callie in Colorado. The only females there were either married or children. But touching Rosie's hands and easing her to the floor, feeling her trust his strength as she lowered herself . . . well, it felt right. Familiar, when it couldn't be. Nice. Real nice.

As soon as he was sure she had settled, he inched into a crouch beside her. Carefully, slowly, he swept his hands around, finding a spot where he could ease himself onto the floor. He found a sturdy shelf behind him to lean against. For a second, Luke wondered if maybe he could get a few minutes' sleep.

"If I die having this baby, I swear my last act on earth will be dragging you down to Hades with me, Simon." Lana Bullard was one pessimistic woman, and clearly not real straight on the commonly held beliefs of Christianity.

Luke gave up on sleep and wondered if Dare had delivered many babies before. Luke only knew of one and that'd been a very strange situation. But Dare had practiced medicine elsewhere since the war. And Luke put hard emphasis on *practice*, because Dare had learned all he knew from practicing on unsuspecting patients and reading doctoring books. Not one hour of formal schooling to train him for his profession.

Rosie shifted in the dark as if she was uncomfortable. Without giving it careful consideration, Luke reached out, turned her back to him and urged her to lean on his chest.

She resisted his guiding hands, and he leaned forward until his lips brushed against her curls and nearly touched her ear.

"Use me as a backrest. I've got these shelves behind me."

She relaxed into his arms.

Luke brushed her tangled hair a bit so he didn't have hair in his mouth and found himself smoothing her hair again and again. And again.

The ruckus in the outer room went on. Luke quit listening because it was just the same thing over and over. Almost like music. Really bad music, salted with screams of pain, threats to Simon, and an almost worshipful tone from Lana toward Dare. But still, there was a rhythm to it.

Rosie's head slipped sideways, and Luke supported her so she was comfortable in his arms as she slept.

He felt the long day catching up with him too, even in this tiny, uncomfortable room. As his head began the swimming just before sleep, he took a second to hope he didn't snore.

He hoped Rosie didn't, either. And he hoped if she woke up before him, she had the sense to be quiet.

CHAPTER 6

Her bedroom door opened.

"Virgil." Ruthy jerked away. "No. Get—"

A hand clamped over her mouth like a vise.

Ruthy reached for the knife she'd started bringing to bed, but Virgil had her wrapped tight in his arms. No escape.

Then, in the lantern light, she recognized Dare Riker. All the fight drained out of her. She was in a storeroom, not her bedroom. Dare stepped into the doorway looking exhausted, furrows on his brow as he gazed down at her. Dare asked, "Who's Virgil?"

Luke leaned forward so Ruthy could see who had her. When she relaxed, Luke let her go, set his strong hands on her waist, and boosted her to her feet. He stood and followed her out of the little room. "So, who's Virgil?"

Shaking the sleep out of her head, she said, "I was supposed to marry him. He drowned in that flash flood."

Dare looked back. "I'm so sorry, Ruthy, I didn't realize. You talked about a flood, but we've been so busy I didn't realize you'd lost someone."

Nodding, rubbing her eyes, Ruthy added, "Yes. Virgil . . . and his parents. My parents."

Dare stopped so suddenly Ruthy ran into his back.

Looking at her, he asked, "Uh, does that make Virgil your brother?"

Ruthy thought of that terrifying moment when the bedroom door had opened. She controlled a shudder. "I suppose he was my brother."

"Where're you from, Ruthy? Because marrying your brother is illegal in Texas." Dare had a lantern in his hand so she could see his face well enough. He seemed pretty confused.

Which was fair.

"I was taken in by Virgil's family when my parents died. The Reinhardts were no relation. Virgil's ma and pa were determined we'd marry." Something occurred to her for the first time. "I think they wanted my family farm. We neighbored them back in Indiana." She thought of what Dare had said for a moment and added, "And marrying your brother is illegal everywhere. But they weren't even adoptive parents. I just lived with them for the last few years. If they're all dead, if they stole my farm, I should get it back now. I might be rich if I can get to Indiana." But they would have sold her farm along with their own when they headed west, and if they'd had money, it would have been hidden in their covered wagon, so she gave up on any hope of wealth.

Since it was a hope that had been born and died in the course of a heartbeat, it was no great loss. Though it was one more thing to loathe about the Reinhardts.

"Well, you can't go to Indiana. Not right now." Luke waved a hand past her face as if shooing Dare on.

"I'm from Indiana, too," Dare said. "What part of the state are you from?"

"Don't you think we should get upstairs while there's no

one here?" Luke didn't like Dare and Ruthy acting like this was some Hoosier reunion. And that was just stupid, but still, Luke thought he and Ruthy oughta get on with hiding.

"I sometimes get patients in the night. When I do, they're always in a tearing hurry. So come this way."

They followed Dare out of the room to a door that opened onto a stairway. "Ruthy, you can stay upstairs, in the room on the far left." Dare shoved a key into her hand. "Lock it. I hope that's proper enough. If it isn't, we'll figure something out, but not tonight."

It was pitch-dark outside. Ruthy had slept some, but she was still exhausted. How long had Dare been with that crazy couple?

"Luke, you'll stay in the attic. There's a stairway you can pull down from my bedroom. But those attic stairs sound like a screaming wildcat when you pull them down. Not even the Bullards could miss that noise. When I bought this house, it was crammed with old stuff. There's just barely room in both places for one person to lie down. You should be able to get some sleep. C'mon, I'll show you. Hurry in case those two come back."

Dare led the way up the stairs. At the top, Ruthy headed for her room. Luke caught her arm and turned her to face him. "Did Virgil inspire you to scream and attack very often, Rosie?"

Ruthy looked into Luke's eyes and realized how isolated she'd been since moving in with the Reinhardts. Virgil's crude attentions had only been recent, and Ruthy had always gotten away. But she hadn't truly been honest with anyone for years. She had a powerful yen to just start talking until every thought in her head had been spewed into the night air.

And then she came to her senses. "We don't have time to talk right now."

"Maybe later, then." Luke's grip on her arm gentled, then fell away.

"Maybe." She went to her assigned room. Dare followed, and his lantern showed the room well enough that Ruthy could see a bed. Everything else was jumbled, night-shadowed stacks of who-knew-what.

"Keep this door locked and don't open it to anyone but Luke or me. If Bullard comes back, sometimes Lana runs him out of the office, then he paces. I wouldn't put it past him to come up here just out of boredom. See you in the morning."

Ruthy locked herself in and collapsed on the bed fully dressed. The room was pitch-black without Dare's lantern. Not even starlight came in, so maybe there were no windows. Or maybe the windows were covered. She didn't care. She had a feeling she didn't want to see what was in there anyway.

She woke up in a room that looked to have seen the business end of a Texas cyclone. Either that or Darius Riker was a complete slob.

There was enough of a mess that it could be both.

She lay in the small bed and listened. There were quiet voices straight below her. Dare spoke in a doctoring kind of voice. His office must have opened for the day.

A look around told her the room did indeed have windows. They were covered with shutters, pulled closed. It was murky, but daylight seeped in.

She wouldn't be visible if she moved around. But would

the floorboards creak and give her away? She remembered no loud creaking when she'd walked the few feet to the bed last night. No sound when she'd lain on the bed. But she'd paid scant attention.

Then she remembered the moment when she'd awakened in that storeroom and thought Virgil had finally caught her. Just thinking about it made terror stoke her belly, even knowing he was probably dead.

She had to do something, keep busy, or she'd let the ugly memories of her last few years take over. She risked sitting up, very slowly, but she couldn't risk walking around . . . so she reached for the nearest stack. It was clothing heaped high enough it might possibly conceal a bedside chest.

It was as if Ma Reinhardt were scolding in her head, telling her she was lazy, an idler, ungrateful to the family who'd taken her in.

Taken her in and stolen her land and treated her like a slave.

The terror and the fact that it wasn't in Ruthy to be idle with or without Ma Reinhardt's nagging made her reach for a wadded-up shirt on the top and start folding it.

As she worked her way down the pile, she realized exactly *what* she was folding. Women's clothes. Where did women's clothes come from in a town with hardly any women? And more important, what size were they? She looked down at her battered dress. It had been in bad shape before she'd taken a long ride on a flooded river.

There was no woman living in this house, of that Ruthy was sure. She'd seen the mess in Dare's kitchen, after all. No woman would put up with that.

Which meant these clothes were very likely unspoken for.

And she could do one more thing in complete silence. Discard the dress she was wearing for this very pretty green calico.

If Dare wanted it back, he'd probably let her wear it while she washed her other one more thoroughly.

With a quick glance at the locked door, which meant she could be completely private, it was the work of moments to change her clothes all the way to her skin. Feeling more decent and orderly, she decided to make everything within reach orderly.

She set to work.

∞

"Let me in, Rosie." Luke rapped on her door. "Dare's bringing breakfast up. His office is empty for the minute." A clicking of the door's lock told Luke she was awake and nearby.

The door swung open. "My name is Ruthy MacNeil. I'm sorry I didn't tell you straightaway yesterday, but I was worried about being found. I've calmed down now, and I'd like you to stop calling me Rosie."

"I like Rosie better." Luke looked at her red curls and couldn't hold back a smile. She'd brushed her hair, and instead of tight ringlets, her hair hung in pretty waves. Her clothes were clean, not what she'd had on before. The skin was peeling off her nose so she was still a little worse for wear, but she looked very nice for a woman he'd fished out of a river just yesterday.

"What have you done?" Dare spoke with sharp surprise from behind Luke.

"She's just letting us in for breakfast, Dare." Luke frowned at Dare's tone just as Dare shoved past him.

"You cleaned this room?" Dare held a metal tray covered with food. He'd piled eggs on one plate, side pork on another. A third plate was heaped with fried potatoes, and he'd set a tin pot of coffee in the one remaining corner. There were spare plates stacked beneath the potatoes. Forks and tin cups were dropped into the spare spaces. Luke's stomach rumbled just from the smell.

Dare set the tray on a small square table. "I didn't even know there was a table in here. I've only been in this room once since I moved in. I opened the door, saw nothing but stacks of junk, and swung the door closed fast."

"It is a complete waste of time to just sit around." Rosie centered the tray on the table. "Idle hands are the devil's playground, you know. Most of the things needed only to be folded and tidied and tucked into drawers or crates that were already here."

Luke saw one wall of the room stacked with boxes. Tidy boxes. He'd bet she did all of that while she was locked in here.

Dare sank into one of three matching wooden chairs set on three sides of the table; the fourth side was pushed up against the wall under a stack of boxes. There was barely room to pass between the bed and the table. A chest of drawers stood beside the bed, cleared off except for a tidy lace circle with a brush and comb and mirror centered on the lace.

"I've had a steady stream of patients for the last couple of hours, which is why I couldn't get up here until now." Dare's voice had more of a bite than Luke liked, especially as it was directed at Rosie. "Someone might have heard you moving around."

"Yes, I realized that." Rosie tugged on the corner of the bedspread, already very neat, but apparently she thought she could improve on it. "If I needed to take a step, I listened for your voice and could tell when you were walking your patients out. Then I'd move to another section of the room and sat quietly while I tidied it."

"You bought this house with this junk already in it?" Luke sat at the table, complete with tablecloth.

"These things belong to someone else?" Rosie seemed very interested in that.

"I mentioned that the families moved out of Broken Wheel. Whoever owned the house left a lot of stuff behind. It all came with the place, so now I own it. I need to get rid of everything, but I've stayed busy doctoring and it's been easy to ignore it."

"Get rid of?" Rosie jumped as if she'd been poked with a pin. "So then if there are clothes of a size that might fit me, I could . . . could . . ."

"You could have them, with my thanks for finding a use for them." Dare made a grand gesture. "There's nothing in this room I want."

"How can you say that when you don't know what's in here? You might be giving away valuable things."

Dare paused, his brow lowered as he thought that over. "If you find a satchel filled with gold coins, I'll kick up a fuss. Otherwise it's all yours."

"I've been through most everything and there's not a speck of gold to be found. But that box right there"—she pointed to a crate sitting by itself—"has women's clothes about my size. I'm wearing a dress, a pair of shoes, and a few other . . . um, garments I found in here."

Since Luke didn't see anything on her but the dress, he decided the garments were unmentionables. He was glad she hadn't mentioned them.

"I would be sincerely grateful for the use of these things—that is, if you're sure."

"They're yours." Dare poured himself a cup of coffee.

Luke was starving and in no mood to talk about the contents of a junk room. He'd just spent the night in a cramped attic with a ceiling three feet above the floor. So he'd been lying down with few other choices. There was so much junk in the attic, he'd been hard-pressed to find a space big enough to stretch out and sleep. And now, as he considered it, it made sense that Dare hadn't accumulated this many things in the two months he'd been living in Broken Wheel.

Luke had to admit, it had never occurred to him to tidy up.

"I did a bit of dusting, but the room needs to be scrubbed. I'll need warm water to do it right." Rosie began dishing up a plate for Luke. He enjoyed her fussing even as he felt guilty over her serving him.

Not that he could have stopped her.

She had an oddly fierce look in her eye, as if an undone task before her was an insult, a sin she was committing by not setting to work.

There were three empty plates. Rosie waved Dare toward the table. "You haven't had time to eat either, unless you got a very early start. I haven't heard you take a break all morning."

Dare sat as Rosie served him breakfast. She asked, "Did that woman come back last night?"

"Nope. But after she and Bullard left, I had a wrangler come in with a broken arm. Got in a fight over at the saloon. I got a couple hours' sleep before my first patient of the morning."

Rosie patted Dare on the shoulder as she set a filled plate before him. That irked Luke for no reason he could understand. But she shouldn't be putting her hands on a man, and especially not Dare Riker. He'd been around a bit too long to be fit company for a young woman like Rosie.

Since she quit touching Dare right away, Luke didn't say anything. Instead, he kept plowing through his breakfast.

"I got a chance to talk with Jonas this morning." Dare picked up his fork. "He's been up all night. Hingle died and his brother needed company. The funeral will be today, so we won't see Jonas until after that's over."

"You didn't get called in?" Rosie asked. "Didn't Mr. Hingle need a doctor?"

"I've doctored him ever since I came to town. He's a lunger, who was a long way gone when I got here. I've treated him to the extent I could. Not much to be done for consumption when a man's as sick as Hingle was. He and his brother knew it and had accepted it. Shame, though, as Hingle was a good man. This town will miss him."

"You all came to Broken Wheel to help me, and you're so busy with your jobs I'm going to make things tough." Luke hadn't meant to visit his trouble on his old friends, but it had happened anyway.

"What you've got to do needs doing, Luke. We need to rid this town of Flint Greer for more reasons than just to get your ranch back and get justice for your pa. I've found out Greer was a carpetbagger who came down from the North after the war. He was just starting out when he killed your pa. Since the day your pa died, he's stolen more land, killed good men, and driven others off their property until he owns almost every square foot of land all the way around town. What he doesn't own is controlled by

Comanches and Kiowas. There's no chance for this town to grow with the current circumstances. You've got right on your side, and I'll be proud to back you while we clear out Greer and his hired guns."

"I mailed all the papers to Jonas because I knew he'd gotten to town. If they got here, Jonas should've seen Vince about them and things should be in order to evict Greer." Luke poured more coffee, thinking of all that lay ahead.

Rosie flinched when Luke poured, as surely as if he'd yelled at her for being lazy. The woman clearly intended to care for all of them—and the rest of the world while she was at it. If she showed signs of boredom, he'd swap rooms with her and let her tidy up the attic, too. That'd slow her down.

"You're talking about the papers including a letter from a judge?"

"Yep."

"They're here, and we're ready to back you when you serve them."

Luke looked at his friend and shook his head. "I should've never let you get involved. It's my fight."

"Couldn't've stopped us, Luke. You were always the kid among the Regulators. You need your elders to help you along."

Luke's head came up, annoyed, but it was an old joke. He'd almost missed being teased by his barely older friends. Almost. "I was doing a full day's work on the ranch when you were still sittin' on your mama's lap and sucking your thumb."

Dare laughed. "Well, you always acted more like a kid than the rest of us."

"Or maybe you all acted like a bunch of old codgers."

Luke pounded a fist on the table and made the plates and cups jump and clatter. "I could take every one of you at the same time, if I had a need to."

Still chuckling, Dare said, "You always were an easy one to stir up, Luke."

"Guess I'd better not slug a man who's putting his life on the line to help me." Since he had no plans to punch his friend, Luke relaxed his fist and went back to his coffee.

"Reckon not." Dare reached for the pot, but Rosie beat him to pouring. "You'll spend the rest of the day hiding."

"I don't care much for hiding." Luke took a long drink from his tin cup.

"Tomorrow morning you'd best get up and out early, hide in the hills during the day until we can get everything in place. I expect Big John to ride in soon."

"What's a Regulator?" Rosie asked.

"It's how we met in the war." Luke knew he sounded curt. She didn't deserve that. She hadn't brought it up. "We were law and order in Andersonville. No time to talk about it now. Dare might get a patient any minute."

"Can I trade places with you, Luke? I'll spend the day in the attic."

Surprised, he forgot about Andersonville, to the extent he ever did. He'd thought of giving her that mess to deal with, but he'd've never suggested it. Maybe it wasn't about working. "Don't you feel safe down here?"

"It's fine, but it's all clean now, short of me scrubbing and hauling wash water up and down the stairs. I can't do that with patients in and out. It sounds like the attic could use some attention."

Luke groaned.

"You're a hard worker before the Lord, Ruthy MacNeil."

Dare laughed and shook his head. "You have got yourself one fine woman, Luke. You planning to hang on to her?"

"No one's hanging on to me. I'm going to take care of myself. Now, if you'll excuse me, I'm going to the attic." She scooped up a small stack of female-looking things. "Can I have a basin of water, Dr. Riker?"

"Sure, if you'll call me Dare."

Rosie shrugged, which wasn't an agreement.

"You expect to scrub the floors up there?" Dare asked, smiling.

"No, well, that's not the first thing I'll do with the water at any rate. First, I'm planning to wash the sleep out of my eyes. Then I'll turn my attention to tidying. Scrubbing floors will come later."

"I'll get it for you, and a towel," Dare said.

"I'm much obliged." Rosie walked out, heading for the attic. Luke heard her steps on the staircase, which he'd left down.

Luke realized he'd been staring out the doorway she'd walked through. But she'd been gone quite a while and still he could see her, like a blaze of red light at sunset that burned into his eye and stayed after the light was gone.

Luke forced himself to look away and caught Dare riveted on the same spot Luke had looked.

Slugging him on the arm, Luke said, "Quit staring."

Dare shook his head. "Imagine how pretty she'll look in clothes that fit and without that sunburn peeling her face."

"You don't need to imagine one single thing about Rosie."

Dare picked up the tray; Rosie had neatly loaded the dishes back on it. "So, *are* you planning to hang on to her?"

Luke was tempted to throw a fist again, because he didn't want to answer. Throw a fist at a man who was risking his own life to regain Luke's ranch. Maybe he wasn't much of a grown-up yet, just like Dare said. But looking after Rosie had given him some mighty grown-up notions.

"Just go get the woman a basin of water." Luke hesitated before he added, "I'll take it up."

Dare left the room with the food tray, laughing.

CHAPTER 7

Jonas Cahill, Broken Wheel's parson, came to visit late that evening, and Ruthy enjoyed meeting the quiet man with the warm smile.

He wasn't given to the teasing between the others, but he was definitely one of them, judging by all the backslapping and smiling.

Jonas was the shortest of the men, an inch or two under six feet, while the others stood above that mark. The preacher had red hair, cut short, though it still curled uncontrollably. It reminded Ruthy of her father.

He was quite a contrast to the others. Vince's hair was short and neat, a rich brown. Dare was a shaggy blond with a slightly darker mustache. Luke's hair was overly long, and so black it looked almost blue in the lantern light.

They met in the kitchen, where Vince took his place by the door as if he were the guardian of the group. His arms were crossed and his clothes were as neat as any big-city lawyer.

Dare paced. He'd locked his front and back door so they'd have time to scatter if anyone came needing doctoring. The lantern burned. Since Vince and Jonas had come calling, there was no need to douse the lights. Only Luke and Ruthy would need to duck upstairs.

Jonas and Luke sat at the table with Ruthy as she poured coffee.

"We've got the papers in order." Vince dropped them onto the rectangular oak table. "These are legal documents, signed by a judge. They should force Greer to leave the premises. Doubt he'll obey them, but serving these papers puts us on the right side of the law."

"I'll deliver them tomorrow." Luke grabbed the papers, his eyes burning with anger. "I hope he wants to fight about it."

"No, Luke, you can't. He's got that narrow canyon into your place guarded." Dare quickly described where the watchmen had stood on the ranch on his only ride out there, nearly a month ago now. "Word is, he keeps lookouts there, armed, day and night. They might let you ride in, but Greer would see to it you never rode out."

"Pa sometimes stood sentries out there. Comanches got restless from time to time, and we had to be on our guard, although we got on with them well in the normal course of things. The Kiowa were friendly most of the time, too. I played with them as a kid, along with my friend Gil. I even went hunting with a few of the young bucks. Anyway, I can get past those guards in the dark." Luke gripped the papers as if he were personally crushing the life out of Greer with his bare hands. "I'll slip out as soon as the town quiets down."

"Sounds good, but not yet." Vince was running this show. Ruthy could tell it, but she wasn't sure the rest of the men noticed. "We've got more to do before we can ride to the Greer ranch—"

"The *Stone* ranch," Luke snapped. "So he's living in my house, is he? He didn't just steal my land, he stole my home."

"Your house was nicer than his. I'm not sure if he moved in there right after he stole the land or not. I heard someone say his own place was a shack, and his wife nagged him into moving out of it." Dare's voice had that dark tone again, just like when he'd mentioned Mrs. Greer before.

Luke wondered if there'd been trouble between Dare and Mrs. Greer. But how much trouble could there have been in the short time Dare had been here? Especially if Mrs. Greer never came to town?

"We've got a few things to arrange before we're ready to face Greer." Vince went back to his planning. "We need to get Sheriff Porter out of town, and we need Big John before I'm willing to ride out to the ranch."

"Greer's got hired gunmen and they're all hard men willing to shoot first and ask questions later. Just the other day, Greer's foreman, Bullard—"

"The man who was here last night with his wife?" Ruthy asked.

"That's the one."

"And you do business with him, Dare?" Luke scowled.

"I thought about refusing him, Luke. I did." Dare shoved his hands deep into his pockets, then almost immediately pulled them free again. Ruthy had yet to see Dare be completely still. "But I didn't want to tip my hand that we're coming for Greer. And I couldn't in good conscience refuse to treat his wife, no matter who he is. You know I learned that in a hard school when I had to treat Confederate soldiers side by side with Union troops."

"Was this in Andersonville?" Ruthy asked. She'd heard

the horror stories of the prison during the war, the terrible loss of life, the starvation and sickness, the cruelty of the Southern captors, and the walking skeletons who'd survived. The bond between Luke and his friends had been forged in that crucible.

There was utter silence in the room. Vince pulled his gun and rolled the revolver with a hard whirl, the gun clicking as he held it at eye level.

Dare stopped pacing, leaned against the dry sink, and crossed his arms. One knee bounced as he stood there.

"That's where we all met." Jonas's voice had a grim quality that didn't match with a man of the cloth. "We were part of the Regulators."

Luke ran his hands deep into his hair. Making a mess that Ruthy wanted to fix. She was surprised—no—shocked at just how badly she wanted to touch his hair, tidy it, run her fingers through it. Giving herself a mental shake, she desperately jumped at their connection as Regulators.

"You said that word before. You said you were law and order inside the prison camp. But you didn't tell me much about what a Regulator is. You have a tight bond."

"We were a group that kept order inside the prison." Jonas spoke quietly. "That made us saviors to a lot of the men because there were varmints locked up in there along with decent soldiers. The varmints stole what few rations there were, stole clothing off men's backs. They called themselves Raiders and they hurt anyone who fought back. Killed more than a few. We got the job of bringing order. Us and a lot of others."

"But there were men who didn't think of us as saviors," Dare said. "More than a few. Yankee prisoners who thought we were helping the Rebs when we rounded up

Union soldiers, no matter what they'd done. After we put a stop to the worst of the Raiders, too many man wanted us dead. So we got pulled out of the prison yard and put to work for the Rebs."

"Which made us even worse traitors," Vince added with a scowl.

Dare resumed his pacing. "It's where I learned doctoring. I got assigned to the camp hospital. Even in there, trying to save lives, I found men who'd risk execution to stab me in the back. They said with pride that they were doing the Lord's work."

"Dare means stab him in the back literally." Luke lifted his coffee and took a long drink of the steaming brew. "He's got the scars to prove it. There were those who decided we were traitors, working for the Rebel guards against Yankees, our own men. We had to watch out for each other for the rest of the time we were locked up. It's a bond between us that's not easily broken."

"'There is a friend who sticks closer than a brother,'" Jonas said quietly.

"That's why we're here." Vince liked to talk, and he was the best dressed and the most civilized of the group. But right now there was cold winter in his brown eyes. "That's why we're backing you, Luke. You'd do the same for any of us. Though I hope you never have to."

"This is old news and it's got nothing to do with what we've got ahead of us. Can we get our plans in order before we have to break this up?" Dare asked, as unhappy as Luke at the conversation.

"You think we'll get a chance at Bullard here at your house?" Luke asked.

"Yep, I think you should keep sleeping here so I have

someone always at hand. You can slip out early in the morning to do your hunting for Greer's men and sleep at my place so we can have two men to bring Bullard down. Bullard always has a bottle with him and he's taken to just leaving it here. He doesn't drink deep. He's too controlled for that. But he nips at it. I've got laudanum, and if I mix it with his whiskey, it'll knock him cold. I don't want to use it until Big John gets to town and can take him into custody and haul him away."

"Big John is a Texas Ranger," Luke said to Ruthy.

"In fact, I can almost guarantee that Bullard will be in here again and again." Dare paced a little faster, as if he could run away from Lana Bullard and her screaming.

They must be done discussing the Regulators, leaving Ruthy with a hundred unanswered questions.

"He's almost as crazy as his wife," Dare went on. "Big John is checking into him being wanted. He needs proof before an arrest and he can't find any outstanding charges in Texas, so he's looking further afield. But no one as ruthless as Bullard can be completely clean. That's probably why he's stayed out here, so far from the law, because he's got trouble on his back trail. John will find what he needs. And as soon as we get our hands on a wanted poster, I'll dose Bullard with the laudanum and knock him out. We'll take him while he's snoring, and Big John will get him on the road to prison."

"And tear him away from his wife and child?" Ruthy's hand went to her throat. "That seems so wrong."

"That baby's gonna have one lunatic to raise it, instead of two. The one it'll be missing is a murdering vermin. I don't see that as a bad thing." Luke glowered at her, and after that she quit asking questions.

"That takes Greer's top man out of the fight." Vince continued with his planning as if no one had interrupted him. "If we take Bullard at night, quick and quiet, Greer might think Bullard ran, deserted him. And if Luke does his job right, honest cowpokes may realize big trouble is coming and just ease away. They might fight for the brand if they're braced, but once they know the kind of skunk their boss is, they won't want any part of it. That leaves Greer real shorthanded."

Luke scowled. "It sounds like you're going to take weeks before I can ride out and face Greer."

"You'll be busy," Vince said. "Ghosting around, thinning out Greer's men."

Luke looked around the room and the other men nodded.

"What about me?" Ruthy asked. "I'm not going to spend the next two weeks hiding in Dare's house."

The men looked between themselves, then turned to Luke.

"You brought her to this party," Vince said. "You got any idea what to do with her?"

Luke looked at Ruthy for far too long before he said, "Oh, I've got me a few ideas."

"What ideas are those?" Ruthy had no idea what these men were talking about.

Luke shook his head. "It's late. Go on upstairs, Rosie."

With a little huff she said to Dare, "If you'll come for me when you don't have any patients in the morning, I can get something on for a noon meal and get to work tidying the kitchen."

"I'd be proud to eat your cooking," Dare said. He pulled open a cupboard loaded with food. "I mostly get paid in potatoes and eggs and other supplies, so I've got whatever you need."

"A nice bit of beef would be welcome."

"I'll get some out of the cellar and have it at hand." Dare shut the cupboard.

"We'll have stew for dinner, and I'll make enough for supper while I'm at it."

"Can I come, Rosie?" Vince gave her a shining smile. "I'd love to eat a meal made by someone who knows what she's doing. I'm not a hand at cooking."

"It's *Miss* Rosie to you," Luke said in a way that drew her attention. His eyes were glinting at Vince.

"My name is Ruthy. Ruthy MacNeil. Try and remember that, especially if you want to eat my stew." She stalked out of the room without looking back. She heard them laughing as she ascended the stairs. When she twisted the key in the door's lock, she couldn't help imagining it was Luke Stone's neck.

"I need a man I can count on. Bullard?" Flint Greer was getting mighty tired of his ranch foreman fussing about his wife. Bullard wasn't the man he'd been when Flint had hired him. Marriage had ruined him. Marriage had ruined them both.

"Lana seems to be okay tonight, but you never know." Bullard pulled a kerchief out and mopped his brow. "Don't ever have a baby, boss. It's a worrisome business."

Flint doubted any babies would come along. His wife was a disappointment in every way a man could measure. He should've never married her. But he'd gotten a wild notion and thought a man as rich and powerful as him oughta have a pretty wife. And his Glynna was pretty, all right. But also stupid and lazy. She'd gotten too skinny to interest him. She couldn't cook to save her own life, and the woman cried over everything. A sniveler like his ma before she died.

Glynna had moved out of their bedroom during one of her tantrums after only a few weeks of marriage, and he'd never let her back in. Even that wasn't enough to keep the woman from wanting to challenge him at every turn. Flint clenched his fist as he thought of all the times she'd as good as begged him to shut her mouth.

Something he was glad to do.

Flint had learned how to teach a real clear lesson from his pa. A boy didn't forget a lesson taught with a hard thrashing. No reason a wife couldn't be trained proper with the same methods. Pa had showed him the way of managing a wife.

"Bullard, what's become of you? You were my right-hand man. You helped me build this spread."

"I helped all right. How many of the new acres you've acquired came because the owners mysteriously died?"

Flint laughed. "While I was in plain view of plenty of folks for an alibi."

Bullard lifted his gun from his right holster. The man always carried two in plain sight. Besides that, he had a gun strapped to his ankle and wore a knife in his boot. And he probably had more weapons Flint didn't know about. Bullard was a man who liked to be ready.

Sounding real casual, Bullard said, "I got word today that they missed in Appleton."

Every ounce of humor Flint possessed shriveled up. "That's about the last place before Broken Wheel?"

"Reckon Stone'll show up here any day now." Bullard glanced up and the flash of amusement made Flint killing mad. His own foreman was laughing at him, as good as calling him a coward.

His fists clenched again. He wanted to hurt someone. Stone wasn't at hand. Bullard would exchange a gunshot for a thrown fist. But the need to hurt someone goaded him. It ate at him the things that'd been said when he'd run rather than serve in the Union Army. As if there were any reason to risk his life over some other man's war, and especially over something as stupid as freeing slaves. It wasn't Flint's fight and he'd taken off out West to evade it. Then he'd come back when the fighting was over and found himself branded a coward, especially by his pa.

That time when Pa had thrown a fist, he'd found a son who wouldn't stand for it. Flint took out years of rage on his pa, then gathered up whatever cash he could lay his hands on and headed for Texas, along with a lot of others from the North looking for easy pickings in the war-weary South. He'd met Bullard along the way; the man was running from a posse and they fell in together. When they'd reached Texas and this rugged, beautiful stretch of canyon, Flint had found his home. He'd wanted it the first moment he'd seen those bleak red rocks.

Broken Wheel was a tired little settlement, with no law around that could stop Flint's land grab.

He'd bought his first place fair and legal. And then in the disarray left by the war he'd begun to expand. He started with Sal Stone, a man alone save for a daughter. Having Bullard kill Stone while Flint was standing in full sight of witnesses miles away, with a forged bill of sale and deed in hand for the S Bar S had worked so well they'd done it again and again until they owned all the land around and Flint had been content. He'd taken particular pleasure in driving off a black man by the name of Harvey Foster, as well as his wife and children. The man stood for all the trouble with the North and South that had led to Flint ending up being called yellow, and Flint would liked to have seen Foster and his whole family dead. But the man had turned tail and run, so there'd been no chance for Flint to get his revenge.

The law still hadn't come to north Texas. There were only a few settlements between Broken Wheel and Fort Worth. But when the law did finally come, Flint planned to present himself as an honest, well-established land baron. For some fool reason, Flint had decided that image he wanted to show the law included a wife.

Then Bullard had come up with a wife, too. They'd have been better off stealing more land.

Flint looked along the road to Broken Wheel. The first stretch of the road was a tight passage, high-sided with red stone stripes. The narrow stretch curved out of sight. In the predawn darkness, it was so deeply shadowed it looked like a tunnel. Flint made sure it was a well-guarded tunnel.

He hadn't ridden it since he'd gotten those blasted legal letters from Stone. It sent a chill down Flint's spine to think of that kid coming—and the chill was for no reason. No one man could stand against Flint and all his hired men.

Those letters were from a judge claiming Luke held the deed, and that made him the owner. The letter stated baldly that Flint had to vacate the S Bar S land. Flint owned close to ten thousand acres and had that many head of cattle. He could've just given Stone back his pa's land, but that would be admitting wrongdoing and, with Sal Stone dead, it didn't take a big leap to think Luke would want more than land. He'd want revenge.

It would take a bullet or a noose to satisfy Luke Stone.

Flint didn't aim to let that happen, and the only way to stop it was to kill the man. Too bad Luke hadn't been there when his father had died. Bullard could've finished off both Stones at the same time.

Luke Stone. Flint had come to loathe that name. Loathe it, and worse yet, fear it. And being afraid made Flint fighting mad. He looked down at his fist and wanted to swing it at someone.

He asked Bullard, "Do I need more men standing lookout?" Two men were always on the high ground, posted round the clock.

"Nope, those two are all you need. I've done a sight of scouting and there's no way to the ranch house that the men can't see. If a rider comes, your men'll fire a warning shot. I'll make sure of who's coming before we let him close. If he runs, our men'll cut him down."

"They should have killed that blasted doctor." It'd been a while ago, but it irked Flint that someone had sent for the doc. Glynna must've shown herself when someone carried in the eggs. She'd probably been crying her fool head off. Flint had been real tempted to fire the wrangler, though it wasn't his fault. No, the fault could be set right at the feet of his worthless wife.

"Now, boss, you can't kill the doc." Bullard was mostly as good a hired gun as a man could wish for. But now he sounded like a mewling pup. His wife was a soft spot, and Flint wished her long gone.

"Lana needs him. I don't know what'd become of her without Doc Riker."

Maybe she'd curl up and die and Flint could get his ramrod back. He needed Bullard, and Flint knew there was no call to shoot the doctor.

It was Glynna who was to blame.

Looking at Bullard, Flint realized he could see the man. The sun was coming up. Another night had passed without Luke Stone showing up.

Flint felt that wash of fear again and hated it. He wanted someone to pay for the fear.

His fist curled just as a lantern went on in the house. His useless wife up to ruin another day. Flint played with the idea of getting rid of her somehow. Those no-account kids would have to go too, and Flint couldn't quite see himself harming a child, even though he couldn't stand having them around.

But while he liked the idea of getting rid of Glynna, he also felt a powerful sense of ownership. And what Flint owned, he kept. Thinking of that doctor with his hands on Glynna was just her trying to provoke him. She had a lot to answer for.

Nope, his wife wasn't going anywhere. The driving need to kill Luke Stone churned all the way to Flint's bones. His rage grew and burned and bled until the whole world seemed bright red. Flint hadn't felt this kind of madness until he'd married. Well, maybe it'd started after he'd heard Stone was heading home. But his anger at Stone and his anger at his wife seemed all tied up together. Before Stone, Flint had taught Glynna lessons with the back of his hand. That'd been enough. But no more. Now, when he was angry, only his fists would do.

It was time to teach her some more.

"Get on with the day's chores, Bullard. I'm going to go explain how things work around here to my wife. Again."

Stalking toward the house, satisfaction grew into triumph. He'd found someone he could terrify and it was surprising how all those worries about Stone faded when he was busy training Glynna.

He swung the door open just as Glynna came into the kitchen. Still limping. Weak. Worthless.

She took one look at his face and knew. The power of it was as heady as whiskey.

"I've got a few things to get straight with you, wife."

A whimper from her lips reminded him he'd married a weakling and it infuriated him. Right now, fury suited him.

CHAPTER 8

Dare didn't get stew for lunch, and he knew just who to blame.

Glynna Greer. Her house was stolen, her children were rude, and her husband, the richest man in the area, didn't believe in paying doctor bills.

Dare fumed as he rode for the Greer ranch—the *Stone ranch*, he corrected himself. He'd had a message sent from the ranch that a doctor was needed. He wondered what it was this time.

He galloped out, wishing he was coming with his gun loaded and his Regulator friends at his side.

Dare well remembered the last time he'd been summoned. And now, this morning, only weeks later, the same hired hand who'd come for Dare last time had ridden up again.

"You need to hurry this time, Doc. She . . . she . . . fell again. She's hurt bad."

That was about the same thing the man had said last time, so Dare didn't get worked up. Most likely the woman hadn't yet healed from her earlier clumsiness.

Tempted to ignore the summons, Dare had only gone because he wanted to see what the woman would say. See if she had any shame for her rude ways. Well, he'd have gone anyway. A doctor couldn't just ignore something like this. But just in case she threw him out again, which he expected to happen, he rehearsed the story of "The Boy Who Cried Wolf." Maybe a fable, well told, would be just the thing to get Mrs. Greer to let go of her snooty ways.

As he rode that last stretch, where the space between the hills got so narrow and the layers of red stone closed in around him, his eyes were on the gunmen standing high above him. They had their guns aimed down at him.

One of them seemed to be smiling, as if delighting in the power he held over Dare's life. Dare looked at those rocks, too. Hanging on to the bluffs more by habit than anything. Some boulders, some huge flat slabs of red stone. Dare wondered if a shot would set off an avalanche. The ground along the narrow stretch was littered with smaller stones that said a boulder could and did come tumbling down from time to time. A good rancher would take charge of this situation by knocking over or dynamiting the large stones deliberately. Yet Dare suspected Greer liked the menacing danger.

One sentry pointed his rifle up in the air and pulled the trigger. A signal.

The stones didn't roll, thank God.

It would be a pleasure to run Greer and his lookouts out of the territory. Dare intended to enjoy every minute of it.

When he rode up and tied his horse to the hitching post just outside the house, the son was waiting at the door, just like last time. That time the boy had tried to block Dare from coming in.

Dare braced himself.

"Hurry." The boy swung the door wide. "Ma's hurt bad."

As if a cracked rib and a sprained ankle weren't bad? She'd had those the last time he'd ridden out here. This time, instead of being sullen, the boy looked sick with fear.

Dare picked up speed.

He found Glynna Greer lying on the floor, sprawled out at the bottom of the stairs. Unconscious.

Dare rushed to her side, feeling guilty for not galloping all the way here. Dropping to his knees, he felt for her pulse. It was strong and steady. Some of Dare's fear eased—but not much. "How long ago did she fall?"

"Uh . . . it was, she was like this when I woke up this morning. It's been two hours . . ." The boy's voice broke. He dropped to his knees on the other side of Glynna, across from Dare, swallowed hard, and added, "She's been like this from the time I sent someone to town. You're not supposed to come out, but I didn't know what else to do."

"Her arm l-looks bad." A quiet voice drew Dare's attention. The girl huddled on the stairs, just a few paces inside the front door. The little blond thing looked at him through the dark oak spindles of the banister. Janet. He remembered this quiet girl from before. Her eyes were wide with terror. Her skin pale. She looked ready to drop over into a swoon, and Dare wished he had time to give to the child, but she'd have to wait.

Dare had been focusing on Glynna's breathing, but the girl's words directed his attention to an ugly misshapen lump on Glynna's right shoulder. Dare saw that her shoulder was dislocated, nothing broken. As he worked his hands over the woman's arms and legs, checking for fractures, he prayed. There was little he could do if a patient was busted up inside. He needed better training for that. For the first time he felt shame that his skills were so limited. But no doctor could open up a patient and hope for much. A few tried, a very few had seen success. Dare wouldn't know where to start. And considering how badly hurt she'd been in the fall, internal damage was highly possible.

Her bones seemed intact, not counting the shoulder.

Her breathing remained steady.

The girl inched over to Glynna's side and dropped to her knees across from Dare.

"I need rags, torn into long strips," Dare said. "Or we might need to tear up a sheet if you don't have anything else. We'll have to put her arm in a sling." The girl didn't move until Dare reached across Glynna to touch the child's arm. Those golden eyes, just like her mother's, were riveted on her badly hurt mom. "Can you do that for me? For your mom?"

The girl looked at him and nodded.

"What's your name?" Dare felt the need to hurry, yet something about this child, who looked so fragile, forced him to take a few seconds to try and help her get hold of herself. He well remembered her name, but he hoped to somehow break through her horror. He wanted to help ease her fears now that a doctor was here.

Doctor, Dare thought with contempt. He had a lot of nerve claiming that now. Glynna might die, and all because of his lack of skills.

"I . . . I . . ."

"My sister's name is Janet. Shouldn't you be helpin' Ma instead of talking?" The boy still had a rude mouth, but he also had a point.

"I'll go for the rags." Janet leapt to her feet and dashed out.

"We're going to need to reseat her shoulder joint." Dare

looked at the youngster and saw, under the orneriness, a boy scared to death. "I'm going to need help. Can you do it?"

"What do you need?"

"I need to pull on her arm. The shoulder's dislocated. But I have to pull hard and it'll be a mercy to your ma if we fix it while she's still . . . fainted." This was no faint. The woman was knocked clean out, but Dare wanted to make it easier on both these young'uns if he could.

"Show me what to do."

"Trade sides with me. Let's do it quick, before your sister gets back. It's not easy to watch. Not for a child."

The boy's shoulders squared a bit to not be included as a child. They quickly got into position.

"Just hold your ma down. Put your hands here." Dare placed the boy's hands just under Glynna's collarbone. "When I pull, don't let me lift her off the floor."

She was unlikely to have cracked or broken ribs that high up. Dare prayed he was right because a broken rib could puncture a lung. Dare might not have formal training, but he'd read everything he could get his hands on and he'd worked alongside some mighty skilled doctors, both during the war and after. Right now all the dire possibilities paraded through his head.

"Have you got her?"

The boy nodded, his eyes riveted on his own hands, spread wide and flat.

Wincing, because he knew how much this would hurt if Glynna were conscious, Dare straightened her arm at the elbow, dragged in a deep breath, then said, "Okay, hold her."

The boy bore down. Dare yanked.

The joint reseated itself with a sickening pop. Glynna cried out in pain.

The boy looked up, furious, as if he'd dive over his ma's prone body to attack Dare.

"Look at the shoulder. It's back where it should be."

The boy turned to look and the worst of his killing fury ebbed. Or at least Dare sure hoped it did.

The girl came tearing into the room with a stack of towels in her hands. She looked at her brother. "What happened? What did he do to her?"

"He fixed her arm," the boy said. "Can't you see it's better? He's helping her."

The girl skidded to a halt, just as the front door slammed open.

Flint Greer.

Dare had met him in Broken Wheel once. Otherwise, the man never came to town. But there was talk, and Dare knew the man to be a tyrant. Greer looked like a wild man. Someone in town said at one time he'd been almost too neat. His hair always trimmed, his clothes clean and well made. He was a Northerner, a carpetbagger, which made Dare ashamed of his part of the country. Greer had come into the area and took what land he wanted. There was no law in north Texas to stop him.

There was nothing tidy about the man now. His hair and beard were long and filthy. His clothes looked like they'd been good quality at one time, but now they were worn near to tatters.

The signal his guard had fired brought him in, as Dare knew it would. The man would be frantic now to see how badly hurt his wife was.

Greer's eyes went first to her, then straight to Dare. "You get off my land."

Of all the responses Dare had expected, that wasn't one of them. "I will not get off your land until I'm sure my patient is able to be left on her own."

Greer whipped a revolver from his holster and aimed it straight at Dare's heart.

Luke raised his head slowly to study the land before him through a row of scrub brush. He saw a pair of riders crossing a long stretch of rich grass. They rode horses with Greer's Diamond G brand.

Luke had been ghosting around all morning, leaving Dare's house before dawn. He'd staked his horse on grass near town and walked. Palo Duro was a good place for ghosting, but a man on horseback had his hands full staying low enough. There were trees to be found, though they were sparse. A man on foot could slither along on his belly through cracks in the ground, duck behind clumps of juniper, scale the red rocks, and study the lay of the land. Luke's time playing with the Indian children had taught him a lot of tricks.

He'd spent the morning getting an idea as to how many cattle Greer ran and how many men he had on the payroll, and whether those men were cattlemen or gunmen. Luke considered how to thin the herd of hired hands on Greer's property and decided to watch a bit longer before he chose a plan of action. The wrong approach could get him shot.

Luke could see the sentries standing on the high ground by the narrow canyon that led to his pa's house. Pa had chosen that spot to build because there were Indians in the area back when they'd settled there. He'd wanted a place he could defend. Now Greer was using his pa's savvy against Luke.

Looking down a long, sweeping slope at the riders, Luke's eyes narrowed on the older of the two men. Even from a hundred yards away, he recognized Dodger Neville. The man had been old when Luke was a kid and a good friend of Pa's. But he was riding for Greer now. The horse had a Diamond G brand. Which meant Dodger worked for the enemy. Luke figured that made Dodger a man not to be trusted.

The younger of the two riders pointed at a divide in the trail, and they rode toward it.

Luke watched them and, knowing his land, walked a rugged trail that threaded between two soaring mesas that would give him a view of the two men at a point farther on. He also kept his eyes open for Comanche. They'd been in the area before his family had moved here and were mostly friendly, but Pa had taught Luke to be mighty respectful of them. Luke knew Broken Wheel was a town for the simple reason that someone passing through had a wagon break down and they'd stayed. Others had settled, but it had never thrived due to the tension with the natives.

The land was dotted with longhorns, all branded Diamond G. Bitterly Luke wondered just how many of them were born to S Bar S cattle. Sal Stone, Luke's pa, had been so proud of that iron with the S Bar S blazing red hot at the end. The calves born to Pa's cattle were now branded to be Greer's.

The land got more rugged and the going slowed, but Luke still reached an overlook in plenty of time to hide behind a man-high jumble of boulders uphill of the riders. He watched them ride up to two other Greer hands and talk a spell.

Four of Greer's men.

Thin the herd.

Luke's hand itched. He knew a good way to make men vanish. He had his Winchester slung over his shoulder and was a dead shot. For the men below, there was no cover for a long way if he wanted to open up on them. But Luke was no murderer. He had right on his side and didn't intend to stoop to gunfire except if it meant life or death to him or to one of his friends.

Or Rosie.

As he stood behind the boulder, a smile stretched his lips. Rosie had been in one beauty of a snit when he'd left this morning. Wanting to come along—of all the harebrained ideas. Dare had ordered her to stay in that upstairs bedroom and hide. Luke had told her she'd get them both killed if she came along with him.

He could just imagine dragging her through the wilderness, spying on Greer's cowpokes. They'd've been found out and shot before they'd been riding an hour.

A snap from behind him had him whirling around, crouching, pulling his gun.

"Don't shoot." Rosie stepped out of a copse of trees, her hands in the air.

Luke dropped to his knees. He'd come within a second of shooting her.

He jammed his gun into his holster and missed, then missed again. His hands were shaking because he knew just how close he'd come to killing Rosie. "What are you doing out here?"

They were a far piece up the hill from the four riders. Luke could scold her all he wanted if he kept the noise down.

"I stepped on a twig."

Words so obvious they didn't need to be spoken.

"How'd you find me?"

With a little huff of a laugh she said, "I've been on your trail all morning. I caught up with you two hours ago and have been following you ever since."

That sent a chill down Luke's spine. He considered himself as good as a man could be in the wild and he'd had no idea he was being followed. But here she was. Living proof.

"How'd you get out of town?"

"I left before sunrise. Dare was called out for an emergency. I heard the man who came to the door say something about Mrs. Greer. Dare told me to forget making stew; he'd be all morning and then some. I had no intention of sitting alone in that little room all day, so I went downstairs, figuring I could have the run of the house with Dare gone. But I couldn't stand it. I couldn't stay in that house doing nothing for another day. I knew you'd sneaked out to where we watched the night we came to town, so I headed that way and set out tracking you."

"I was careful not to leave a trail." Luke had covered miles this morning on the rugged, rocky soil covered with clumps of low-growing grass. It was a hard place to pick up a footprint.

She shrugged one cute little shoulder. "I managed to find it. And you didn't go fast."

Luke had stayed to rocky or wooded areas and rarely stepped onto a path bigger'n what a white-tailed deer might follow. "I can't believe you tracked me."

Rosie glared. "I'm here, aren't I? You think I just happened upon you? And I would have stayed hidden all day if those men hadn't distracted me. I was busy watching them while I eased closer. I didn't see that stick."

That reignited his annoyance, but he put that aside for now because honestly he was impressed. "Where'd you learn to track like that?"

"I learned for a couple of reasons. I was a hand at fetching food for my family when I was young. I was the only child, so Pa let me tag around after him more than he might have if he'd had a son." Her face relaxed into a smile that made her eyes flash with pleasure as she talked of her father. "We hunted together a lot, and he said often enough I could slip up on a sleeping deer and steal its antlers and never wake it up."

"You said a couple of reasons. What's the other?"

Her smile vanished. He'd seen this level of tension in her only once before: when Dare opened that storeroom door in his office and Rosie jerked awake and cried out the name Virgil.

"When I was at the Reinhardts', Virgil was always pestering me. Even when I was far too young, he was . . . was giving me . . . attention. I didn't like it ever, and as I grew up I learned to hate it. In the last year or two I learned to fear it. I did a lot of outside chores, and he'd try and catch me alone. I learned to listen for him coming and run for the woods. There were heavy woodlands around our property, so if I was quick and quiet, I could stay out of his way. I got very good at sneaking around. I'd listen for Pa Reinhardt to come near. I'd get to his side and Virgil wouldn't bother me anymore."

"Then the other night when you were sleeping"—Luke almost said *sleeping in my arms*, but he didn't think it was wise to mention that now—"and Dare woke you up, were you dreaming of being in the woods?"

"No, Virgil wasn't above trying to get into my bedroom

at night. After the first time it happened, I jammed a chair up against the doorknob and slept with a knife."

"Didn't your ma notice?"

"I was always last to bed and first to rise—not counting Virgil's nighttime wanderings."

"Why?"

"Why what?"

"Why would a child be last to bed and first to rise?"

Rosie frowned and crossed her arms. She glared at the ground as if the dirt and rocks annoyed her. And maybe they did. She liked things tidy and heaven knows this canyon was a mess. He was trying to figure out how to goad an answer out of her when she said, "Ma and Pa Reinhardt never quit reminding me I was living off their charity. They insisted I work to pay my way, and I worked hard. And it seemed like the harder I worked, the less they did, until toward the end I was doing everything."

"Everything, really?"

Rosie nodded. "Way too close to everything. The daily chores, inside and out. All the cooking. I planted in the spring. I hunted in the summer. I harvested in the fall. I cared for the stock all through the winter. And I did it all with the Reinhardts slapping at me and calling me lazy. And now that I've finally grown in a brain, I'm more than sure they stole my pa's land. They didn't farm it; I'd have noticed because they'd have probably made me do the work there, too. I suspect they sold it, claiming they were acting as my guardians, then kept the money for themselves, all while working me like a slave."

"So is that why you're forever cleaning? You got in the habit?"

"No, I'm forever cleaning because your friend's house

is a pigsty. He shouldn't be allowed to practice medicine in that place. He should—"

"Get your hands where I can see 'em." The sudden hard voice, combined with a pistol being cocked, shut Rosie up. Luke cursed himself for being distracted by the woman as he slowly raised his hands and turned to look death right in the face.

CHAPTER 9

Dare looked death right in the face. He lifted his hands from Glynna's body, keeping them where Greer could see.

Glynna moaned with pain from Dare's treatment of her shoulder, but Dare didn't let it distract him from Greer. "You really want me to leave your wife, even though she's unconscious? She could be dying."

This wasn't a man making idle threats. He held that gun as if it would give him great pleasure to pull the trigger, almost like he was looking for an excuse to kill someone. The killing rage in Greer's eyes was irrational. Dare remembered what he'd heard about Greer's temper. How when he was in a rage, he was a madman. How could Greer find his wife on the floor like this and order the doctor out? An ugly suspicion reared its head.

Had Mrs. Greer fallen down the steps or had she been pushed? Greer wouldn't be surprised if he'd already known his wife was lying there. Dare thought of his other visit to see Glynna. Maybe this wasn't the first time.

"No man touches my wife but me." Greer pulled back the hammer on his Colt.

"Flint! No!" Glynna threw up her hands to cover her face. When she moved her injured arm, she cried out in pain and clutched her right shoulder with her left hand. "I'm sorry! Flint, please stop!"

Dare looked at Glynna, and the terror in her voice was impossible to ignore. And every condemning word she said reduced Dare's chances of walking out of there alive. Especially now that Dare knew he needed to take Glynna and her children with him. Greer would never let that happen.

Glynna's cry of pain drew Greer's attention, too. But rather than acting worried, Greer's lips twisted in annoyance, like his wife caused him one problem after another. But the gun finally lowered and went back in Greer's holster with a smooth motion that told its own story of Greer's deadly skill with a gun.

"Do I go," Dare asked, doing his best to keep the fury out of his voice, "or do I wrap the ribs she broke . . . falling down the stairs?" Dare wasn't sure if Glynna had broken ribs, but Greer didn't know that.

Glynna's cries of fear descended into sobs that wracked her battered body. There would come a time to make Greer pay for this, and every other crime he'd committed. Dare was mighty tempted to make today that day. He didn't have his gun. His Winchester was out on his saddle, but that might as well be a thousand miles away. And what if he could get it? Or get Greer's gun from him and kill him? To shoot a man with children looking on—it seemed like the kind of thing a man would have to answer for at the pearly gates. But leaving a woman in this man's clutches would be its own ugly sin.

God, give me wisdom to handle this.

Jonas was the one with the wisdom amongst the Regulators. Dare wondered what Jonas would do right at this moment. Pray, which Dare had already done. But what else? No still, small voice whispered any suggestions.

"Help! I hurt. Help me . . ." Glynna's crying distracted Dare. He was there to heal, not kill. And maybe that was God's answer. The fury in his heart wasn't what he should heed. He needed to care for Glynna.

Dare studied the deep scrape on her chin and glanced over to see a heavy ring on Greer's right hand. The hand that even now was clenched into a fist.

Had Greer really knocked her down the stairs, or had he done all this damage with his bare fists?

"You kids get upstairs." Greer switched his attention to his children. No, not his children if Mrs. Greer had only married him in the last year. "You're too lazy to work, then you're not gonna eat. Now git! And don't let me see your faces until tomorrow!"

It was still midmorning. Did that mean the children would go without food all day? Did Greer hit them, too? If the young'uns weren't Greer's, he might be even more apt to hurt them.

The belligerent look on the boy's face hardened into hate. This boy knew exactly what Greer had done, and he wanted to protect his ma. Dare had a sick feeling that the day was coming when the boy would either kill Flint Greer or become just like him. Or both.

"Go." Dare realized he'd never learned the kid's name. "I'll take care of your ma."

With a long, heartrending look at his mother, the boy turned, caught his little sister's wrist, and dragged her up the stairs. Long, broad steps with a sturdy railing—not that easy to fall down.

A door slammed upstairs, and Dare turned back to

Greer. "What'll it be, Flint?" Dare did his best to sound professional. Glynna needed him. She moaned and clutched her shoulder, still semiconscious. "She needs her shoulder in a sling. Her ribs have to be wrapped."

Dare needed to come up with something that Greer couldn't do himself.

"Anytime someone is knocked unconscious, they most likely have a concussion." Dare pictured Flint's heavy fists striking the delicate woman, wrenching her shoulder out of its socket.

Dare had to look down or Greer would see death. Dare hadn't been around women much. His ma of course, but they'd lived a long way out. It was almost a surprise just how powerful were the instincts in Dare's heart and mind and soul to protect a woman. To stand between her and danger. Right now it was taking every ounce of his self-control to not lunge at Greer and rip out his throat. And since Greer was standing about five feet away with a gun, that meant Dare would die.

Which wouldn't help this woman out at all.

But Dare thought of Luke and the trouble Luke was bringing, and Dare relished settling justice on this vicious bully.

"Sometimes there's bleeding in the brain and there needs to be treatment for the patient to wake all the way up."

"I been knocked cold before—more'n once. I came out of it without a doctor."

"Yes, but you're not a delicate woman. Things are different for women." Not true. Leastways not from what Dare had learned in the medical books he'd gotten hold of. Men and women, in this case, were the same. And since he'd had little experience with women patients, mostly just the madwoman, Lana Bullard, Dare didn't really know what he was talking about. But then neither did Greer.

What Dare did know was, he'd do anything to stay there and take care of Glynna Greer, and then he was going to find a way to get her and her children out.

"I need to make sure her vision isn't blurred. She could be nauseated and dizzy for days."

A look crossed Greer's face that made Dare wonder if the polecat hadn't had some of these symptoms when he had his concussion.

"And we need to keep her awake." Dare looked down and wondered how to keep a woman awake who was already asleep. "Once she regains consciousness, she can't be allowed to sleep for"—Dare took a chance, making up an excuse for him to stay a long while—"twenty-four hours."

Then he had a better idea. "It would be best if I took her to my office so I could observe her closely and make sure she's responding well."

And then he just made the next part up. "She could lapse into a coma."

"A coma? What's that?" Greer pulled off his hat and tossed it at a hook on the wall. He didn't come close to getting the hat to hang up. When Greer turned back, at that second, he resembled an ape Dare had seen in a picture book. Greer had hair on his head, his face, his neck.

The backs of his hands were so thick with black hair it looked like a pelt. He had shaggy brows that almost drooped over his eyes. And those eyes—they were so wild they seemed to jump around in his head.

His nose was too flat. It looked like it had been broken so often it barely had a shape anymore. Maybe Greer had been a fighter earlier in life. His forehead was so prominent the ape comparison was almost too close. Dare wondered what Glynna Greer had thought when she'd stepped off a stagecoach and seen Greer for the first time. Had she realized instantly that she'd made a terrible bargain? But Dare had heard Greer used to be tidy, clean-shaven and well dressed. Maybe this was what a man looked like who'd spent a year descending into brutality.

"A coma is a deep unnatural sleep. They can't be awakened from it. It's different than being unconscious. But it can come later, after a blow to the head, such as your wife has received."

From you, you filthy sidewinder.

"Can I tend her while we talk, Greer? She needs treatment, and the more I can do while she's unaware the better. She'll be in terrible pain when she comes around."

Flint clenched his fist and looked from Dare to Glynna for too long. Then he slashed his hand in the air, the bulky ring glinting in the light. "Do whatever you want with the lousy trollop. Should've never gotten mixed up with a woman. Nothing but a nuisance since she set foot in my door. I should've just let her keep going the first time she ran off."

It made Dare sick to think of Greer catching her and dragging her home.

"But she's mine. I got her, paid what was owed, and she belongs to me. Ain't nuthin' gonna change that."

Dare saw the look on Greer's beast-like face. The man enjoyed having someone small and defenseless at his mercy. He wasn't letting her go. "Can I take her into my office in Broken Wheel? I should get back so I can see my other patients."

"She doesn't leave my land." Greer's snarled words were

more animal than man. "I've got a guard posted, so don't try and leave with her, not if you want to live."

Greer grabbed his hat off the floor and stormed out of the house. He slammed the door behind him so hard the glass in the nearest window rattled.

The door's loud crack seemed to finally reach deep enough into Glynna Greer's battered mind that it woke her. Golden eyes flickered open, the rarest color he'd ever seen.

"You've got to get out of here." Her voice cracked. She swallowed hard. "Get out before he comes."

Dare didn't know how to tell her it was too late.

"Keep turning, but make it mighty slow. If you're thinkin' of trying to get a shot off, make sure you know my first bullet goes into her."

Carefully, his hands in plain sight, Luke turned to face Dodger, his father's old friend. When he faced Dodger fully, the old-timer's eyes narrowed. "Luciano?"

"Reckon it's me, Dodger."

"You've come home at last."

"You gonna use that gun?" Luke nodded at Dodger's weapon, still aimed dead center at Luke's chest. For all Dodger's threatening words about shooting Rosie, this was a man with a code that didn't stretch to hurting a woman.

"Nope." Dodger holstered his gun, then rounded the boulder where Luke had stood watching him. When he got close, a smiled stretched on his face and he grabbed Luke's shoulders. "I've missed you, boy. It's good to see you."

Luke was still leery of trusting him. But he needed to start somewhere and Dodger saying "home at last" sounded hopeful. "I've come to start trouble, old-timer. I've got papers to prove I own my ranch, not Greer. I mean to have him hanged for Pa's murder."

"Murder? You think Greer killed your pa?"

Luke lifted a shoulder in a casual shrug that didn't begin to reflect his true feelings on the subject. "I know I own this ranch. Pa sent me the deed before he died, naming me the owner. Pa said there was trouble coming at him and giving me that deed protected the S Bar S. Greer ain't tellin' the truth about Pa selling out to him. That makes my pa's land stolen, and Pa being dead ended any dispute about the sale. That may not be a murder charge that will hold up in a court of law, but in my eyes, Greer is guilty as sin."

Dodger's faded blue eyes sparked. "I never knew, Luciano. I'd have *never* hired on with Greer if I had. I've always hoped that if I stayed around the Greer place, I'd see you or your sister again. I was mighty fond of both of you when you was young'uns. Where's Callie?"

"Callie's married to a good man. She's living on his ranch in Colorado and has a baby and another one coming. Pa wrote when he sent me the deed. The letter was a while catching me. He said Callie'd married some Yank soldier who'd abandoned her, left her with a baby on the way. All Pa knew was the man's name and that he was from Rawhide, Colorado. I rode out to Colorado to make the man do right by my sister and found Callie there. She'd hunted him down on her own."

Without her worthless brother's help. "Her husband, Seth Kincaid, seemed like a wild man, but a hard worker and right fond of Callie. She's happy."

"Good to know. I've spent time wondering if I should've gone tracking her. But I wasn't on the ranch when she left.

I came in and found you all gone, your pa dead. I've surely wondered what became of you, but I've never heard even a whisper about Greer not owning the ranch. I heard you took off and your pa sold out before he died."

"I've got a judge who's seen my deed. Greer doesn't own this land. Any deed he's got is forged. It stands to reason he had a hand in Pa's killing."

"Greer's a hard man, but there are a lot of hard men out West. I reckon I'm one myself. But there's no denying he's made a lot of savvy land buys. Men who looked dug-in just up and sold to him. But then this is rugged land—I could believe a rancher would sell out and leave the country. Maybe men ran or they died. Tell me what you need from an old friend to find justice for your pa, Luke."

Justice. The word didn't quite suit Luke. It was too civilized. When he pictured Greer, he saw the man dying in a blaze of gunfire. Luke's gun. It gave him so much pleasure to imagine it, it had to be a sin.

"And then," Dodger said, nodding at a spot behind Luke, "introduce me to your lady friend."

Once he'd recognized Dodger and been sure he wasn't going to open fire, Luke had forgotten Rosie was even there.

He turned to introduce Dodger, and she arched one pretty red brow at him and said, "Luciano?"

"I'll explain later." He hadn't been called that for years. "Dodger, call me Luke."

❦

As soon as the door closed behind Greer, the one upstairs opened. The children came rushing down.

"What can we do to help?" The boy glanced nervously

at the door. Greer coming back was a frightening prospect for all of them, Dare included.

"Are all the bedrooms upstairs?"

"No, there's one down here that Ma sleeps in."

Glynna Greer didn't sleep with her husband. Dare got cold satisfaction from knowing that.

Dare slid his hands carefully under Glynna and lifted. Glynna's lips clenched tight but a small moan of pain still escaped.

"Janny," the boy said, "you go get bread and some apples and get it up into the bedroom. Next time we won't starve if we have to stay locked up a few days."

"I'll hide them so he can't never find 'em." The little towheaded girl with golden eyes like her ma dashed for the kitchen.

"You need to leave before Flint comes back." Glynna rested her left hand on Dare's chest, and he felt it burn through his shirt.

Dare exchanged a look with the boy, then stood, holding Glynna close to keep from jarring her shoulder. "Let's go."

The boy headed in the same direction his sister had gone, rushing alongside the stairway. They walked past a door to the kitchen on the right, where the girl was frantically gathering food. The boy then turned left toward an open door, Glynna's bedroom.

Dare saw with one glance that the woman was sleeping in there alone. The room contained only women's things. Her clothes hung on pegs. Her brushes and bottles were on a chest beside the bed. Not a mark of a man anywhere. Glynna had put what space she could between her and her husband. But it hadn't been enough. All he had to do was look at her to know that.

"I need more rags. If you don't have big ones, bring me a sheet I can tear up."

"No, I'll be fine. Go back to town." Glynna's hand clenched his shirt front. To Dare, it looked like she was holding on to him. Her words and her actions didn't match at all. Her eyes closed and her head rested more fully against him.

The boy wheeled to leave, but then paused beside his mother. "Will she be all right?"

Dare knew better than to promise anyone anything. But he couldn't stand the look in the boy's eyes. "Yes. What's your name?"

"It's Paul. Named for my pa and grandpa."

"How'd you end up out here, so far from family?"

"They died. There was no one left and no money, and trouble from Pa and the war that . . . that made us need to move. Ma answered an ad and we all thought it was going to be the saving of us." A one-shouldered shrug seemed to say it didn't matter, that it wasn't important. But Dare knew it was.

"I'm going to take care of your ma's injuries. Then I'm going to get her out of here. I may not be able to take her—take all of you—today. But I'll find a way. You're not staying here with Greer. Will he hit her again?"

"Not for a while. He seems to work out his need to hurt her, and then he's calmer for a time. She might not make a mistake that angers him for a while neither. She tries so hard to not set him off, but no one can be perfect enough to keep from upsetting a rabid dog."

"Unless me being here sets him off." Dare wanted his gun. He wanted his friends at his side. He wanted the whole Union Army to come down like raining brimstone on Flint Greer. He now knew just how Luke felt.

"Thanks, Paul. We'll figure it out. I'll not forget, and if Greer stops me, I'm a man with friends. We'll get you out of here and get you somewhere safe. Now get those rags and get back here."

The boy had gleaming hope in his eyes as he jerked his chin and rushed out of the room

Dare laid Glynna down and her eyes fluttered open. "I heard what you said to my son. You shouldn't have."

"Shouldn't have what?" Dare needed to get on with his doctoring, yet he couldn't stop looking at those beautiful tear-stained eyes.

"Shouldn't have promised him we can get away. We can't. I've tried."

"Greer said you'd run off before."

"I snuck away and got the children to town after he hit me the second time, not long after we got here. I went to the sheriff. He held me there until Greer came. I screamed for help so the whole town could hear and no one would help me. I had a bruised-up face and I told them he'd hurt me. They all just watched as Greer dragged me onto his horse and rode out of town. He had men with him that brought the children."

"Does he hit the children, too?"

"No, not yet. But that's only because I stand between them. I find I have a gift for drawing his rage to me. Paul is ready to kill him. My boy is so full of hate it's going to destroy him. Janet barely speaks. I was such a fool. I thought a rancher would be an honorable man. Flint wrote letters full of promises. I think now someone wrote them for him. He can barely sign his name."

"Why didn't you tell me this when I was out here before?" Dare began unbuttoning her dress; it was blue calico sprinkled with white flowers.

She didn't protest, which told Dare just how dazed she still was. If her head had been clear, she might insist this was caused by another fall.

Sounding so hopeless Dare felt the ache of it in his bones, she said, "I was terrified you'd tell Greer every word I said, and everyone in town has to have heard about me that day—the screaming, the sheriff holding me for Flint. Why would I believe you didn't already know? Why would I believe you'd help me?"

"All you need to know is I will." Dare spoke it with all the fierce passion of a vow before God. He meant it just like that. "Whether you believe me or not doesn't matter because I *will* get you out of here. You can believe it when it happens."

He slipped her dress over her left arm, then very carefully eased it down her right arm. A few quickly suppressed moans of pain escaped her pursed lips.

Paul came in with the rags just as Dare got the dress pulled down. He saw his ma at the same time Dare did. The bruises on her arms, one in the perfect shape of a man's crushing hand.

A wild growl came from the boy as he set the rags down on the bedside chest and studied his battered mother.

"Go on, son," Dare said quietly. "Get in your room before Greer comes back and punishes you or Janet for not minding him."

Rather than obey or object, Paul said, "There're men posted at the front and back doors. That low-down sidewinder's not going to take a chance that you'll leave with her."

Dare had expected nothing less. "I'll have to go today, without you. But I'll be back."

The boy's eyes were riveted on his mother, who closed her eyes as if she was ashamed of being too weak to stop her child from seeing the bruises.

"Paul!" Dare drew the youngster's attention. "You have my word."

It was sickening to see such fear in a child's eyes. The boy had lived with hopelessness for too long to risk believing there was a way out. Dare looked at Glynna and her eyes flickered open. Hers were gold and Paul's were blue, but the defeat in them matched.

"I swear it on my own life. I'll come back. I'll get you away from Greer."

Glynna's eyes fell shut.

Paul stormed out of the room.

Dare reached for the rags and, with rage made worse by his impotence, tore the rags in strips, trying to take his frustration out on a helpless piece of cloth when he wanted to tear a strip off Flint Greer.

No, that wasn't quite true. He wanted to rip Flint's head off.

CHAPTER 10

Ruthy watched the town lights die. Luke was beside her in the trees behind Dare's house. Mostly watchful, but he'd throw her an occasional irritated glance. Which she noticed because she was glancing at him at the same time. With the same irritation.

"Why are you still so upset? I never came close to giving us away."

"I caught you, didn't I? You gave yourself away that once. What if I'd been Flint Greer or Simon Bullard?"

Ruthy clenched her jaw. "I wouldn't have gone up close to them. I do have some sense, Luciano."

"Do *not* call me that."

"It's an old nickname? Is that it?"

Crickets chirped.

A coyote howled at the rising moon.

For some reason, Luke's annoyance with that name eased her tension. She fought a smile.

"It's my name, but it's not."

She decided to wait a little longer.

He cracked. "I'm Italian, but my parents changed their names to sound more American. They wanted to belong more fully in this country. Leastways that's the story they told me. I think their names just took too long to spell."

"So your parents gave you an Italian name and a real name?"

"Italian names are real."

Ruthy sniffed just to torment him.

"My parents were Perlita and Salvatorio Pietra. They were both born in Italy and were married before they came here. Ma called herself Pearl and Pa went by Sal. And in Italian the word *pietra* means stone. So they changed their last name to Stone. They gave my sister and me Italian names, but we never went by them. We were always Luke and Callie. Somehow Dodger found out our real names and sort of teased us by calling us that. Luciano and Calandra. I don't mind it so much, but don't you start."

"But I think Luciano is a nice name." She didn't like it as well as Luke, but where was the fun in admitting that?

"Quiet." The light in the last house near Dare's blinked out, and Luke rose slowly from where they crouched in the juniper and mesquite surrounding Broken Wheel. "Let's get inside. Dare's probably decided you're dead."

"I told you I left a note." She decided to save Luciano for some time when he was really annoying her. Of course, he was really annoying her right now. "He went out before the sun was up so I had no way to tell him when I decided to leave. And there aren't any lights on in his house and we've seen no sign of patients coming and going. Dare is probably out on a doctoring case and has better things to worry about than where I got to."

"I believe that, because if he'd been there, he'd've stopped you from leaving, locked you in your room, and not let you do such a harebrained thing."

"You brought me along to fight a land war, Luke Stone. Now you're acting like I'm an idiot for taking a small risk." As she spoke she felt the anger grow. "I don't think you can pretend the danger I might face is anyone's doing but yours."

Turning from his watchful study of the town, Luke looked at her, let out a heavy sigh, and lowered his head. "I know I've brought you to a bad situation, Rosie. I know and I'm sorry. I just didn't know what else to do. I couldn't leave you and I didn't have the days and days it would've taken to get you to another town."

"I've wanted to be free of the Reinhardts for so long." Ruthy swung her arms wide and almost hit him. "I don't mind turning my hand to a chore and seeing it well done. But I hated doing it for them, being little more than a slave. I've hoped and prayed to be free to pour the strength of my back and the skills in my hands and the knowledge in my brain to building something for myself."

"And instead you've been forced to turn aside. You've been dragged into a fight that's not yours. I know you're hard-pressed to sit idle, but if we are careful, we can keep you out of this fight completely. You can lay low while my friends and I clean up this mess. When it's safe, I'll get you to a bigger town and find you a place to live and a job."

A pang hit hard as she listened to Luke. "Stay out of your way now and you'll get rid of me for good later, is that it?" Which was wise and probably what she wanted. The fact that it hurt her feelings was ridiculous.

"I wouldn't put it that way. I just wish you didn't have to get mixed up in my troubles."

"Well, you couldn't have left me floating. And there's no town big enough for me to hope to find work for days in any direction."

127

Luke shrugged. "But you don't have to add more risk to your life by taking such dangerous chances."

Ruthy felt twisted up inside and wanted to argue with Luke. She wasn't sure about what exactly; she only knew she was upset and she didn't see any reason to keep it to herself.

Before she could find a new way to nag him for something that was most likely her own fault, Luke said, "Let's go," and dashed across the open space.

Ruthy sprinted to keep up. They hurried past the small corral and the building where Dare stabled his horse. Normally the horse would be outside grazing.

Luke reached Dare's back door and turned the knob. "It's locked? What's going on?"

"It was locked when I left this morning and I didn't want to leave it unlocked. I climbed out right here." Ruthy pointed to a window that led into Dare's office.

Luke quickly raised the window so that Ruthy could scramble through. Then she held it for Luke. She was starting to slide it silently shut after Luke just as someone came rushing up. Vince.

She jumped back and squeaked in surprise. She saw Luke draw his gun and whirl toward the window just as Vince lifted it open again.

Luke holstered the gun. Another man Ruthy didn't recognize climbed in behind Vince.

"What's going on?" Luke asked. "Where's Dare?"

"We saw you run in; we've been watching for you." Vince moved into the room to make way for the second man. "Leave the lanterns off."

"Big John, good to see you." Luke slapped the newcomer on the back. In the dimly lit room, Ruthy could barely make him out. He was unusually tall and lean. His hat shaded his face so she saw no details. He had a star pinned on his chest that reflected the bit of moonlight from the window.

"Dare's been out at the Greer ranch all day," Vince said.

"The Stone ranch." Luke scowled. "Try to remember that, Vince. What's he doing out there?"

"I only know he headed out and never came back." Vince shook his head and fell silent for a few moments. Then he said, "Big John Conroy, this is Ruthy MacNeil. Shall we sit down and talk about whether we now have to go rescue Dare? The kitchen has enough chairs." Vince, with a grand gesture, swept his hand toward the kitchen. "After you, Miss Ruthy."

"Thank you, sir." Ruthy hurried toward the kitchen and went straight for the stove. She stirred the embers, added kindling, and set to work making coffee.

Luke dropped into a chair at the table. Big John sat across from him. Vince stood sentry at the kitchen door.

She'd barely gotten the grounds measured and the coffee started to brewing when a horse came riding up. They all tensed as it went past the front door. Vince vanished from where he'd been leaning and was back in seconds. "It's Dare. He's putting his horse in the stable."

A whoosh of breath told Ruthy that both Luke and his friends had been imagining something bad. They were probably right. Whatever had happened, it wasn't bad enough to keep Dare from finally getting home.

All three men left the kitchen.

The coffeepot hissed. Ruthy hadn't seen Luke eat anything but jerky all day. Dare might not have had a regular meal, either. The other two, though there was no reason they should be hungry, were men after all. Men would usually eat.

So Ruthy got to work. Clanking a skillet onto the iron stovetop, she found a side of bacon and began slicing it. She dropped the first few slices in the pan, and soon they were popping and sizzling. The warm, savory smell made her stomach growl as she loaded the pan with pork. It wasn't only the men who hadn't eaten much today.

She heard voices in the hall, Dare's among them. It took everything in her to not give in to curiosity and leave the stove. But there was work to be done.

The bacon crackled nicely. She pulled another skillet out, poured grease off the bacon, and began slicing crisp potatoes into the heating oil. She was eager to know what was going on, but she couldn't leave the quickly cooking food. In a moment of inspiration she plucked a towel off a hook and waved it over the frying food, sending the aroma toward the men. Less than a minute later, they wandered into the kitchen.

Ruthy concealed a smile. The smell of food was a more effective lure to most men than a woman politely asking, or even nagging.

"I tell you Greer beat her half to death." Dare's words stilled Ruthy's slicing and erased the pleasure she'd taken in drawing the men to her.

"Beat who?" Ruthy asked. Not counting herself, there were only two women around—Lana Bullard and Glynna Greer.

"His wife, Glynna." Dare's words were sharp enough to bite someone's head off. "I got called out there this morning and found her unconscious. I've been there all day tending her. I should never have left her." Dare slugged a fist into the wall with a harsh thud. "But I pushed my luck way past reason to stay as long as I did. Greer was in and out all day, raging at me to leave. He was ready to shoot me to get rid of me, and he threatened it more than once. He had guards on both doors. I'd have died trying to take her, and I'd have risked it if I'd thought there was any chance of getting away. But Greer was on edge like no man I'd ever seen. He'd have shot me, or ordered someone to do it. Then she'd end up still trapped with him once I was dead." The venom in Dare's voice was frightening. "Besides, I want to go back when I have my Colt."

Greer battered his wife? Ruthy felt plenty of venom of her own.

"We're going out there tomorrow and we're getting her and her children out." Dare lit a lantern. Ruthy noticed the kitchen window had its shutters closed. Dare must have done that yesterday.

"Will he hurt her or the children before morning?" Big John's voice was deep and smooth. He wasn't happy about a woman in danger, but he was thinking, and calm. A lawman must see terrible things and learn to keep his head.

There was a long, seething silence coming from Dare. Ruthy turned back to the food just to keep her hands busy.

Finally Dare said, as if he hated to admit it, "The boy told me Greer doesn't do it too often. We probably have some time. But she's so scared." Dare stopped pacing and shoved both hands deep into his shaggy blond hair. "He hurt her bad. And those kids are all torn up inside. We can't leave them out there."

"Then we need to set things in motion as soon as possible," Big John said. "I've got a prisoner transport paper I'm going to use to get Sheriff Porter out of town. Broken

Wheel's sheriff has a reputation for greed. There's money enough in moving this varmint between Fort Worth and Memphis, Tennessee, where he's wanted for murder. The pay's good. Porter'll do it."

"Good riddance to that varmint. Glynna told me she ran away from Greer once, and when she got to town, Porter held her until Greer came and hauled her back home."

Looking grim, Big John said, "I found wanted posters on Bullard. I'll have to take him in myself. I need four days to get Bullard hauled to a jail that's run by a man I trust, get him locked up, then get back here. And I want you to wait for me. I want the law involved in this."

"I don't know if we can wait." Dare spoke through a clenched jaw.

"What about Greer's men, Luke?" Vince was back at his place by the door. "Did you make any headway there?"

"Yep. I talked with one old-timer, name's Dodger, who was there before my pa died."

"He stayed on after Greer killed your pa, and you trust him?" Dare sounded like he was looking for an excuse to punch somebody.

"He was gone from the ranch while all the trouble happened. When he came back, he believed Greer's story about buying the ranch. But Greer has always been a hard man to work for. Dodger's ready to believe the worst. He said others working for Greer aren't happy. The main trouble is Greer's wife. Dodger knows she got hurt once, but it was blamed on a fall. Not everyone believed it and that was before today. She almost always stays in the house, but there's been talk."

"What kind of coyote works for a man who abuses his wife?" Vince pounded the side of the door with a closed fist.

Dare paced, dodging around Ruthy at the stove. Even his normal boundless energy was just a ghost of what was driving him today. "They know she's being mistreated and they just put up with it?"

"Dodger said a man challenged Greer about it when he saw a bruise on Mrs. Greer's jaw. Trouble was, it was one of Greer's hired guns who issued the challenge; he wasn't a well-liked man. At the time they believed Greer's story about a fall. The man vanished. No one's seen him again, and no one's missed him."

"Dead?" Big John asked.

"They can't prove it. Dodger and most of the regular cowpokes were out riding the range. The men in close when Greer got challenged aren't talking. Bullard was there when it happened and he got the drop on the man who faced Greer and put a stop to the fight. Then Bullard wasn't seen for a while. He's fast and deadly as a rattlesnake and not afraid of killing."

"That's the honest truth," Big John said. "I've got wanted posters on him from Louisiana, Arkansas, and the Indian Territory. He's wanted for murder. I'd say he picked this lonely spot and stayed here because he knew he'd be arrested if he was seen by any honest lawman. I won't have any trouble keeping him locked up in any town with an honest sheriff. And now Bullard's backed Greer against a man who wanted to put a stop to Greer abusing his wife. There ain't many men who will stay quiet and watch a woman be hurt. Even the lowest of the low-down varmints draw the line at hurting a woman."

"Since the gunman challenged Greer, Glynna only steps outside to use the privy, and she never speaks to anyone," Luke said. "Dodger said he couldn't believe Greer would stoop so low as to hurt his wife. But Greer's a tyrant to work for and some of the hands have already drifted. More are inclined in that direction."

"A cowpoke from the Greer place has come for me twice to go and treat her." Dare began pacing faster. "The first time I believed her when she said she fell. I should have known better, but she told me herself. I thought she was clumsy and rude. Instead she was beaten and terrified into silence."

The loathing in Dare's voice sounded like he'd decided to batter himself.

"Dodger knows we're bringing trouble." Luke looked between all his friends. "I told him about the deed and how the ranch was stolen and my pa killed. Dodger said he's going to whisper in a few ears and he thinks a good chunk of Greer's hands will drift. A lot of men are ready for an excuse to ride out. There may be a few that will even switch sides and back us. Dodger couldn't have known about whatever happened today. He'd have mentioned it. So Greer is keeping it quiet."

Luke paused long enough it drew Ruthy's attention, and she saw guilt etched on Luke's face. "Can we wait until we can take Bullard out of the fight, get the sheriff out of town, and Big John can get back? Will she be safe?"

Dare didn't answer for a long time.

"If we had a few more days," Luke went on, "it might make the difference between saving her and just getting us all killed. I don't want you all to pay with your lives for helping me. I'd go in tonight, right now, the four of us against them all, if I thought he was going to touch her again. No matter whether it meant I got the ranch back or not. I'd rather die trying than sit here while she's being hurt."

"There's no way we can get through that canyon un-noticed," Dare said.

"I think I can get past those sentries. There's a game trail I know that might work. I'll need to scout it out to be sure, but I'm willing to risk using it tonight."

"Food's ready. Is everyone eating?" Ruthy pulled a stack of plates off a shelf.

The men, even agitated as they were, all said yes with such enthusiasm it was as if they hadn't eaten in days.

Or maybe they were building up their strength to fight a private war.

She divided a small mountain of bacon and fried potatoes between them, taking a smaller portion for herself, but still enough. She needed to keep her own strength up, because she was going to be part of this.

Dare joined Luke and Big John at the table. Vince took his plate and went back to the door.

After she poured them each a cup of coffee, she decided to make her intentions known. Talking to Luke before they'd come into Dare's place tonight, she'd been upset at being pulled into the middle of a gunfight. No more.

Now she knew exactly what she wanted. Her goal was as clear as the Texas sky and as straight as a Comanche arrow. She sat beside Luke at the table straight across from Dare, with Vince standing behind Dare at the door and Big John sitting across from Luke. She waited until their mouths were full, which took no time at all.

"I'm going to be right in the middle of this fight or I'll know the reason why."

Dare choked on a chunk of potato. Vince spit coffee onto the floor. Big John's Texas Ranger badge flickered and flashed until it matched the fire in his eyes.

Luke slammed down his fork with a sharp clatter. "I'll give you a reason why—"

"I'm good with a rifle." She cut him off. "If there were plenty of us and it was a fair fight, I'd stay out. But even if you wait for John, and a lot of Greer's cowhands ride away, you're still outnumbered and Greer's got a well-defended home. It'll be hard to flush him out. I won't hide while you all risk your lives."

"It's no place for a woman." Dare tapped his fork impatiently on his plate. Even sitting the man could not be still.

"I've been slapped too many times in my life to let another woman endure that, not if I can stop it. And I was harassed too often by that stinking pig Virgil to sit safely at home while a woman puts up with worse than happened to me."

"Miss," Big John Conroy said, sounding so wise and reasonable it was all Ruthy could do not to dump his cup of coffee over his head, "this is best left to—"

"I'm going to help. You can leave me here, locked up, unarmed, but I'll get out. I'll arm myself. I'll find the fight. I'm good with a gun. I'm good in the woods. I can be of use to you. Tell them, Luke."

Luke acted as if she were pouring hot coals down his throat when she asked him to side with her. "Tell 'em what? That this is a plan hatched by a half-wit?"

"Tell these men how I handled myself in those woods." She turned to meet his eyes dead on. "If you won't honestly admit I'm a sight better than you, then I'm saying, out loud, to every man here that you're a liar."

All four men froze at the insult, even Dare. In the West, to call a man a liar was to ask him to meet you at high noon. Land deals were struck on a handshake. Thousands of dollars' worth of cattle changed hands just on a man's word that he'd pay what was owed. A man with the reputation of a liar was ruined. No one would do business with him. He had to leave the state and find a new home and hope his reputation didn't follow him.

Ruthy knew that very well.

One by one, the men at the table turned to Luke.

"That true, kid?" Vince asked. "She's better'n you? Cuz you're all mighty good."

"Will you admit it, Luke? It doesn't matter if you do or not. I'm in this fight to stay."

"She's good. No denying it." He glared at her, hornet mad to admit the truth. "I never saw her with a gun, but just like I ain't a man to lie, neither is she a woman to do such. I reckon if she says she can hold her own with a fire iron, it's the truth."

So, Luke wasn't a liar. He was a stubborn, bad-tempered mule hungry for revenge.

But not a liar.

Ruthy's heart pounded as she waited for the men to decide whether to include her in their planning.

"Your family really hit you?" Luke asked quietly. The whole room fell silent.

"They weren't my family. They just took me in when my folks died. But yes."

"And Virgil . . ." Luke said his name in a way that made a chill race up and down Ruthy's spine. "He's the one you had to lock the door against by night and hide from by day?"

"I had no lock, but I had a chair I wedged under the door, and I slept with a butcher knife under my pillow."

"And you say Virgil is dead?" From his tone, Luke

seemed to promise that if Virgil wasn't dead, Luke might want to go have a long, hard talk with him.

"I saw his broken body floating down the flooded river. He's dead."

Luke nodded for far too long. "It seems you know better than any of us what that woman is going through."

"I do. And before God, I will not sit in safety while she needs help. I want you to get your ranch back, Luke. But more than that, I want Flint Greer crushed, and I'd be proud to involve myself in the crushing."

"That's mighty bold talk for a pretty little frontier woman." Vince had humor in his voice, but Ruthy wasn't in the mood for it.

With a sigh, Luke looked between his friends, his eyes settling on Vince. "What do you think?"

This wasn't the first time Ruthy noticed that in a group of strong men, they all seemed to look to Vince.

"I think since she plans to come anyway, we might as well find out where she'll be the most use." Then Vince looked straight at her. "But we're trying to protect a woman in danger already. If we save her but get you hurt, we haven't done one bit of good. Tell me you understand that, Miss Ruthy. Promise me you'll listen to us and take the precautions we ask. We're all tough men who've been to war and back. Tough as you are, you're barely more than a girl. If you won't think to your own safety, then think about the terrible scar it'd leave on our souls to let you be harmed if we fail to protect you."

Ruthy gave a firm nod of agreement. "I'll let you make it safe for me. You have my word I'll listen to your instructions and follow them." Then she added, "Who knows? I might have a few instructions for the lot of you before I'm done."

Big John frowned, clearly not happy about Ruthy's help, but done arguing. "That's settled then. We wait now until we can take Bullard out of the picture. Then we make our move to get rid of the sheriff. You keep working on the hired men, Luke. Thin the herd. Take your little scout with you so we can learn the extent of her skills in the woods."

"You're talking about days, John." Dare started pacing again. "Glynna Greer might not have days."

"How big a chance is there that Bullard won't show up here in the next couple of days with that loco wife of his?" Luke asked.

"Almost none." Dare's voice was so dry, Ruthy thought she heard a cactus bristle scraping his throat.

"Then when he shows up, we make our move. Do you want us to jump him?" Big John went back to eating.

"That won't be necessary." Dare picked up his fork.

"You'll have your hands pretty full," Luke said, going back to eating with less enthusiasm than before. "You think you can handle him and his screaming woman?"

"Bullard has taken to bringing a bottle along with him to these doctor visits. He drinks while he waits. He left a half-full bottle last time, and I've already got it laced with laudanum. He'll be asleep before he's been here an hour. He'll be groggy before he passes out, and I'll be able to get him out of the office. Then you can get him out of here, John. Hide him somewhere until you get those transport orders to Sheriff Porter and he hits the trail. Then you take Bullard and go. We'll wait as long as we can. But if I get word Mrs. Greer is in danger, we're riding in and taking her out of there, and I don't care how many men I have to face."

John nodded. "He brings whiskey to visit the doctor?"

"Yep." Dare took a long sip of coffee. "You haven't met Lana Bullard. I'm almost ready to make Simon split the bottle with me, and I don't even drink."

There was a long silence and then the men broke into laughter. It almost seemed as if they needed to laugh to break the terrible tension.

But Ruthy couldn't find a laugh anywhere.

CHAPTER 11

It had been nearly a week since he'd met up with Dodger the first time, and for the first time some of Luke's tension eased. "How many men are left?"

Dodger sat down and leaned back against a rock. He could ride past those sentries easy enough. He had to do it every day to check the herd, and afterward he'd wind around a mesa out of their sight and meet Luke and Ruthy. "We're past roundup, so the hands were thinning out anyway. Greer hires on a lot of drifters in the spring, then later they move on. I'd say he's down around ten hands right now. Half of those are hired guns, loafers who take turns standing sentry and do little else. Five of us, along with Greer and Bullard, do all the work—ride Greer's range that goes on for miles. I've been spreading the word about Mrs. Greer's injuries and how she got 'em. I thought the men might just take the fight to Greer himself when I told them everything, but I convinced them to hold off by telling them about Greer stealing land and how we're trying to get him arrested, which would keep him away from Mrs. Greer forever. I expect more men to head out before long. If they don't, they'll side with me if I brace Greer."

Rosie pulled cookies out of the folded cloth she'd

brought along. Luke took one—with plans to have a few more. But as he munched, he wondered why the woman didn't start tidying up the rocky ground. She could *not* relax. She'd baked cookies last night after they'd gotten home. Long past time for her to have been ready to quit for the night. They'd been out on the trail all day every day from before sunrise to after dark.

"And Mrs. Greer is all right?" Rosie asked.

"I've got one of the men assigned to take eggs, milk, and vegetables into the kitchen. She ain't been outside at all for near on to two months, since before the doctor was out the first time. My man got a glimpse of her, though. She was staying out of sight for the last week, but he saw her in the kitchen yesterday. She's healing. He's gotten the little girl to tell how things are going. But Greer's guards keep track of how long a man stays inside. So my man can't learn much. We're all working double shifts because so many of Greer's men are hired guns. The long hours keep us away from the house."

Rosie held the plate of cookies out to Dodger.

He took a handful as he talked. "Greer seems upset about losing the men, and if he gets upset enough, he might take it out on her. We're watching, Miss MacNeil. I promise you we are. I'm prepared to go in there and stop him myself if there's more trouble. The little girl's window faces the bunkhouse. My man gave her a bright piece of blue glass and told her to hang it in the window if there's trouble. We'll come a-runnin'. I'm hoping you're ready to face Greer before we need to do that. If your plan works and he goes, she'll be safe."

"They're married." Luke ate another cookie. "If I can't make an arrest stick, Greer will think his wife should stay with him wherever he moves on to."

"Yep, they're married, and Greer's mighty possessive of his missus. But you're gonna make the arrest stick, unless he runs. If he runs, he's gonna have to leave her behind. And if he stays, he's gonna be locked up for life."

"Either way, she's safe," Rosie said with a grimly satisfied nod.

"I want to show you where the sentries are." Dodger finished his last cookie.

Luke stood and gave Rosie a hand up. "These men are loyal to Greer, so be mighty careful of them, Rosie."

"My name is not Rosie." She narrowed her eyes at him.

"I don't think I can stop calling you that."

"Let's go do some scouting." Dodger led the way.

Luke regretted Dodger's company. He'd've rather spent time alone with Rosie.

❦

"Riker, we got a problem, you and me."

Dare whipped his head around expecting another scene with Lana and Simon Bullard. Instead there was only Simon, leaning against a post in front of the general store.

A chill slid down Dare's back at the look in Bullard's bitter cold eyes and the way his hand flexed right next to his gun. Dare had his holster on and his gun loaded; he'd taken to wearing it all the time since that day at Greer's. But he also had a crate full of supplies in his arms.

"What's this about, Bullard?"

Simon Bullard was a massive man. Over six feet tall, heavy and running fat, but rock-solid fat, and he had fists like hams and a gun that never lost its shine. He was probably fifty years old, but there was no sign that age was slowing him down, or if it was, he made up for a lack of speed by being deadly accurate.

"It's about my boss not wanting anyone sniffing around his woman. He told me to come in here and make sure you understood that." Bullard's eyes shone like blue ice. He had a black hat pulled low on his forehead that shielded his eyes from the sun and helped him make every shot count.

"Let's take a walk." Dare started down the board-walk, and Bullard hesitated. Dare wondered for a second if he wasn't asking for a bullet in the back.

Then Bullard moved and began stalking along beside Dare. "I've been put in a bad place by you," Bullard told him.

Dare kept moving. If Bullard was walking and talking, he wasn't shooting. Dare knew he probably oughta keep his mouth shut. He could pretend like he didn't know what Greer had done to Glynna, but a reckless fury drove him to speak. "Because your boss wants to be able to batter his wife, and he doesn't want any doctor knowing he's done it . . . but you need me to take care of Lana. That is a bad place."

"That's about the size of it."

A man stepped out of Duffy's Tavern a few paces ahead of them. His eyes went straight to Bullard, and he ducked back inside like a scurrying rat.

"You look to be a mighty fearsome man, Simon." Dare was counting heavily on Bullard's wife at the moment. Now that Dare wanted to get Bullard and his wife into his house, the woman hadn't been in all week screaming about the baby.

"I get paid real good to be fearsome, and no one can say I don't earn my money." Bullard pulled his gun.

Dare's heart sank.

Bullard spun the revolver on the pistol, checking the

chambers. "My wife, well, I never should've gotten married. But I can't get her out of my blood. No woman's ever gotten her hooks into me like Lana's done. I wanted her, and I took her, and now I'll protect her with everything I've got. And right now protecting her includes keeping a doctor in this town."

Done checking his load, Bullard holstered his weapon.

"Does Greer know you feel that way?"

"Greer and I understand each other. I've got my own cabin on Greer's land. I keep Lana away from him, and more than that I keep her away from his wife. Greer expects me to back him when there's trouble. Right now, to Greer, you qualify as trouble."

"I'm not sniffing around Greer's wife; I'm doctoring her. Do you hold with Greer putting his hands on his missus? A lot of men draw the line there." Dare had more to say, but just then another door opened, this one across the street at the jail. Sheriff Porter stepped out, but rather than see Bullard and turn tail like most men would, he walked across the dirt street to join them. He walked with a strut that seemed only to underscore what a weakling he was. Seeing the law coming should have struck Dare as a good thing, but Porter was Greer's man, bought and paid for just like Bullard. And Glynna had said Porter handed her over to Greer, so there was no pretending this man would protect a woman.

They stopped walking as the sheriff reached them. Standing down on the street, Dare and Bullard towered over Porter on the raised board-walk.

"Trouble here, Simon?" The sheriff was the opposite of Bullard: short, skinny, shifty. The lawman had brown eyes that skittered around like nervous vermin. The way he talked first to a brute like Simon showed a man who was ready to take orders with no interest in truth or law and order.

To Dare's way of thinking, there wasn't much lower than wearing a badge with no interest in justice.

Porter wasn't a man Dare feared facing, but he was worse in his own way than Bullard. The sheriff was a man to shoot someone in the back, from cover. A coward as dangerous as a Texas sidewinder.

Silently, Dare apologized to the sidewinders he'd just insulted.

"No trouble, Sheriff." Bullard turned his cold gaze on Dare. "Is there, Doc? Not as long as you stay out of Greer business."

"Then we've got no trouble," Dare said. He expected in the next few days to bring a cyclone down on Greer business. He kept that to himself.

"You should put the gun aside, Simon." Dare knew he was wasting his breath, but he had it to waste. "You've got a child on the way, and that child needs a father who'll care for him, teach him how to live a decent life. Do you want your son to be a gunman?"

Simon turned to face Dare, blocking his way. "I'm real proud of who I am, Doc. If it's a boy, I'll teach him everything I know."

As they stood there, Dare's stomach sank because of what he saw in Bullard's eyes. Sharp intelligence and cool viciousness—a lethal combination.

"My boss didn't say I needed to rid this town of you, but he did want me to give you a message. It's this: Stay away from the Greer ranch and stay away from his wife."

"And if I get a call to come out to Greer's place, I'm supposed to ignore it?"

"We've found out who asked you to come and we've dealt with him. You won't be asked again."

"I need to come and check on how her shoulder is healing."

"Stay away if you want to live." Bullard's cold-blooded threat stirred up something hot in Dare's belly. His hands, full of supplies, itched to make a fist and shove Bullard's threats down his throat.

But now wasn't the time. Soon. Very soon.

"You hear that, Doc?" Sheriff Porter asked.

"I heard my life being threatened. Is that what you're asking if I heard, *Sheriff*?" Dare emphasized the title to make sure the sheriff caught his scorn. "I'll stay away, Bullard. Or if I do come, it'll only be because someone needs me to come real bad."

Bullard didn't like that, but Dare didn't care much about what Bullard liked. He hadn't come to shoot but only to pass on a warning. With a jerk of his chin, Bullard stepped aside.

Dare walked the short distance to his house. An itch between Dare's shoulder blades kept him from forgetting for one second that one of the fastest gunmen in the state of Texas was watching him take every step.

❦

The scouting took all day, but Luke enjoyed hunting around his ranch. Dodger gave them enough warning before he headed off to do his chores, so they knew where to hunt and where to avoid.

Only trouble with that was, the spot Luke was aiming for—the one that led to the ranch by a way not visible to the guards—was at the top of a cliff.

"We have to *climb* that?" Rosie looked up the almost sheer rock wall.

"I know of a couple other ways around. If those guards had been posted in a different spot, this would have been easier. But the guards are where they are so, yes, we have to climb that." Luke had known this route would probably work, but he was hoping he could find something easier. The sentries had a view of more than just the narrow canyon trail; they could watch the ranch for miles around.

"Are you sure this is the only way?" Rosie plunked her little fists on her hips and looked disgruntled. And the woman was a worker, so Luke looked back up the cliff and wondered if he was risking their necks.

"I haven't climbed this since I was a kid. But we can do it. If you want, I'll go up first and then lower a rope for you."

She narrowed her eyes. "If you can climb it, so can I."

"It's the pure truth, Rosie. I haven't found a single thing this week that you can't do every bit as well as me. Hiding from your no-account brother all those years is coming in handy now."

"Just the same, I'd have preferred him to not be such a worthless skunk."

"I'd find him and whip him good if he weren't already dead."

Nodding, Rosie said, "I appreciate it."

Probably because he was putting off scaling the cliff, Luke leaned on the red rock and said, "When this is over, are you . . . are you . . . what do you plan to do? You have no family anywhere?"

"None I've ever met. My folks went west to Indiana a long time before I was born. I know they had some brothers and sisters but I've never met them and I don't know how

I'd go about finding them. And if I did find them, they'd be strangers to me."

Luke nodded. "When my folks came west, they left everything behind, too."

"We're going to have to stop stalling and climb."

He laughed and realized he didn't want to move, and not because he was dreading the climb. No, it was because he liked talking to Rosie. Reaching up, he caught one of the curls that had escaped her bun and now danced in the light breeze. "You're sure a pretty little thing. You should stay around Broken Wheel. You could get to know me and my friends when we *aren't* planning a war."

"I think I know you all pretty well." She jerked her head at the cliff. "Let's go."

"Rosie, do you ever stop looking for work?"

"Call me Ruthy." She'd told him so many times, even she knew better than to expect it.

"Rosie suits you." Luke leaned toward her, then stopped. What was he doing? He might be dead in a few days. And here he was thinking of kissing a woman. That wasn't the way an honorable man had oughta act.

"It does not."

"Rosie red hair."

"You only call me that because I was sunburned when we first met. My hair was drab brown from floodwater."

"You were pretty even soaked in mud." With a sigh of frustration he turned to the rocks. It was probably thirty feet high, and the ground was soft. If one of them fell, they might not even get hurt . . . too bad. "All right. Let's climb this stupid cliff."

One step at a time, Luke inched his way up the rock, searching out handholds and toeholds, some of them so narrow a rolling piece of gravel might knock his grip loose. Halfway up, he stopped to catch his breath and looked down. She wasn't following.

"What are you waiting for?"

"I think I'll let you get to the top. Then, if you fall, you won't knock me off the cliff on your way down."

She had a point. He was most of the way up before he looked down again and she'd started. He could tell she'd tucked her skirt into her waistband and was scrambling up as smooth as a wily mountain goat. The woman was right handy with everything she put her mind to.

The ledges were narrow, and clinging like a burr to the side of the cliff was harder than when he was a kid. Luke finally reached the top and rolled over the ledge onto a mesa with a decent stand of trees to use for concealment. Breathing hard, he turned to look down at Rosie. She was climbing faster than he had, if he cared to admit it. Which he didn't.

He lay there catching his breath a minute, watching his little mountain goat tackle the cliff. She was close enough to hear him. "I clambered around in these hills a lot as a kid. I found out I could get around that trail this way. There were a couple of trails besides this one, but the lookouts can see us if they look just right. I might risk it. But we need to try and figure a way out for Mrs. Greer and her two children. There isn't an easier way. I've given it a lot of thought. I made a game of it when I was a kid—sneaking around, hunting deer, playing with the Indians. I learned all the tricks a few of the Indian kids could teach me, and I know these canyons like I know my own name."

"Your name? You mean Luciano? Do you really know your name all that well?"

Luke smiled.

"This is going to be a mighty slow way to get to your ranch when we go throw Greer out." Ruthy wasn't even breathing hard as she neared the top.

"Maybe we could string a rope. Leave it behind so that the day we come we can move faster."

"Good idea, unless they find it." Rosie got close enough to reach his outstretched hand. She took a moment to untuck her skirt for modesty's sake, then grasped his wrist. He hoisted the little lightweight the rest of the way. She rolled onto her belly beside him. He was glad he'd had a chance to rest before she saw him. "Why can't we just go however Dodger goes? We're meeting him in secret."

"Because he rides away from the ranch in full view of the lookouts. When he gets out to where we meet, he can get out of their line of sight. But we can't get in or out of the ranch house unseen any other way than this. Through these trees there's a good place to study the sentries, and a trail that leads to the house. It's tough but passable. Now stay low."

Luke crouched behind a line of scrub junipers. He and Rosie were far enough away that they could talk quietly with no risk. A soft wind gusted toward them, which cut down the chances of their voices carrying. The sound of the swaying trees and the birds chattering in the branches covered small sounds.

"There's one." He pointed to the closest watchman about a hundred yards across a deep gorge on their side of the trail to town.

Rosie crawled up beside Luke. "And the second guard is over there." Another man was almost a half mile away on the far side. Both were sitting, leaned back against a boulder, lazing in the sun.

"They're not real watchful." Luke would've fired them on the spot. Which told Luke a lot about how Greer ran his place.

"Dare said they were plenty alert when he rode in and out." Rosie dropped to her knees, frowning.

"They had a lot of time to see him coming. Any rider on that town road is visible for a mile or more."

"Why post a sentry at all?" Rosie looked at him. "Is it because of you? You said Greer had a posse on your trail, so he's worried about you showing up."

"He knows I'm coming." He dragged his attention away from the guards to look at his pretty partner. "Maybe that's why the guards are posted. I don't know what Greer told these men, but either they're poor guards or Greer didn't impress on them that I'm a serious threat."

"I could pick the nearest one off from here with a good rifle." Ruthy sounded confident. "But I don't hold with shooting a man in the back."

Earlier, Luke had found a place for Rosie to demonstrate her shooting. She was a surprising mix of dead shot and skilled tracker. Also a woman who knew a sin when she saw one.

Luke found the combination hard to resist. "Now that we know just where the men are, we know this back trail will get us past them. It's a steep walk from here but it's all hidden from the guards."

"We can't do it on horseback, and we've been half a day walking and climbing to get here," Rosie said. "And we need to haul Greer out of there, either unconscious or tied up. We can lower him with ropes down that cliff we just climbed and tote him all the way to Broken Wheel. It won't be easy."

Luke decided they looked to be there for a while and he might as well get comfortable. He lay down on his belly studying the terrain.

Rosie watched beside him. "I think what we need is a way to get Greer out of here. Lure him to town and grab him there."

"I don't know how often he goes to town."

"Then what can we do to get him to go?" Rosie stretched out beside him.

Luke tossed Ruthy's question around. Then he remembered a tiny detail about the Stone ranch that no one else might know. "I have an idea."

"Tell me." Rosie looked away from the guards, curious.

"Let me think about it awhile." Luke frowned. "We'd be taking a long chance with Mrs. Greer's safety, and I need to consider all the things that could go wrong." Luke watched the guards and considered further.

"Is there an unguarded trail out of here that goes south, away from Broken Wheel?" Rosie seemed to prefer to do the thinking for both of them, and out loud. "John could take Greer over that trail. Lock him up for stealing the ranch. Maybe under questioning he can be tripped up and he'll admit to killing your pa."

Watching Rosie use all her skills to sneak around was impressive. Watching her consider angles and determine how best to hurt Greer worked him up, too. And since she wouldn't quiet down long enough for him to study on his plan, he got to thinking about her. And how pretty she was and what a big old lonely ranch he was going to have in his possession in a few days. Which made him turn to his home.

"Look at it." The ranch was within sight, though still far

away. It was log and stone, made out of the materials that surrounded it. Two stories high. Smoke curled out of one of two chimneys. A neat front porch stretched the length of it. A log barn stood behind. Horses grazed in the corral. The sun was getting low in the west and beginning to cast a reddish glow. It was near time to head back. They'd take a more direct route now that they knew exactly where to go, but they still needed to move carefully. They'd be hours getting back to Dare's house.

"It's as pretty a place as I've ever seen," Rosie said quietly. Her presence there was nice. "This whole canyon is beautiful. Rugged, not lush like the land back in Indiana, but it takes your breath to look at it. The red rocks jutting up out of the ground, changing colors with every foot. Those big slabs of stone that seem to have been built on sand and now the sand's been blown away."

Ruthy pointed to one of the strange rock formations that appeared now and then, irregular and jagged.

"Those are scattered all over this canyon. I called that one God's Lookout Tower." Luke smiled at the childhood memory. "Staying standing the way it does seems miraculous. I liked to imagine God was watching over us."

"Were you born here?"

"I was. Pa and Ma moved here before I came along. They had a farm back East, but there was a fire and two older brothers died."

"There's so much sadness in the world."

"Ma said with her sons gone, there were too many memories. They lost the house in that fire. Lost most everything, so it was easy to sell the land and start over out here. They were on the Sante Fe Trail and were mighty wary of the stretch of desert ahead. They heard about this pretty country with the layered red stone and decided they'd gone far enough west. So my pa took a chance and left the wagon train."

Pointing to the striped stone the sentry stood on, Luke said, "Those strange lines looked to Pa as if God made the earth one layer at a time. He'd taken the name Stone and it just seemed meant to be. He found Broken Wheel, a run-down little town, the same as now, some hardy folks who traded with the Comanche and Kiowa, and a few ranchers running cattle in the area. They called this Palo Duro Canyon.

"Pa picked the spot to build a house and settle down, knowing it was easy to defend. I was born here. Callie came along a few years later. Then Ma died birthing a baby when Callie was about ten."

Rosie made a sound of sympathy, and Luke turned to study her instead of the rocks. "After that, our family changed. Pa'd always been stubborn and I reckon so was I. Ma stepped in between us and kept the peace. Without her, we just went at each other all the time. Looking back, I know some of it came from both of us being so sad about Ma dying, but I couldn't see it at the time. Callie rode with us, doing ranch chores until she was as good a hand as Pa or me. A crack shot. I didn't like her being out and running wild. Pa thought it was fine. That added more things for us to bicker about."

"I never had any brothers and sisters," Rosie said. "And I lost my folks to scarlet fever when I was twelve. I had it first, brought it home from school. I lived through it. My folks didn't."

He reached over to rest his hand on hers. "That's when those polecat Reinhardts took you in?"

Nodding, Rosie closed her fingers around his. "The fever hit the school first. So it spread almost everywhere. It'd done a lot of damage, so there weren't many people able to take an orphaned child. The Reinhardts stepped in to help. At the time, it seemed like an act of kindness. At first I was so miserable missing my folks, I didn't much notice how they treated me. Nothing would've made me happy. Then they put me to work. I spent years working from before sunup to full dark, and all that time I was dodging their fists and their no-account son."

Luke shook his head. "Tough way to grow up, but you managed to become a fine woman." Her hair had gotten mussed throughout the day, though those curls would be hard to control under the best of circumstances. He saw the softness, remembered how the curls felt and couldn't resist touching them, enjoying the silk under his callused fingers.

The world ebbed away. The cackling birds seemed to go silent. The cool wafting of the wind faded to nothing, until all he was aware of was one woman. Soft skin. Soft hair.

Without planning to . . . exactly, he raised up on one elbow and closed the small distance between them and kissed her.

When her hand gently settled on his shoulder, he put inches between them so he could see what was in her eyes.

He liked what he saw and kissed her again. Longer this time. Finally she pulled away, and he found his hand sunk deep in her shining red curls.

"The sun's getting low," she said. "We'd better get on for home now." She slipped out of his grasp, not looking at him, her cheeks pink as the sunset.

They crawled back to the ledge, where Luke stood to his feet. As she rose beside him, his first thought was that he needed to get nearer to her. But he let the world back in and remembered where they were and what they were doing there.

"Long past time to head in." Luke rubbed the back of his neck. He had a warm spot left by her caressing hands. He looked at her and saw that her hair wasn't even pretending to be pulled back in a knot at her neck. He'd let it free and it gave him a deep pleasure to know he'd mussed her up a bit. He hesitated, but it felt right so he reached out and took her hand. "C'mon. Let's go."

They made the long climb down and started the journey back to Broken Wheel in silence, holding hands as they walked. Luke relived the kiss. He had no idea what was going on in her mind, but he hoped it was the same thing that was going on in his. The one thing he knew about women was, a lot of them liked to talk everything to death.

He sure hoped Rosie wasn't like that.

"Luke, we need to talk." The light-headed joy Ruthy had gotten from kissing Luke had eased enough she could think a few clear thoughts. "Can I ask you something?"

Together they watched and waited as Broken Wheel went to sleep.

"Sure." He was whispering, so he leaned in closer, and when he spoke, warm breath tickled her ear and sent a shiver up and down her spine.

"The thing is, up until what happened—"

"You mean up until I kissed you?"

She swallowed hard to hear him say it out loud. "Yes, until then. The thing is, you've acted all week as if you didn't even care for me."

"That's not true."

"You were furious when I said I wanted to help fight Greer. You've snarled at me every time I asked to come along. You yelled at me when I—"

"Okay. Yes. I've acted . . . well, I've been rude. A few times."

"No. Constantly."

"But it isn't because I don't care for you."

"You think I'm a pest. You think I'm slowing you down. You think—"

"It's because I can't get near you and not want to kiss you."

For a second she was struck dumb.

"Whenever you're around, which is all the time, I catch myself thinking of how pretty you are and how sweet." He lifted her hand and kissed the back of it.

She shivered deep inside. She should tell him to stop. There wasn't any hurry in saying it, though. "I reckon I have had me some thoughts too, Luke. But you've got a lot to deal with right now. We can talk more about such things as kissing when you've put your troubles behind you."

"And why is that?" There was a surprising spark of temper in his question.

"Why is what?" She turned to look fully at him. "You want to know why we should wait to see if you get yourself killed in the next few days?"

"You know, it occurs to me that you've been living almost as a prisoner of the Reinhardts ever since you were a kid. Now, all the sudden, here you are—a pretty woman in a town full of men. You may be thinking you can have your pick."

"You really—?" Ruthy stumbled over her words when

she realized she was going to ask if he really thought she was pretty. Begging for a compliment. There had certainly never been any indication from those around her that she was anything other than homely. If she hadn't been holding his hand, the surprise might've tumbled her into a heap on the ground. "You think I could have any man I wanted?"

It was a heady feeling. She, who had feared for years she was going to be forced to marry that horrid Virgil Reinhardt, could now have her pick of men. She was beginning to really love Texas.

"Just never you mind about other men," he said.

"I'll mind whatever I please to mind, Luke Stone. Until this afternoon, there was no man I was of a mind to kiss."

"Not even me?"

He sounded almost like a little boy, and she found it so endearing she melted. "Well, maybe you. A little."

His temper vanished and she wondered what had sparked it. Jealousy? Was that possible?

The sunset turned to dusk, and dusk to full darkness as they waited in their hiding place behind Dare's back door. An owl hooted. The leaves rustled with the evening breeze. The smell of juniper and rich loamy soil mixed in an alluring way with the scent of a strong, quiet man. And there in the dark, as they settled in side by side, his hand reached out and touched hers much as it had while they'd walked.

And now as then, she held on.

CHAPTER 12

Dare slammed the side of his fist against the kitchen table so hard the table slid and hit Luke in the gut. "I'm giving this one more day." Luke didn't need to be reminded that Dare was losing his mind worrying about Glynna Greer. "You don't know how she looked!"

"Now, Dare," Luke began, "we've got Dodger watching—"

"I know it." Dare surged away from the table. "But if Greer turns his fists on her again, even if Janet signals for help, Glynna might not survive another beating. I know we need Bullard out of the picture and the sheriff out of town."

"A few more men left Greer's ranch." Luke wanted to go in as badly as Dare.

"We're more concerned with not taking a risk than we are with protecting that woman." Dare slashed a hand like he was wielding a saber.

"There'll be no protecting her if we get ourselves killed, Dare." Big John rarely moved when he could avoid it, but he was a man Luke wanted in a fight. Big John never quit. He wasn't as ruthless as Vince. He wasn't as fast with a gun as Luke, and in all modesty, Luke figured he, Dare, and Vince were all smarter than Big John.

But John was solid, brave, and as strong as an ox. He had no quit in him. He never panicked. Even in the midst of madness, John never lost sight of right and wrong. He made a perfect Texas Ranger.

"We're cowards." Dare was trying to goad them into action now even if it meant he took a fist in the face.

They let him have his say, because Luke understood how he felt.

Jonas might've had some words of wisdom, a handy quote from the Bible that would have calmed Dare down, except Jonas had been called away again. Being a parson appeared to be a more demanding job than being a doctor, lawyer, Ranger, or rancher.

"We're waiting to get all the advantages we can so we can win." Big John lifted the coffee Rosie had made for them all and took a deep drink.

"Yes, and our waiting may get her killed." Dare wasn't a man to sit around on the best of days, and today was by no means the best. He stormed out of the kitchen.

Luke heard him stride toward the front door as if he could force Lana Bullard to show up just by wanting it so bad.

Dare came back, fuming. "Why did that lunatic decide to be reasonable about having her baby now of all times? Since I came to town, she hasn't gone a week without begging me to save her. Sometimes I think she just wants to come and visit me. I don't like the way she looks at me and hangs on every word out of my mouth."

"When is her baby due anyway?" Rosie asked.

Trust a woman to ask a question that didn't matter. "She says she's around six months gone with the baby." Dare ran his hands deep into his hair. "Three more months

MARY CONNEALY

I've got to put up with her. And then I'll hand her baby over and feel like I'm consigning the poor little one to a nightmare. Its father'll be locked up, maybe hung. Its mother will be a foam-at-the-mouth madwoman. Oh yes, that's going to make delivering my second baby ever a real pleasure."

"You've only delivered one baby before?" Rosie looked shocked. "When was the other one?"

Luke remembered it all too well. As shocking an experience as he'd ever had.

Dare stopped pacing. And he never stopped pacing. "Can we focus on what's important here?"

"Let's talk about going in." Luke clenched both hands into one big fist on the table in front of him.

Dare jerked his chin down in agreement. "Tomorrow. We'll just have to tackle this mess with Bullard and the sheriff involved."

"No. We wait," Big John said.

"What if we get the word he's going after his wife?" Luke asked. "His lookouts will mow us down if we go in on the main trail, but I can get us past them."

"You're sure?" Vince straightened from the doorway, his eyes narrow.

Big John leaned forward, listening close.

"I'd want to get there about dawn, and I'd figure it's about two hours on a bad game trail, some climbing. But we can do it. So we'll make an early start. We'll leave Rosie to stand guard and hike the rest of the way in. If those sentries realize what's going on, she can come a-runnin'."

Dare started moving again. "With a back way in, we could go and arrest Greer tonight."

"Getting to the ranch, we'll have to face maybe ten men,"

163

Luke said. "There are four of us. Five if Jonas goes and he's saying he's in."

"Preacher man shouldn't go to a gunfight." Vince shook his head. "Gotta be hard on a parson to shoot folks, no matter how deserving."

"It's hard on anyone." Luke had done plenty of fighting in the war and he knew the scar it left. It could sneak up on a man, invade his dreams, haunt him until a man believed in ghosts.

"So instead of two apiece, we'll each take three," Dare snapped. "And Jonas'll be able to hold a prayer service for us while we do all the work."

"Ten men against three." Luke was ready. They'd put it off too long. "Dodger'll throw in on our side. I think a couple more Greer hands will too, or at least they won't fight for Greer. That'll mainly leave us to face Bullard and Greer and a handful of others—all of them tough, dangerous men."

"If we pin them in the house, they can threaten Glynna and the children." Dare looked sick thinking of Glynna, threatened, trapped, her husband killing mad.

"I'll slip in a window," Vince said. It was just the kind of thing he was best at.

Dare shook his head. "They don't know you. If I get inside, they'll know I'm there to help."

"I'm a sight better at sneaking around than you," Vince said.

"I know, but you lose the advantage if you have to waste time with explanations. You might need to convince them you mean no harm, which could cost us crucial seconds."

"That's a detail we can figure out later," Luke said.

"Let's do it. Let's go tonight." Dare rubbed his hands together.

Luke could see he was already mentally running for the trail.

"No." John spoke with the weight of a mountain. "Not tonight. If we give up on Mrs. Bullard coming back in so we can take Bullard out of the fight, we still need to get the sheriff out of town. That's one detail we've got to get in order. I'll get the sheriff moving tomorrow. Luke, send word to Mrs. Greer through your friend Dodger that we're coming. We'll go in after Greer early the next morning."

Dare looked hard at each of them. "Are we going in or not?"

"Let's do it." Luke crossed his arms, determined.

"I say we wait," Big John repeated. "We can give it a few more days. Bullard is a ruthless gunman, fast and deadly. And he's a leader, too. We've got a lot better chance of getting everyone through this without a lot of killing if we take Bullard out of the fight." John had common sense on his side. Right now common sense was irritating.

"I'm tired of waiting," Vince said. "But I suppose one more day to get the sheriff out of town makes sense, and then we'll go—"

Squeaking buckboard wheels rolled up to Dare's front door.

"Doc, help me! It's time. It's for sure." Simon Bullard shouting from outside.

They all shot to their feet. This was it.

"Luke, Ruthy, get upstairs. Big John, you go up too and be ready to grab Bullard when he's had enough to drink. Vince, stay here and wash up these coffee cups so he can't see we had a crowd in here."

Luke was already on his feet. It was a sign of how worked up Dare was that he told them to do what was obvious to everyone. Go upstairs, keep quiet. Be ready to help. It was insulting.

Dare dashed out and came right back to look square at Vince. "If Bullard offers you a shot of whiskey, for heaven's sake say no."

Dare ducked out of the room again, heading for his front door.

Luke grabbed Rosie by the arm, but she was moving so fast she ended up dragging him instead of him dragging her. Like most things with this woman, Luke had to hurry to keep up. She tore up the steps, heading for her bedroom.

Luke turned to Big John, who was hard on his heels. "We need to be in the room at the end of the hall. There's a lock on the door, and sometimes Bullard wanders while Dare tries to calm his wife down."

They moved fast and had the upstairs door closed just as Dare swung his front door open with a loud bang.

And the circus began. The shouting—that was Bullard. The tears—Lana's. The calm laced with sarcasm—Dare.

Big John leaned close to Luke. "I'd like to go down and arrest them just for being this stupid."

There oughta be a law, no doubt about it.

"Here's your bottle, Simon." Dare definitely pitched his voice to be heard on the second floor. "You left it here last time."

Lana started caterwauling as if Bullard having a drink were a sin against their marriage vows.

Which maybe it was. But the least of Bullard's sins.

More yelling from Bullard, mixed up with Lana's occasional worshipful tone aimed at Dare. A long stretch passed with the same volume coming from both Lana and Simon. Then slowly Bullard got quieter.

Luke whispered, "Bullard is slurring his words."

"How much of that stuff did you drink, you old fool?" Lana being a sympathetic and supportive wife as always.

"How's it going in here?" Vince asked.

"Get that man away from me!" Lana screamed as if Vince had charged in bearing a knife.

"Mrs. Bullard, you're fully clothed. Vince can see nothing. Vince, why don't you help Simon to the kitchen and get him a cup of coffee?"

"Don't leave me, Simon!" Lana suddenly broke into wrenching sobs. It would've been heartbreaking—if she hadn't done so before five or six times.

"Has Dare considered pouring some of that whiskey down Mrs. Bullard's throat?" John whispered.

"He thinks whiskey might be bad for the baby," Luke replied. "And that was before he laced it with laudanum."

Big John shook his head. "That's gonna be the least of the kid's problems."

A soft knock on the door at the base of the stairway drew Luke's attention. "Move quiet."

"Stop insulting me." Big John shoved Luke out of the way and moved so quiet, Luke couldn't believe it of such a big man. Luke looked at Rosie. "Stay here. Please."

She scowled. "Of course I'll stay here—stop insulting *me*."

Luke followed John, conscious of every creak. Good thing Lana was pouring her heart out to Dare, talking to him with a fervor that sounded almost reverent. She broke into loud sobs every few sentences. Honestly, a buffalo herd could probably stampede down the stairs and it wouldn't shut her up. When Luke got downstairs, Vince had Bullard sitting in a chair in the kitchen. Sleeping like a baby.

167

Lana screamed. "I think it's coming, Doc."

"You're not even in labor, Mrs. Bullard. Try and calm down."

"Can I have a drink of whiskey? Get Simon's bottle!"

"Don't tempt me, Mrs. Bullard, please don't tempt me." Dare groaned.

"Grab a leg," Vince muttered as he slid his hands under Bullard's arms. John and Luke both grabbed a leg. They had him outside and around the house as fast as they could move. Once in the woods, John stripped Bullard of his guns and checked him for hideout weapons. There was quite a stack by the time John was done.

"I'll be right back with the horses." Vince ran for the stable behind his house at the far end of Main Street, which wasn't real far away.

"Tie his feet. I'll get his arms." John threw Luke a length of rope.

Vince was back only minutes after they'd finished.

"Vince, I planned to stash Bullard somewhere and hand those papers to the sheriff tomorrow before I headed out, but if you'll talk to Porter, I can get on the road right now. You're wanting to get this cleared up fast, so if I head out tonight, I'll be most of the way there before this coyote even wakes up."

"Good thinking. I can get rid of Porter." Vince and John draped Bullard over the saddle. Vince added, "You watch this one. Just because he's loco over his wife doesn't mean he isn't dangerous."

"Believe me, I know just how tough Bullard is. I've seen his wanted posters. I'll be ready for trouble." John straightened his hat, mounted up, and took the reins of his own horse and the one Vince had fetched. "Listen, both of you.

Dare is half crazy worrying about Greer's wife. Try your best to get him to wait until I come back. Give me four days. I'll push as hard as I can and try to cut it shorter, but I want to be here. You need another gun on this raid, and I want it to be mine."

"Four days." Luke figured they'd have their hands full with that. "We'll try and hold him back. I wonder how he's going to explain to Mrs. Bullard where her husband went."

"I'm glad he's the doctor and not me. I heard that woman. Arresting outlaws is a sight easier way to make a living." With that, John turned and rode away.

Luke and Vince watched until he vanished into the night, then hurried back to the house.

CHAPTER 13

"How long did you say you've been expecting a baby, Mrs. Bullard?" Dare didn't feel right making a personal exam of a woman's body. If there was a baby coming, then fine, but there most certainly wasn't. In fact, Dare had a very strong suspicion about this whole thing.

"Where's Simon? I wish he'd stay at my side like you do." The sobbing from Lana was the same as always. Lots of noise and drama, no tears.

"When did you say you were . . . ?" Dare had been at doctoring too long to let a personal question embarrass him. But he hadn't treated women much, and certainly not in a private manner.

She grabbed the lapels of his shirt. "You have to save me, Dr. Riker."

Too bad he couldn't figure out from what.

"How long gone are you with this baby?" Dare thought that was a safe question.

"I know when I missed my monthly. A woman in my profession knows. I'm about six months along. Simon!" Lana's voice rose to a scream. "You get in here, you low-down, belly-dragging sidewinder!"

Lana had blue eyes that went soft when they beseeched

Dare for help and lit with fury enough to shoot lightning bolts when she shouted at Simon. "I want my husband. He made me belly full, and he should be here when I need him."

"Lana, please forget Simon for now." Forever probably, but Dare knew better than to give Lana that piece of news. "Simon was drinking. I'm sure he fell asleep somewhere. He'll be of no use to you for a while."

"Get me off this table. I'll find that man. He'll be useful or I'll know the reason why." Lana struggled to get up. She showed no sign of any pain.

She also showed no sign of any pregnancy. Dare hadn't had much practice, but he'd read a lot and he knew the symptoms of a woman bearing a child. Lana Bullard had only one of them—granted it was a big one.

"Lana!" Dare got so close she couldn't look at anything else.

Finally she quit shouting for Simon and settled back on the table, turning adoring eyes on Dare.

"Lana, stop worrying about your husband and listen to me." Dare stared into her eyes, searching for a connection. He thought she was finally seeing him.

She nodded.

"How old are you, Mrs. Bullard?"

"I'm forty-five years old, if it's any of your business." She said it with vanity, of all the unimportant things at the moment.

Dare upped her age by three years, maybe five. "Mrs. Bullard, I don't see a single sign that you're in the family way. You are not expecting. You are getting older. If your . . . your monthly time stopped, it may be because of the . . . the . . . ." Dare felt himself blushing. He could not believe he had to talk with a woman about this. "Because

172

of the change of life an older woman goes through. You would be showing some by six months and you're not, not a bit. There's no movement, and a baby should be moving inside you by now."

He'd read that plain as day in one of his medical books. "And your belly should be round by now." Lana's belly was round but that had nothing to do with a baby and everything to do with overeating for fifty years. "You're not going to have a baby." Dare didn't think he could say it any more clearly.

Lana's arms trembled.

Dare said more quietly, "I'm sorry. It's clear that you wanted this baby." It wasn't clear at all, but nothing about Lana Bullard made much sense. "But you're not going to have one."

"Yes. Yes, I am. I'm going to have a son." She sounded distraught.

Dare wondered if he'd done wrong. Maybe he should have let her spew her bile over Bullard's disappearance. By forcing her to admit there was no child, he was layering terrible disappointment on an already explosive situation.

"We're going to call him Simon. Simon Bullard Junior. Little Simon." Lana smiled and began to hum. She lifted the little pillow from under her head and hugged it as if it were a baby. She pressed the pillow against her cheek while she crooned.

Dare didn't know what to do. "Lana?"

She didn't respond.

"Lana, you understand me, don't you?"

The humming grew louder as if to stop him from speaking.

"There won't be a child. I'm very sorry, but—"

"'Sleep serenely, baby, slumber.'" Her voice rose. She showed no sign of hearing Dare. "'Lovely baby, gently sleep.'"

Dare recognized the old lullaby. His mother had sung it to him. He had to say the words. Say them now before she fell any deeper into whatever confused place she was sinking. "Lana, I'm sorry—"

"'Tell me wherefore art thou smiling, smiling sweetly in thy sleep?'"

Dare glanced up as Vince poked his head in the door. Dare looked at Lana, then arched his brows at Vince, hoping for some help.

Vince ducked back out of the room, the yellow-bellied coyote.

"There's no baby, Lana." Dare didn't know how else to say it. He gripped her shoulders and gave her a firm shake. "There is no baby."

Those blue eyes, so wide and so hurt, locked on his. "Are you telling me my baby is dead?"

"No, there was never a baby. You were mistaken. These things happen."

"Do something, Dr. Riker. You've got to help me."

"There's nothing to be done. There was never a child."

Lana shook her head as if she were dizzy and couldn't focus. Slowly, her head still shaking, she swung her legs around and sat up, dropping the pillow to the floor. She looked around the room as if she'd never seen it before. Her eyes landed on Dare and sharpened. Her hands flexed into claws.

"You killed my son." She'd always nearly worshiped him, which had made Dare very uncomfortable. Now she was blaming him with the same ferocious strength she'd

174

put into reverence. What did a person do when their God betrayed them?

"You killed my son!"

He backed up, expecting her to attack.

She jumped off the table, whirled, and made a dash for the door.

❦

Glynna's eyes shot open as her door clicked.

He's here. Flint is here.

"Ma, wake up."

Her whole body shuddered. She'd been coiled to fight, even though the pain in her arm and ribs, her battered face, and her aching, wrenched muscles made every move painful.

It was Paul. Her son. Her poor son. What had she brought him to?

"What is it?" She didn't even bother trying to sit up. She could do it if necessary, but it hurt. Breathing hurt. Thinking hurt. Loving her children, whose lives she was destroying, hurt.

The door closed silently. "That old cowpoke found a chance to talk to me earlier in the day." Paul's low whisper in the darkness spoke of the lessons he'd learned since moving into this house. "He says the doc's going to get us out of here."

Glynna hated hoping. It was too awful when the hope was crushed. But she felt it happening. Was it possible this nightmare could end? "Flint will kill him."

"The doc's got a plan. He needs a few more days, but the old guy, Dodger, said if we can see Flint working himself up to attack you, we're to let him know and they'd come sooner."

Sometimes Flint struck with no warning. But usually that was just a shove or a backhanded slap. As a rule they had a calm stretch after a bad episode, often a month or more before he blew up again. Glynna had the sick feeling that he liked seeing her bruised and hunched over with pain. Once the bruises started to heal, it would eat at him and his temper would start to erupt, shouting insults, shoving and slapping her. And it had been getting worse. He'd only really done damage these last two times.

"I know when he's on edge and needs to take it out on you with his fists." Paul's voice was soaked with hate. He'd been such a good boy before they'd come out here. But hungry, always hungry. There'd been little to eat and even that bit was drying up fast. They'd lived in an area that was hunted out, and anyway Glynna was no hand at hunting if there had been game. The scandal attached to Glynna's name had ruined any hope of a paying job.

"How can we help?" she asked. "Did Dodger want us to do anything to prepare?"

"We've got a signal arranged. One for if Flint starts into one of his rages, we'll signal from the house. Another from Dodger when we need to be ready for the doc to come. And we—"

Heavy footsteps upstairs struck terror into Glynna's heart. "Get out quick! Hide in the pantry."

Paul gave her a look of such fury and hate and failure it nearly tore a hole in her heart. It was ruining her son not to be able to protect her.

"He won't hit me." Glynna fought down the need to scream at her son to run. "He might yell, but he's never come after me when I was hurt." Of course who could tell what a vicious brute might do? "Go, please. I can't stand thinking he might hurt you too, Paul. He won't spare me even if he does take after you."

Paul grabbed the doorknob, gave her one last agonized look, and slipped out. The boy had learned to be as silent as the tomb.

Flint's tread hit the stairs, and Glynna braced herself to take whatever she had to, to distract Flint from finding Paul. The children weren't supposed to leave their rooms at night. Flint liked making rules, then waiting to see if anyone would break one of them.

Her door crashed open. Flint, lantern in hand, filled the frame. She tried to stay calm.

Let him rage. Don't say anything to give him an excuse to strike.

He looked more like a beast than a man. He'd been so tidy when he'd come to Little Rock. He'd insisted that she not travel alone. A thoughtful gentleman, or so it seemed. They'd married immediately, then traveled home. Glynna realized after long days of a rugged journey that Flint had to come and get her or she'd have never found Broken Wheel. But she'd wanted to leave her life behind so she hadn't complained. They'd taken the stage back to Fort Worth, then in Flint's buckboard they'd come the rest of the way, riding for days north to the Texas panhandle.

"Did I hear talking down here?"

"I might have been talking in my sleep." She'd learned to keep her excuses short. He was mostly just waiting for her to speak so he could call her stupid. The man didn't limit himself to stupid, though. He was also fond of scrawny, ugly, clumsy, weak, and lazy. Glynna had kept track at first, but she'd stopped paying attention a long time ago.

"I'm gonna check both of those kids' rooms, and if one of 'em is out of bed, they'll pay for it and so will you."

Paul would hurry, but he'd have to go into the kitchen, come around the far side of the steps, and then creep up. The stairs weren't squeaky, but even a tiny creak would give her son away.

"Why do you want me here, Flint?" She knew she was taking a terrible chance challenging him in any way. But she had to protect her son.

"You're mine, that's why."

"But you hate me. You never stop saying I'm a lousy excuse for a wife. Why don't you throw me out? Let me take my children and go. I make you so angry. Wouldn't you be better off without me?"

Flint stepped into the room and slammed the door. Glynna flinched at the loud crash. He came toward the bed and set his lantern on the table. Glynna didn't worry about him inflicting husbandly attentions on her. He'd shown no interest in such a thing almost from the beginning. She wondered if whatever stopped him from wanting her in the night was what kept him angry.

The first time he'd shoved her, she still had a backbone and so moved down to this bedroom in a huff, thinking to teach him a lesson. He'd never invited her back upstairs. And he hadn't learned a thing. But she had.

"How'd I get myself stuck with such an ugly wife?" Flint grabbed her chin and turned her face one way, then the other. She didn't have bruises on her face anymore, not often anyway. After she'd run off to town, marked by him, Flint had been more mindful to make sure clothing hid her bruises.

She thought she heard a muffled sound on the stairs and

knew Paul was near the top. Glynna held her breath and prayed Flint wouldn't notice. Her husband's attention stayed fixed on her.

Paul would be in his room now. She started breathing again. All that remained was to turn Flint's attention away from her. His sneering had a light tone. His touch, though rough, wasn't violent. If she could just keep from setting him off.

She didn't speak further. Let Flint say his worst. She'd take it, and when he left, she'd pray. The possibility that the doctor might come gave her the first true hope she'd had since she ran away to town after the first time Flint had punched her. She'd put up with him at the beginning, the shoving, even a backhand. She'd made excuses for it all. She'd blamed herself and twisted herself into contortions trying to please him. But when he'd landed a punch, she'd waited and watched and bided her time. And the next time he was away from the ranch, she'd gone to the barn and politely requested three horses be saddled. She'd ridden for Broken Wheel with her children.

She'd arrived to find every door closed to her. The sheriff refused to listen to her plea for some type of sanctuary.

Flint had come and carried her home over his saddle, leading her horse, leaving her children behind for his men to bring back to the ranch.

Dropping his hand from her chin, he grimaced as if touching her disgusted him. Well, the feeling was mutual.

He turned for the door and swung it open. Looking back, the lantern swung in his grip and cast an almost demonic glow to his brutish features. Glynna knew she was looking at a true servant of the devil.

"I sent Bullard to have a talk with that meddling doctor,

and I've fired the cowpoke that went for help. Next time either of 'em shows their face on my land, they'll die."

Flint slammed the door, leaving her in darkness. His pounding feet thudded up the stairs. She listened as he opened and closed both doors to her children's rooms, but he only stayed long enough to look, then went to his own room. Glynna thought of the handsome doctor who had treated her with such kindness. She thought of the older cowhand, Dodger, who was helping them right now. She thought of her children.

Flint would do anything to keep her, though it made no sense when he hated her so. That meant trying to help her might get others killed. The thought was too painful.

She'd already done too much damage with her decision to answer that stupid mail-order bride advertisement. If she believed the doctor's rescue would work, she'd let him try. The price she'd pay didn't matter; she'd given up worrying about her own life.

But the doctor . . . the price he'd pay would be his life. And what about the price her children would pay if she were dead and they were left here at Flint's mercy?

It was unbearable. She had to get word to Dodger for the doctor to stay away.

CHAPTER 14

"Vince followed her and she stood in the middle of the street staring into the sky for a while. Finally, she went to the boardinghouse and checked in. Vince waited for a few minutes until he heard her snoring." Dare slipped into the woods before sunrise with Ruthy and Luke. "We'll have Jonas go talk to her this morning."

Luke didn't envy Jonas. The more he learned about his friends, the more he thought ranching was the perfect way to make a living . . . if he could just get his ranch back.

"She never even asked about Bullard? Where he went?" Luke asked.

"Nope." Dare looked asleep on his feet. "Vince is giving the letter to Sheriff Porter right now." Dare rubbed the back of his neck as if he were in deep pain. "We'll hold off for four days if possible so Big John can get back. You go talk to Dodger."

"I intend to. I've got a message I need to get to Mrs. Greer."

"A message?" Dare narrowed his eyes. "What are you going to say to her? I want to know." Dare seemed way too interested in Glynna Greer. And that was saying something, because all of them were mighty worried about protecting her.

"I think I've mentioned that Greer is living on my land."

"About six thousand times."

"Well there's one good thing about that."

"No there's not," Dare said.

"I know the S Bar S as well as I know my own name. I was born there, and I ran wild there all my growing-up years. I know every acre, every hill and valley, every game trail." Luke's eyes flashed like black fire.

"Okay, fine. I believe you. You know your own land. What are you going to say to Glynna?"

"And I know every hiding place."

The silence was broken only by the gusting of the wind.

Finally Rosie said, "Hiding place?"

Luke nodded. "And with that hiding place, I think I've figured out a way to keep us all alive and get our hands on Greer without flying lead."

"Without putting Glynna or her children in the line of fire?" Dare asked.

"Especially that."

"Tell me what you've got in mind."

Luke smiled. "It started with a Texas cyclone the year I was born, followed closely by a worrisome visit by a Comanche band."

A thunder of hooves drew their attention and they watched Sheriff Porter go tearing out of town. A man on a mission that would take him out of Broken Wheel for two weeks.

Vince came around the corner, and even though they were deep in the thicket, he looked right at them and smiled.

Luke gave his head one firm jerk of pleasure at the sight of the polecat sheriff leaving. Then he finished his story.

❧

"Where's Bullard?" Flint slapped his gloves in his hands, wishing for someone to punch over all his cowhands riding off.

Dodger shrugged. "I ain't seen him this morning."

Payday had been a week ago and he'd had a short group then. More had drifted off right after he handed them the month's cash money.

It was because of Luke Stone.

Flint slapped his gloves again, bringing them down with his left hand to smack his right. He wished it was someone's face. Today that someone was Simon Bullard. Except to hit Bullard was to die. Since Bullard wasn't here, Flint didn't have to fight the urge. Flint glanced at the house and knew who he could hit.

She was worthless now, though. He'd have to go into her room, where she was always lying down, to teach her a lesson. No fun in that.

His gloves hit with a sharp whack again as he imagined it.

"I ain't seen him for a couple days." The old coot, Dodger, was a solid worker. Slower than he oughta be, age taking its toll.

The old-timer hadn't looked Flint in the eye lately. There were a few of his men acting like that. The ones who'd hired on recently, brought in because of their reputations with their guns, were loyal, but Flint had a bad feeling about Dodger and a few of the others. Flint would've sent them all down the road if he wasn't so shorthanded.

Dodger pulled his own weight and that of another man or two. But he was slow about it.

Things would change around here once Flint had finished with Stone.

Slap.

Stone and Glynna. Somehow this was his wife's fault. Things had been fine around here without her. The ranch ran well. The men worked hard. Flint was making good money. But when she'd shown up, Flint's luck had changed.

Somehow Luke Stone coming home was all tied up with Glynna, and it made Flint killing mad that he'd ever been so weak as to want a woman of his own.

Slap.

"I'm gonna ride out, boss. Maybe Bullard'll show up later. If Lana didn't come home, then it figures he's with her. Give him time." Dodger seemed more than normally interested in the dirt in front of his toes.

"He'd better show up." Flint didn't bother to mutter words about firing Bullard. He oughta. It helped to rule this ranch if he kept the men a little scared all the time. But threatening to fire Bullard was so out of the question that Dodger wouldn't believe it, and that'd make Flint look weak.

Dodger turned for the barn. As he went in, it occurred to Flint that he should give Dodger the job of tending the house. Taking in milk and eggs and garden vegetables for his wife to burn to a smoldering ash heap.

Slap.

No way this slow-walkin' old man could take an interest in his wife.

He saw Marty heading for the house with a pail of milk. Marty was another one of the men who didn't meet Flint's eyes.

But the men loyal to Flint were shifty. He didn't want

them to even get a peek at Glynna. Better to let this young-ster do the chores.

Or switch to Dodger. He saw Dodger ride out to the west. Well, he'd switch men tomorrow. Flint had a long, hard day ahead of him, worse than ever without Bullard, who did his share of the hard work if his wife wasn't cutting up.

His irritation with Bullard grew and Flint thought of Glynna and wished she were on her feet again. He liked to face her when he had a lesson to teach.

Slap.

His hand stung and he realized how hard he was hitting himself. Better to hit someone else hard. He wished he'd ordered Dodger to take over tending the house. He should have done it before the old man left.

Marty came out of the house. Flint had men standing watch. If Marty stayed inside too long, Flint would hear about it. But the kid came and went fast.

❧

"Dodger, is that you?"

Ruthy saw the white-haired man emerge from the bushes. It was the beginning of the second day since Big John had left. He should be turning Bullard over to the law sometime today, and then he'd run for Broken Wheel. Big John would be here in two days. It was almost time to act.

"How is Mrs. Greer?"

Ruthy shuddered to think of anyone married to a man who had mistreated her to the extent Dare described.

"I haven't seen her. I got assigned the job of hauling supplies in for the family. I've talked with the children and they say she's better. She didn't get out of bed for a week, but now she's on her feet, not in top shape but mending."

"Can't you get in to see her?" Ruthy hated this. She thought of how hard this land had been on Lana Bullard, who was still at the boardinghouse, nursing whiskey and occasionally coming out to buy a new bottle. Jonas had asked the saloon to stop selling to her, but they wouldn't cooperate.

Jonas and Dare had both tried to talk to her, but she started singing lullabies whenever they talked and acted as if they weren't there.

Now here was Glynna Greer, trapped with a brute for a husband. And Luke was taking Ruthy to a gunfight.

"I only have a minute when I take in the vegetables and later go in with the eggs and milk. There are men paying attention. I have to be in and out fast. The kids talk a little, but they're real scared to break any of Greer's rules."

Luke had a note ready. "I need to get this to Mrs. Greer."

Dodger took the folded piece of paper.

"We've got a plan to lure Greer into town. Mrs. Greer needs to help. If she's willing, she has to wait for us to tell her it's time."

"I haven't liked the way Greer is acting." Dodger stuck the note in his pocket without reading it, which might mean he respected Luke's privacy. It might also mean he couldn't read. "I think he's heard you're close to home. That's why he never leaves the place. Of course, it's a busy time on the ranch and he's shorthanded."

"Has he asked about Bullard yet?"

"Yep. Threw a fit over Bullard running off. He's still hoping the polecat will come back. I told him I heard tell Lana was staying at the boardinghouse and all Greer could say was good riddance. He figures Bullard ran off to escape his pecking wife. But Greer is real upset to lose Bullard."

"Has he lost any more hired men?"

"He's got eight men left. But three of them won't back Greer in a fight. Me among 'em. But the five left who will back him are hard, dangerous men. They spell each other on lookout and always stay close to the place, which makes the rest of us work even harder. Greer at least is working his cattle. He's out of the house for long hours every day. And he's put out the word for more men, but none have come along yet. I think he's too well known for his hard treatment."

They heard a galloping horse approaching and all three of them turned and threw themselves toward the shelf of rock that shielded them.

No one in sight.

"I've gotta get back on my horse fast." Dodger left in a near run.

Ruthy knew the old man's joints hurt.

"We need to cover our tracks and get out of here." Luke grabbed a fallen branch.

"Dodger might need help. We can't just abandon him." Ruthy was shocked at Luke's decision to desert someone in danger.

"No, Dodger'll have a story spun if someone catches him walking. But if they're suspicious and they come up here and find tracks, that's when he'll be in danger. Let's go." Luke caught her upper arm and dragged her along. "Head down and wait for me on that rock shelf. I'll cover our trail."

"Dodger, hold up." The voice that hailed Dodger rang with authority rather than friendliness.

"I know that voice." Luke worked over the tracks with equal parts speed and care. "I haven't heard it since I was seventeen. That's Flint Greer. Get out of here, Ruthy, and make it fast."

It didn't suit her but she could see no other choice so she hurried away, hoping they hadn't put off this final move against Greer until it was too late.

Simon Bullard hung limp over the saddle, waiting for a chance to strike. He looked at the boulders where they were stopping and saw the perfect weapon if he could only get his hands on it.

Flexing his tightly bound wrists to fight off numbness, he coiled his muscles like a rattler ready to strike. He'd been waiting for his chance for a day and a half. The Ranger was a mighty careful man.

As the big man dismounted, back turned, Simon kicked the blue roan mustang he was draped over, hard in the flank. The horse reared and jerked at the reins tied to the Ranger's saddle. The Ranger's black stallion pranced sideways, snorted, and threw its head.

"Easy, boy." The Ranger moved fast to calm the mustang as it wheeled. The roan's rein snapped, setting it free. The Ranger's horse lashed out iron-shod hooves and reared, ripping its reins out of the Ranger's hands. The stallion took off running. Leaping for the reins of Simon's horse, the Ranger finally came close enough. Simon lifted his hands and brought them down hard on the Ranger's head, knocking the big man to his knees. Throwing himself to the ground, Simon grabbed a rock he'd already spotted, small enough to fit in his bound hands, large enough to crush a skull.

He reared up and swung with every ounce of strength

he possessed and smashed the Ranger in the head. He got a powerful blow in, but the rock went tumbling out of his bound hands. With a grunt of pain the Ranger slumped forward, stunned but not unconscious. Not dead like Simon had hoped. The Ranger shoved himself to his hands and knees.

With Simon bound hand and foot, the Ranger only had to get space between them to put a stop to this and regain the upper hand. Simon couldn't let that happen.

There was a knife in the Ranger's scabbard, and Simon crawled clumsily forward, grabbed the knife, and stabbed the Ranger in the back.

"You low-down sidewinder!" The Ranger rolled sideways, the movement tearing the knife from Simon's hand. Stumbling to his feet, the Ranger staggered away from Simon, out of his reach. Then the Ranger fell again. Blood flowed from his head and back. Simon took savage pleasure in the sight.

To finish this, Simon crawled to where the knife had landed, snagged it, and slashed at the leather strips binding his hands.

With his hands free, Simon hacked at the ties on his feet. The Ranger got to his knees and staggered toward the nearest boulder, clawing for his gun. The man wore a pair of Colts. If he got his wits to working, it'd be knife against gun. Simon didn't like those odds.

His feet now free, Simon stood and nearly fell. His legs weren't working after being bound tight for a day and a half. On unsteady feet he dove after the Ranger, who dragged his gun from his holster. Simon landed on his stomach, wheeled his body around, and kicked the six-shooter out of the Ranger's grasp.

The man went for his other gun and Simon stomped on his hand. Their eyes met. The big Ranger, blood pouring out of him, disarmed, met Simon's eyes and a chill of fear rushed down Simon's spine. Why would he feel fear when he was in control and the Ranger was seconds from death?

Because Simon saw a brave man, an honest man, a lawman.

A better man.

And Simon hated it.

To dispel the uncomfortable sizzle of fear, Simon raised the knife so the Ranger could see death coming. Enjoying the victory, enjoying knowing justice and courage, law and honesty were going to lose.

A sudden motion turned Simon's head to see the Ranger's stallion charging. A shrill whistle cut through the afternoon breeze. Simon threw himself behind the boulder the Ranger had tried to get to for shelter. The stallion wheeled and came at Simon again. Simon scrambled up the rocks. The horse stopped, standing guard over his master, bugling a challenge. The Ranger caught the reins and wrapped them around his wrist, his last act before he slumped to the ground unconscious. Maybe dead.

Simon could stab the horse, and he was so enraged he almost did it just to deal out pain. But no simple stab wound would put down a horse. Stuck on his perch, Simon looked at the mustang he'd been riding, spooked away, now standing at a distance and watching the fight.

The Ranger had passed out. He lay with his life's blood pouring from him, dying, Simon was sure. But there was no way for Simon to plunge one last certain blow into the man's heart. Even the guns Simon had knocked out of the Ranger's hand were within reach of the black's heels. Simon couldn't get them.

Furious, he looked from the Ranger to the roan mustang and decided he'd done enough. Scrambling around on the boulders, he put a lot of yards between himself and that black demon. When there was enough space, Simon stepped out of cover. The stallion took a step as if to charge, but he was stopped by his reins hooked to the Ranger's wrist.

With a smug smile, Simon said, "You outsmarted yourself, Ranger. You've got your horse to protect you, but you've stopped him from getting me."

There was no response from the Ranger.

Simon caught the mustang and threw himself on the saddle, only now really feeling the pain in his wrists and legs. How had he ended up in custody anyway? He couldn't remember much except getting Lana to the doctor.

Simon's mount reared and fought the grip on the reins and only then did Simon realize he was holding the horse with cutting force. He relaxed.

With one frustrated look back, Simon saw the horse nuzzling the Ranger. There was a rifle in a scabbard on the horse's saddle, and the Ranger was bristling with weapons. Two Colts and one more knife. Simon was lucky he'd been able to hang on to the knife he'd stolen.

Giving up on the weapons, Simon turned his horse and spurred it toward Broken Wheel. He been gone most of two days and would be that long getting back. Greer would be mad, but it weren't nuthin' on how mad Lana was gonna be. He kicked the horse harder, as if hurting the brute could make the time Simon had been away vanish.

Greer was gonna threaten to fire him.

Lana was going to threaten to kill him.

With a cruel smile, Simon admitted he didn't mind that.

It was one of the things that had kept him bound to her. As long as she didn't complain too loud when she failed.

⸎

"Ma, I got a note." Paul slipped into the room.

Since Greer had begun complaining of being short-handed, he'd taken to working long hours. He was gone before Glynna woke and came home after dark—usually. Glynna knew better than to relax.

"A note?" Glynna's ribs were still very tender, but they'd stopped the worst of their aching. Her arm was out of its sling now, though it remained sore as blue blazes and she had to favor it. At least she could move it a little now, as the swelling had gone down. "Let me see." She reached for the note with her good arm, the left one. Unfolding it, she saw a name that had only been whispered since she'd come to town.

Stone. It was signed by Luke Stone. The man who had kept Greer so close to home for the last two months. She suspected Luke's threatened homecoming had spurred the beating Glynna had been dealt, because Greer was furious and, worse yet, scared. He'd taken it out on her. And now this mystery man, this whispered name, had contacted her.

She read quickly. It gave her equal parts terror and hope. Folding the note, she said, "Follow me, children."

They went to the closet under the stairs, and she found exactly what Luke had said would be there.

The back door slammed open. Glynna quickly, silently, closed the closet door. "Get upstairs."

"I'm not going." Paul's face twisted with hate.

Glynna thought of the note and was terrified Flint would see it. "Take this, tear it into tiny pieces, and swallow it if you hear him coming." She thrust the paper at her son.

Paul then realized the danger and grabbed the note. Shoving Janet ahead of him, the two ran for the stairs.

Glynna limped to the kitchen. She clutched at her chest. She was feeling somewhat better, but Flint liked to see her hurting, so she moved as if she were in agony.

He strode toward her, meeting her as she stepped into the kitchen. "Where's my dinner?"

If the food was ready, he complained it was bad. If the food wasn't ready, he complained it was late. He always had some complaint, some reason she deserved what he did to her.

She'd even believed it at first, though her first husband had always remarked on what a good cook she was, so she knew the food was decent. She did have a tendency to overcook things, but who wanted something raw? And who minded a bit of scorch on a potato?

But no lack of skill in the kitchen justified the things Flint said, the foul names he called her. And she shouldn't have put up with it for even a moment. She always wondered if she'd stood up to him right from the first, would things have been different?

She'd never know.

"I have leftover roast from last night. There's bread on the shelf, baked this morning. I can try and get you a sandwich, but I'm moving slow. My right arm won't work."

"Get away from that bread. I'll do it. I'll be here all day if I wait for you."

Glynna felt a surge of relief as he confined himself to insults. She moved to the table and sat down.

For better or for worse.

Those vows covered a lot of territory.

In sickness and in health.

Well, a cracked rib equaled sickness, so it was like the

parson was gunning for her, guessing at her complaints and making her vow to endure.

Glynna refused to believe, even after taking vows, that God wanted her here, trapped, hurt, her children being twisted by fear and hate.

The vows a wife took had to be matched somehow by the husband. She'd read a lot of the Bible, but she hadn't found the exact spot that talked about how a marriage worked.

Maybe someday, when she'd read the Good Book all through, she'd find chapter and verse. She knew God well enough after years of prayer that she believed He'd give His blessing to her escape.

She sure wasn't going to wait until she found the right Bible passage before leaving.

"Sit down, Flint." She knew what he expected of her. A polite lady. Polished. He'd never heard of the recklessness of her life or he wouldn't have married her. Why had she been so stupid as to not tell him everything right from the first? Because he'd seemed nice. She hadn't wanted to discourage him. She'd been desperate to leave Arkansas.

Flint came to the table with a sandwich that was two slices of bread cut as thin as he could manage. The roast beef he'd filled it with had been chopped roughly before it went in between the bread.

"Where are you working today?"

"I changed the man delivering milk and eggs so you've lost the man you're flaunting yourself with."

Glynna frowned. She hadn't expected that, since she hadn't seen anyone for a long time. "I've stayed in my room all week. I've never even spoken to anyone who came to the door." She asked, "Who is the hired man you're speaking of?"

"Don't act like you don't know his name is Marty."
Flint slammed a fist on the table.

Glynna jumped.

"I know he's got notions about you and you're leading
him on."

She braced herself for Flint to turn that fist on her. He
was working himself up to a temper.

"You talked about hiring a Marty a while back. Didn't
you say he's just a boy?" Glynna barely knew the men
who worked here. Flint was so jealous, she avoided all of
them to not give Flint a reason to strike her or punish them.

"I didn't like the way he acted when he brought supplies.
I know you talked with him, batted your eyes at him. I'd
fire him right now if we weren't so shorthanded. And he
ain't no boy. He's old enough to want a pretty woman.
I've got someone new to do the chores you're too lazy to
do. An old man whose head won't be turned when you
swing your skirts."

"Let anyone you want bring in supplies." It was all
Glynna could do not to snort. Pretty? Bent over like an old
woman? "I don't remember ever speaking to the boy." She
did actually. She'd been in the kitchen twice when the boy
came in. Both times he'd looked at her and seen her pain.

The first time he'd said, *"I'm going to get you out of here,
ma'am. He can't go on hurting you like this."*

Glynna had told him to leave her alone and get out. That
was the first time Dr. Riker had come.

She'd tried to get Dr. Riker away for the same reason.
To save his life.

The second time the boy had seen her was since Dr.
Riker's second visit. He'd come in and said nothing, but
it was there in his eyes. His wish to protect her. The note

proved he was in communication with Luke Stone and probably Dr. Riker. If Flint found out, he'd kill them all.

God, what do I do?

She thought of that note sent from out of the blue. Luke Stone. Back. Glynna knew nothing except his father had sold the ranch to Greer.

But did she even know that? She only knew what she was told by a man who was the worst kind of evildoer. Lying would be his way. She would assume then that Flint had stolen this ranch and Luke was here to take it back.

Dr. Riker, swearing to help her.

Luke's note with a plan to protect her and the children. They had to be connected. Either that or she had two rescuers working independently. She prayed they knew about each other and could work together. They'd need their combined strength.

"As soon as my arm is better, I can milk the cow and gather eggs and tend the garden. I don't need anyone running those errands. I'm not afraid of hard work."

"I'm not letting you near my animals. And I'm not giving you a chance to flaunt yourself in front of my men. You stay inside, you . . ." Flint called her a vicious, profane name.

She didn't react. An honorable woman would say something. She would demand he treat her with respect, but he was too brutal, and she'd heard it too many times before.

She'd decided earlier that she couldn't ask Dr. Riker to risk his life for her, but now, today, she changed her mind. She'd risk her life, Luke's life, and anyone else's life to get out of here. To stay was to watch Flint destroy her children, even if he never laid a hand on them.

Glynna sat there not speaking. Waiting for whatever cruelty Flint would deal out to her, wondering how she'd been swept into this life.

CHAPTER 15

"We can't wait any longer." Dare slammed both fists on the table.

"Where's John?" Luke surged from where he sat. Usually he could keep himself still, but not today. It had been five days. "He should have been back by now. I'm sick of waiting."

Vince leaned in the doorway, yet his eyes flared with satisfaction when Luke spoke of action. Jonas sat at the table, a picture of calm. Luke was tempted to punch the man of God just to get a reaction out of him.

"And I'm sick of hiding." Luke grabbed his coffee cup. He'd be pacing and running into Dare if he didn't get hold of himself. "It makes me feel like a coward, a rabbit hiding from a wolf."

"I'm done. If it was just your land, we could wait." Dare looked Luke in the eyes. "You know that doesn't mean your land's not important, but we could get it next week or next month. The end would be the same—you'd have it back. But Mrs. Greer is in danger."

Luke looked at Vince. "If we wait any longer, the sheriff could come back."

Vince nodded. "Something's happened to John. Let's get this finished so I can go hunting for him."

"Jonas, you got anything to say?" Dare asked it as if he would turn violent if Jonas disagreed with him.

Jonas held his cup in two hands. Luke realized Jonas was strangling his coffee, more worried than he let on. "I'm ready, too. You're right. Something's delayed Big John. It might just be work. Some job he got assigned that he couldn't get out of, but I doubt it. He wouldn't let much stop him from coming back. So we need to finish this and go help him." Jonas looked up. "Maybe we need to go help him first."

"What about Glynna Greer?" Dare spoke quietly.

He was crazy to go rescue that woman. But Big John—Luke thought of all the times Big John had stood with them, shoulder to shoulder. He'd even personally fought off a man who'd stabbed Dare one time, then pulled the knife out of his back and staunched the bleeding.

"We have to get her out first," Luke said. "I send the note tomorrow, telling her we move the next day. Then we wait for Greer to come to town, killing mad, thinking to drag her back home. That's our chance to grab him without putting Mrs. Greer and her children in the crossfire."

Luke looked at Ruthy. "You stand guard on that overlook. Probably some of Greer's men will abandon their posts and come to town with him. Dodger says he can control the rest of the varmints at the ranch. I'm trusting you to go in there and get Mrs. Greer and her children out and bring them overland home."

Even as he said it, he felt sick with fear for Ruthy. He looked at Dare, then Vince. "It's not right. Ruthy shouldn't be doing this alone."

"Are you willing to go with her and leave catching Greer to us?" Dare asked.

"I oughta." Then his eyes swung to Jonas. "How about you? You go with Ruthy and leave the three of us to handle Greer."

"No," Ruthy said. "All of you need to be here."

"Greer will be riding to town, probably with a few of his men. The fight is here." Jonas looked at Ruthy. "Are you sure you don't want backup? I'll ride with you if you want."

Luke plunked down in the seat beside Ruthy, almost slopping his coffee over the brim of his cup. "If Greer doesn't bring his men with him, or Dodger can't control the ones that stay behind, then you can't get in. You'll have to wait for us to handle Greer, get him locked away, and come to help you. Mrs. Greer should be safe until we get there. What do you think?"

Ruthy's eyes brimmed with determination. "I promise to use good judgment. If it's not a situation I can handle, I'll leave Glynna until I have help. If I think I can get in, bring her out, and get her hidden, then I'll do it."

Luke believed she would. "There's just one more thing." He knew his tone was deadly earnest by the way everyone turned to him.

Vince said, "What?"

"I want Ruthy to marry me. Now. Tonight. Before all this happens."

"Luke," she began, "what—?"

"If I die," Luke said, cutting her off, "I want you to have my name. I want to rewrite my will. I want you to have a home."

"So then I have to pick up the war you've started? If you die, it stands to reason Flint will live."

"No he won't," Dare said with utter assurance.

Luke started again. "If I die—"

"Stop saying that!"

"If I die," Luke repeated, "I want us to be married. My will right now leaves everything to my sister, but she doesn't need this ranch. You do. You need a home, Ruthy. Why not take mine? You know you're going to marry me sooner or later."

"I do not."

Luke's dark eyes held her gaze. "I'm telling you we're doing it sooner. Tonight. Jonas will perform the ceremony. Vince and Dare can be witnesses. Vince can update my will."

Ruthy shook her head. "Luke, please . . ."

She was going to say no. Luke's stomach swooped. He thought he was asking her for practical reasons. He wouldn't mind having a wife and here was a handy woman, pretty and right close by. He liked kissing her and she was a good cook. Why not get married?

But watching her shake her head told him there was a lot more to this than being practical.

He looked at his friends, who all were watching him with intense interest and a fair amount of pity. "Can you leave us alone for a few minutes?"

Vince grinned and slipped out the door with a single step. Dare paced out of the room on Vince's heels.

Jonas stood and gave them both a solemn look. "Marriage is a serious business. It takes two people who are committed to make it something God will bless. Don't do this on a whim, Luke."

Luke met Jonas's eyes. "This is no whim."

Jonas seemed to search around inside Luke's head for too long. He must've seen something he liked because he

gave his chin one jerk down and up. "All right. Good luck."
He left the room.

Luke sat beside Ruthy, who had furrows on her smooth
brow, a frown on her face. But she hadn't started hollering,
and he took that as a good sign.

He needed to do this right. He didn't know much about
women, but he'd heard they were notional critters and there
was probably a right way to propose. Luke reckoned he
hadn't found it so far.

Taking her hand, he tried his very best to be . . . he
struggled for the word . . . uh . . . *romantic*, that was it.

He hadn't practiced this and it was a mistake on his part.
Now he had to think and talk at the same time. And Ruthy
already looked impatient.

"It'd be stupid not to marry me right now in case I get
shot." He smiled. There, that had to be enough romantic-
ness for any woman.

Her eyes narrowed. Which was about as far from *Yes,
I'll marry you* as an expression could get.

"What's the matter?" He tried to figure out where he'd
gone wrong.

"You just called me stupid and talked about getting shot.
Is that supposed to convince me of anything?"

"I said you'd only be stupid if you *didn't* marry me. It
isn't like I insulted you or nuthin'." Judging by the way
her frown had just converted to a snarl, he thought maybe
in her twisted womanly mind—he'd heard talk of how
contrary a woman could be—he'd said something wrong.

Or more likely she'd taken it wrong. Drawing in a slow
breath to give himself time to think, a spark of an idea came
to him. "You like kissing me, right?"

The snarl eased . . . some. Just in case she'd forgotten,

he pulled her right out of her chair and landed her on his lap. Then he kissed her to remind her of how nice it was. Then he kinda forgot about reminding and just kissed her like a house afire. The door to the kitchen opened and he just happened to have his eyes open for a second, because mostly he had them closed.

Dare looked at them, smiled, and ducked back out. The man seemed to think things were going well. Luke had to agree.

Ruthy stopped kissing him, and Luke rushed in before she could start yapping about something that made no sense, like how a woman could kiss a man and sit in his lap and then not marry him.

"You have the most beautiful hair, Ruthy." Luke ran a hand deep into it.

He slid his hand around to support the back of her head, just as his other arm was busy holding her around her waist, keeping her pinned to him.

"I want you to be mine. I want you to be my wife. I can't think how I'm ever going to find a more perfect woman. Marry me, Ruthy. Tonight."

"Luke—"

He cut her off, not liking her tone. A few more minutes spent kissing her and he pulled away again. He could keep doing this just as long as she kept ignoring the obvious. When he looked at her, she still had her eyes closed. They flickered open. Their bright blue seemed to beckon him. Her sunburn had all peeled off and her skin was fair and coated with freckles.

"I've never seen anything so pretty in my life. Please say yes. You know we're going to get married eventually, don't you?"

"Well, probably, but . . ."

"Then why wait?" He took another kiss and when it ended he saw that she'd been swayed.

"I'll marry you, Luke. I can't have a man around I want to kiss as much as I want to kiss you and not be married to him." She shined a bright smile at him. Maybe the brightest smile he'd ever gotten from her. "You're right. It *would* be stupid not to marry you."

"And no woman as hardworking and trail savvy and smart as you could ever be stupid. Let's get Jonas in here and get us hitched."

He boosted Ruthy to her feet, stood, and went to the kitchen door. When he pulled it open, all three of his friends were stepping away from the door, too slow to cover up that they'd been listening in on the whole thing.

Luke rolled his eyes. "You half-wits can come in now."

They all smiled and trooped in, not bothering to deny their eavesdropping.

"Jonas, Ruthy and I are getting married." He went back to her side, took her arm, and hooked it around his elbow, all formal-like. "We'd like you to perform the ceremony."

Smiling, Jonas said, "It would be my pleasure."

Vince and Dare stood beside Jonas as if all three of them were doing the vows. His best friends in the world here with him, witnessing his marriage to the prettiest woman he'd ever seen. It suited him right down to the ground.

He looked forward to getting this marriage over with so he could go shoot Greer without having to worry about what would become of his sweet Ruthy. Then go find Big John and hopefully save him from whatever trouble he was in.

He wasn't sure, because women were a mystery, but he didn't think he should tell her that right now.

"Dearly beloved . . ." Jonas began talking and distracted Luke from trying to make sense of his new wife.

❧

Ruthy had the dreadful feeling that Luke was just marrying her to get some chore out of the way so he could turn his attention to whatever else he had on his list.

She wondered if the idiot she was marrying was preparing to check her off. Still, she wasn't a woman to kiss a man she didn't have serious intentions toward, so of course they needed to get married.

She squared her shoulders, looked at the trio of grinning fools who seemed to think they were all acting as parsons, and resigned herself to a husband who made Virgil Reinhardt look like a low-down, belly-dragging razorback hog. Which of course was exactly what he'd been, no need for Luke as comparison, except that Ruthy figured she'd done well for herself.

The absence of any mention of love was demoralizing. Her parents had genuinely loved each other, and Ruthy wanted that for herself. But she'd seen no sign of that with anyone else. So she'd marry Luke and set to work making him love her.

The encouraging thought helped her stand up straight and speak her vows with conviction.

The ceremony was over about the time she'd squared her shoulders, no fussy words of romance for the men in this house. At least at no point in the ceremony had she been called stupid.

Luke shook hands with his friends. Dare grabbed Ruthy, his eyes twinkling with mischief. "I think the bride should get a kiss for congratulations, don't you, Luke?"

"Get your own woman if you want a kiss." Luke dragged her out of Dare's arms, which Ruthy appreciated.

"So, tomorrow you tell Dodger we want to move the next day, right?" Dare asked.

Ruthy felt a flash of annoyance that her marriage had been pushed aside already. It seemed like a fairly important event to her.

Luke nodded. "Yep, I'll send the note tomorrow telling Mrs. Greer it's time."

She was clearly alone in that.

"Ruthy will head out early the next morning, and we'll wait in town for Greer." Luke looked at Ruthy, frowning. He was worried. She decided it meant he cared—not that he thought she was incompetent. With a mental shrug she decided that if she had to read his mind to discern his feelings, she might as well imagine he was feeling something she preferred.

"We need to write up a will before you go, Vince."

Luke—checking things off his list again.

"I wrote it up while you tricked the poor little lady into marrying you." Vince shoved the will under Luke's nose. "It's a simple will leaving everything to Ruthy."

Luke read all three paragraphs thoroughly.

"What did you think? That I was going to slip in there that you were leaving me your horse?" Vince grinned.

"Nope, I just wanted to see what it looked like. A man oughta know what he's putting his name on." Luke signed. "You sign it too, Ruthy."

She hadn't been listening all that close, but she was pretty sure she'd just taken an oath before God to obey him. She had no memory, though, of a vow saying she had to like it.

"Dare and Jonas, you sign as witnesses." Vince had everything in order. "Time to call it a night." Vince slapped Luke on the back and left without another word. It seemed very sudden to Ruthy.

Jonas nodded and there was a bright flush on his freckled face. "We've got a big day tomorrow. I'll see you then."

That wasn't really true. They had a big day the day after tomorrow. Tomorrow was just for telling Glynna they were moving the day after. Vince and Jonas could sleep all day if they wanted to. But before she could tell Jonas that, he was gone.

Dare said, "I'll go ahead and take Ruthy's room tonight to sleep. My room is bigger. Bring the kitchen lantern up to light the stairs, Luke."

Before Ruthy could say good-night, Dare vanished.

Ruthy turned to Luke. "Didn't you and your friends need to discuss a few more details about the next couple of days?" He was looking at her as if she were truly the most beautiful woman in the world. Which Ruthy knew was hogwash.

"Let's go on up," he said. "We don't want a patient to show up at Dare's door and see us." Luke grabbed the lantern.

"No, of course not."

Luke took her arm in that same formal way he'd done during their wedding, which reminded her they were married. Honestly, she'd have thought she'd feel differently after a wedding ceremony. It was a big step and yet nothing had really changed.

As they reached the top of the stairs, Dare came out of his own room with a stack of clothes. "I put a few of your things in there, Mrs. Stone." Dare said the name with unusual emphasis, then gave her a strange smile, rushed away, and shut himself in the far bedroom.

Ruthy's bedroom. The one she'd been staying in since she arrived in Broken Wheel. The one with the lock and key.

As Luke rested his hand on her back to guide her into Dare's room, she saw a clean dress and nightgown, both of which she'd found in that spare room. Luke urged her forward and shut the door, with him on the *inside* of the room.

With her.

And her nightgown.

And that's when she realized just how married she really was. She was feeling something now.

She tried to form a clear thought because she definitely needed to have a talk with Luke. Sure, they were married, but that didn't mean—

Luke turned her in his arms and kissed her, and she couldn't remember what exactly she'd wanted to say to him.

And not long after that, wrapped in his arms, she didn't have a solitary thought in her head except how much she liked her brand-new husband.

CHAPTER 16

Ruthy couldn't remember the last time she'd been held—
not counting the other times Luke had done it, of course.
But before Luke, in her life with the Reinhardts, they hadn't
touched her except to slap her, or in Virgil's case, paw at
her.

Waking in Luke's arms, she felt an almost desperate
pleasure in being close to another person. That it was her
husband was all the more wonderful. She didn't move.
They needed to get up and get on with the day. It was
still dark, but they always rose before sunrise and got out
of town. They didn't have long and yet it was impossible
for her to move just yet. So, for a few more minutes she
would lie here and be held.

She'd never really noticed the lack of contact until this
moment. But his touch on her skin felt like water in the
desert. It was as if she'd been dying of thirst for years.
And now, as he held her, she let herself be drenched. She
soaked in the glory of it. Could a person be hungry to be
touched? Hungry for contact with someone?

An odd notion, yet that's what it felt like. It was a feast
she couldn't end just yet.

She looked up at Luke, and his midnight brown eyes were open, studying her. There was a look on his face that fed her even more.

"Good morning, wife." It was dark, but her eyes were fully adjusted and she could see his generous smile. She'd made him happy. It was a heady feeling. She let herself revel in it. And truth be told, he'd made her happy, too.

Rubbing her hand over his chest, Ruthy said, "I didn't know how lonely I've been since my parents died. I didn't know how much I needed family. And now I have you."

"So you're getting used to the idea that we got married?" His lips touched hers as if he wanted the kiss to influence her answer, but it wasn't necessary. Her answer should thoroughly please him.

"I'm very glad we got married. I don't know if I'm used to the idea. I'm enjoying it too much to say I'm used to it." Ruthy didn't want anything to break into this quiet moment, but her thoughts were too strong to stay inside. Stroking one hand along his powerful shoulder and down to his elbow, marveling at being held in such strong arms, she said, "I want you to be safe."

"I know." Raising himself onto one elbow, his hand went to her hair and his fingers sank deep until he held the back of her head and leaned close. "Your safety is so important to me that I know how you feel."

"We could just ride away." She ran a finger down his cheek and felt the bristle of the morning's growth of beard. The scratch on her finger was something she'd never felt before, never wondered about. Now she found herself fascinated by it. "We can homestead and start building a ranch with our own two hands. I'm not afraid of hard work."

Luke laughed gently. "That is the honest truth. You are

the workingest woman I've ever known, and you're going to make a fine rancher's wife."

"It doesn't have to be *this* ranch, Luke." Even in the dark, she saw how serious he looked, how intense and sincere.

"I can't just ride away; you know that, don't you, Rosie? I can't let a man kill my father and steal my ranch and not stand up to him. In the war I risked everything to do what I thought was right. I did it in battle, and then in Andersonville. I didn't realize how torn up I was from the war. When I rode away from Pa and the ranch, I was hurting from all I'd seen. All the death, the horrible wounds, the starvation. But instead of facing it, learning how to handle what was boiling inside me, and stick with my pa and my home, I ran. I ran and my pa died. It's my fault my pa is dead. Maybe I couldn't have stopped it, but maybe just being there—with Greer knowing Pa had a son who'd gone to war and came back knowing how to fight—might've stopped him."

"Or maybe Greer would've killed you both."

"It could've happened that way. I'll never be sure, and it can't be undone. But Greer should still pay for what he's done. I have to do this or I can't call myself a man. Can you understand that?"

"Yes, but the thought of losing you when I've only just found you hurts until my heart seems to be stopping. I can barely breathe."

He kissed her, long and deep. When it ended, he said, "What happened with my pa is in the past, and no matter what happens we can't bring him back. With you at my side we could find new land, turn a homestead into a fine ranch. But what about Mrs. Greer?"

That reason was one Ruthy couldn't deny. If Luke

walked away, Ruthy couldn't go with him. She'd have to stay and find a way out for Glynna Greer. And it would add up to the same fight and the same danger, whether for the ranch or for Glynna. There was no way to avoid what they needed to do, and there was no way to keep Luke safe.

"You're right about Greer needing to pay for killing your pa, and about taking back what was stolen. And you're right that we can't leave a woman and her children to be harmed while we ride away to somewhere safe."

"I like it that you would balk at risking our lives for the ranch but would insist on risking them for the safety of a person. I think that makes you a very fine wife, Mrs. Stone." Luke kissed her again.

"My name really is Mrs. Stone, isn't it? I need to say it out loud a few times to get used to it. Mrs. Stone, Ruthy Stone—"

"If you can't recall that you're a married woman, I can think of a better way to remind you."

He was a long time reminding her, and it was much too late when they finally left the house. Dawn was approaching and they risked being seen.

But all that risk couldn't wipe the smile off Ruthy's face.

☙

Glynna had fretting down to an art form.

She was sure there were Bible verses about never being afraid, and others about never worrying. Well, she was doing both and mixing that up with prayers for forgiveness, so in an unfortunate way her worry about worrying and her fears about being afraid were sins on top of just her plain worries and fears.

She suspected God wasn't impressed.

With Flint shorthanded and not coming close to the house most days from dawn till dark, she'd thought of something new to worry about, and she'd written Luke Stone a note to warn him. She felt like she was risking everything to send a note back. Could she trust Flint's cowhands? Maybe if the boy came back, but not anyone else.

"Paul, Janny, we need to plan." She sat at the kitchen table with Paul across from her and Janet at her side. She looked from Paul's resentful expression to Janet's fearful one and prayed and worried and prayed some more. "I told you that any day now we're going to get a note saying when help is coming. I've told you what we have to do, and we've done what we can to be ready. Do you understand what's expected of you? Can you be as patient as I need you to be?"

"I'm not a kid, Ma. And I want out of here as bad as you." Paul crossed his arms as if he was angry with her for questioning him. And he probably was. Angry for the questions, angry that he'd been forced to leave his home, angry that she'd married Flint to begin with.

"Most of all, we're going to have to be quiet. Can you do that?"

"Of course I can be quiet. Worry about Janny crying like a little baby." Paul seemed to want to fight.

"Good, Paul. I'll count on you. Janny, honey, how about you?" Glynna used her good arm to pull Janet close. Her little girl was much more likely to just curl up in a corner somewhere and be completely silent. Glynna hated that her daughter had turned into such a timid child. She hadn't always been like that.

"I'll be quiet, Ma. I can hide for a long time." Janet leaned into Glynna's side.

"I just want to warn you. It might be for hours. Maybe even days. And we're not going to give up, no matter how hard it is."

Janet tucked her head under Glynna's chin and sighed.

Glynna had gone over the plan several times. She pulled her children close just as the kitchen door swung open.

Fighting down the urge to shove her children behind her back, Glynna relaxed when she saw it was the old cowpoke, Dodger, who'd recently begun bringing in the milk and eggs. Had he been chosen because he was more loyal to Flint?

How would she ever get the note from Luke if this man had taken over? Then the old-timer set the food down and reached into his pocket. "I've got another note from Luke, ma'am."

He extended a hand and Glynna was terrified to take it. Was this a test? Did Flint know about the notes and now he'd written one to see how she acted?

"I don't know anyone named Luke. Just leave the food and go, please."

The man looked steadily at Glynna. There was strength in him that tempted her to trust him.

"I can't think what to say to make you trust me. And it's mighty sensible of you not to. Mr. Greer took the boy off the job of delivering to the house and now, if I stay about one minute longer, I'll be taken off, too. I've been meeting with Luke every day. I'm the one who brought the note and gave it to Marty. I'm responsible for the fact that your husband's been losing hands. When the day comes, and it's coming soon, that Luke rides in here to reclaim his land, I'll be backing him because I used to know his pa. Your husband probably murdered him, or hired it done. If Luke needs to know anything about taking back his ranch and you can help him, this might be your last chance."

The man was quiet for a while before adding, "Luke told me about his plan. Told me what you were supposed to do." The old-timer repeated Luke's plan word for word.

"If you're in on this with Flint," Glynna said, "then we're already doomed because this would mean Flint knows everything." She thrust the note she'd prepared into Dodger's hand. "Flint's gone long hours. Luke is counting on Flint running to town when he can't find me. But my husband won't know to chase after me if he doesn't come home until late. So Luke's fight may take place after dark. Flint might even wait until the next morning to ride after me, figuring no one in town will help me and there's no hurry. Luke needs to know that."

Dodger nodded. "Obliged, ma'am. You've done the right thing. I won't see you hurt by Flint, not one more time. I'm not one who can stand for a man laying his hands on a woman to hurt her, and I'm ashamed I didn't realize it was going on long ago. I mean to put a stop to that while I'm helping Luke regain the land that was stolen from him."

Glynna couldn't resist one more question. "Does Dr. Riker know about this? Because he offered to help me."

"I don't know. Luke's never mentioned the doctor's name, but I'll make sure he knows. Now I've gotta go. I've been in here far too long."

As the old man left, Glynna knew Flint would hear about how long he was in the house, even though it was mere minutes. But whatever was going to happen, it was going to be soon. Maybe Flint wouldn't hear about it in time.

She read the note. "It happens tomorrow."

Janet actually smiled. Paul didn't, but his eyes shone and

his chin lifted. She saw guarded hope. She almost regretted it because hope, if it was shattered, would destroy her children and it might well destroy her. And what about the men who were planning to save her and her children? How many of them might die?

"Come here and let's pray." She rested her hands, one each, on her children, noticing her shoulder was working much better. She was going to be able to do this. And if she needed to fight, she'd be ready and willing.

"We'll ask God to protect us and the brave men who are coming. Let's pray no one is asked to pay too high a price for their kindness."

CHAPTER 17

It was time. They'd finish this today or die trying.

Ruthy slipped out of Dare's house while it was full dark. She'd gone out nearly every day but always with Luke, except the first day when she'd been trailing him. But even then he'd been with her, even if he didn't know it.

Luke was with her now, but only until she got on the trail. He'd helped her pack a bedroll and a good-sized pack with food enough for a night on the trail and extra rope to get the Greer family down that cliff.

"I've got you ready to go." Luke gave her a lingering kiss, then pulled back, frowning. "This is all wrong. I should at least walk to the lookout with you. From what Mrs. Greer said, Flint probably won't even ride into town until tonight, maybe tomorrow. I'll go tell Dare we changed our plans."

Ruthy wrapped her arms around his neck. "You know I've got nothing today except a long walk and a long wait. You know that. Now go on back in before the sun pushes back the night." A rooster crowed on the far side of town. A lid slammed in the blacksmith's shop. "You've got to get into Dare's and hide until Greer shows up."

Luke shook his head, and for a second she thought he'd

refuse to let her go on her own. It was insulting. And she'd tell him that if she didn't feel so glad for his protection.

"I know you can handle yourself." He gave her one last awkward hug, the pack getting in the way. "But I'm going to be worrying about you all day."

"Fair enough. I'll worry about you, too. That'll keep things even."

He gave her a lazy salute, and she finally turned and strode away down the trail. She could cover a lot of ground on foot before sunrise. Once the sun was up, she'd need to keep to cover and move much more slowly. Before the narrow trail twisted, cutting Luke off from her line of sight, she looked back and he was there, a silhouette in the dark, watching her. She couldn't see his expression, but she felt sure his worry matched hers. And earlier his smile had matched hers. Maybe even his love matched hers.

She was finding marriage to be a most wonderful arrangement.

"Where've you been?" Greer had a look on his face that'd make a man run for cover, but Simon didn't have time.

"I'll explain later." Simon had been a while getting Lana settled back in the cabin, then riding out to find Greer. "I had trouble and it took me a couple of days to straighten it out. If you want to fire me, then do it. But I ain't got time to talk. I got back last night and found Lana in Broken Wheel and brought her home. She had a run-in with the town doctor."

Greer's anger turned away from Simon to focus on Riker. "That man came to the house when he wasn't needed. He had his hands on my wife."

Simon almost told Greer what Lana had said, about the doctor killing Simon Jr. But it didn't sound right. Why would the doctor kill a baby? Simon decided it must've been an accident during the birthing, which still made it the doctor's fault and the man was going to pay.

"He treated my wife wrong, and I'm going to make sure it never happens again."

"You can go do as you want with the doctor. He oughta be run out of the country as far as I'm concerned."

"I won't be long, boss." Simon reined his horse to head out.

"While you're in town, put out the word I'm looking to take on more hands."

Simon almost twitched with impatience. "The word's out already, but I'll make sure they know you're still hiring."

"You don't need to be all day about it," Greer said. "I need you riding this range. And keep your ears open for any word about Luke Stone. I've got my money out there convincing people to grab him if they see him, but I haven't heard a word since they tried to frame him for robbing a stagecoach a week or so back. They had a posse after him, so I'm hoping the kid's quit the country."

"He ain't no kid, boss. When we shot his pa, he was a kid, but not anymore."

"Not we, Bullard, *you*. *You* shot his pa. And if you let Stone get too close, I'll make sure he knows where to aim his gun proper."

Simon faced Greer, and for a second he could see himself drawing his gun. A bullet slamming Greer to the ground. Greer had never been a tough man. He hired his dirty work done. He put up sentries, hired gunmen, then left his safety to them. He trusted others to protect him because he had money. To Bullard's way of thinking, that made Greer a weakling and a coward. The money had been good, so Bullard had stayed, but no more. The Rangers knew about him, and with one of their own dead, this area would be too hot for Bullard to stay. He'd never killed anyone west of Texas, so after he had it out with the doctor, he'd pick up Lana and head for New Mexico or even California.

"You reckon Luke Stone is gonna see you hiring a man to shoot his pa as being different than shooting him yourself?"

Rage swept across Greer's face, and Simon thought it might come to a showdown. But Greer needed him more than he needed Greer. Greer must've known that because he didn't draw. Or maybe he was just yellow.

"I need a man I can count on, Bullard. You tell me right now if you're that man."

Simon planned to ride to town, shoot that worthless doctor just to make Lana happy, then collect his wife and ride away, all before sunset. What he'd done to that Ranger left him no choice. But Simon wasn't about to make Greer killing mad, then turn and ride away. He might get a bullet between his shoulder blades.

"I'm your man, boss. You can trust me." When Simon rode off, he could feel the itch in his spine. Then he heard Greer's horse come trailing after him.

Reining up, he let Greer catch him, better than to have the coyote at his back. "Did you forget something?"

"Nope, I'm just thinking about my wife and that doctor. I don't like it. If you're gonna shoot the doc, it'll give me pleasure to tell that to Glynna. I'd like to see her face when she hears. It's time my wife learned a lesson about being a hussy."

Simon knew Greer liked to put his hands on his wife in anger. From Greer's tone it looked as if today was one of those days. Mrs. Greer was going to pay for being a bother to her husband. Simon figured it was none of his business.

With a hard nod, the two men set off for the ranch.

CHAPTER 18

Glynna took one frantic look out the window and saw Flint riding up at a full gallop.

Simon Bullard, the brute that backed Flint whenever there was trouble, rode alongside. Her single glance saw Bullard split off from Flint without slackening his pace. Riding for town.

"Children, get in the cellar. Now!" Glynna hadn't a second more to try and figure out what was going on.

Paul came from the kitchen, hustling Janet along in front of him. He swung open the closet door, then moved to lift the small trapdoor that led to the cellar. "Get down there, fast."

Janet scrambled down so fast she almost slid.

"Go, Paul."

"No, Ma. You go next."

There was no time to debate him, so Glynna nodded and went down the ladder.

After closing the closet door, Paul clambered down into the cellar after her, pausing to pull the trapdoor firmly shut. Glynna heard the slide of a bolt on the door and then Paul was on the floor beside her. Only at that moment did she realize what dark really was.

"Silence, children. Absolute silence."

The back door slammed open.

"Glynna, get in here!" Flint's voice was thick with wrath. She'd heard this tone before, always followed by his heavy fists. Flint cursed her, and Glynna wanted to pull her children close and cover their ears. A child shouldn't hear such filth.

"Where are you, woman?" Flint stomped through the main floor, crashing open doors, shouting her name. The children's names. Roaring. Threatening. Swearing.

The search went on and on. Flint thundered up the stairs, his rage building, his threats more brutal and ugly with each passing minute. If he found her now, she knew with certainty she wouldn't survive.

He came tearing back down the steps, stomping around, opening and closing doors again. Then he came to the closet that sheltered them and wrenched that door open.

"Glynna Greer, you get yourself out here or you'll be sorry."

Had he found her? Had his earlier rage just been for the pleasure he took in cruelty? She had no guarantee that he didn't know about the cellar. He'd never mentioned it to her, and it was made in such a cunning way that she'd hoped he'd never noticed it. But how could she be sure until this moment—this life-and-death moment?

Her hiding place felt like a coffin and she was buried alive.

She stood there, hiding underground like a frightened rabbit. And she hated it. How had her life brought her this low?

She felt dizzy. For a moment she thought she might collapse, and that noise would be all it took to bring Flint through the trapdoor and into the cellar, pull them all out, and have them at his mercy.

God, please protect us. And please help me find a life that is pleasing to you, where my children will be safe. Please . . .

That's when she realized she wasn't breathing. Slowly, silently, she pulled breath into her lungs and her head cleared.

More seconds ticked past as she carefully drew in each silent breath.

At last the closet door overhead slammed shut, and Flint's heavy feet thudded toward the kitchen.

Realizing how still her children were, she whispered, "Breathe."

She heard them both inhale and knew that, just like her, they'd been frozen with fear.

Flint continued to bang around upstairs. He searched the entire house a second time, still shouting, his fury growing. Things began to crash, glass shattered, wood broke, heavy objects banged against the walls and floors as if Flint, unable to harm her, had decided to destroy the house instead.

The back door opened, then slammed with such violence she wondered that the door didn't break as she heard him storm down the few back steps, yelling for his men.

Glynna pulled her children tight against her and then began what was probably the hardest part of their plan. They waited.

Ruthy pushed hard for her lookout post, wanting as much of this journey done before sunrise as possible. It was a winding trail most likely made by deer, and even pushing hard it was slow going.

As the dawn turned to daylight, she neared a spot where

she had to cross the well-worn road from Luke's ranch to Broken Wheel. Luke had studied a few crossings and picked this spot. It was closer to the ranch than he liked, but the sentries could see down this road for a long way. Right here trees stretched all the way overhead for just a few yards. She could cross unseen.

She got to the edge of the road and stopped to listen for riders coming or going. Ruthy heard only the breeze stirring the trees and an occasional blackbird cawing overhead.

Not that many riders came and went here. She was likely safe, but caution made sense, so she used it.

Planning to move fast, she stepped onto the trail and felt herself yanked back. Twisting, expecting to see Bullard or Greer, she saw a bough snagged on her pack. She tugged against it, but it was a twisted juniper branch, shoved through a strap on her pack as if it had reached out and grabbed her. She tugged harder and got slapped by the bobbing branch.

Then galloping hooves pounded on the road. They were coming from Luke's ranch. Where she stood at the edge of the trail, she was clearly visible. She pulled out her razor-sharp knife to cut the branch free.

The road curved sharply a few yards down. The rider should be rounding that curve any moment.

There was no way to get out of sight as long as the branch was hooked. She slashed at the branch. It was tough and green, and didn't give on the first try. Cutting again and again, the rider raced toward her at breakneck speed.

Ruthy cut at the branch and finally it snapped. She ran for the nearest boulder, dodged behind it, and looked back at the road. She saw the branch she'd just hacked off lying on the road, its cuts unmistakably fresh. There was no time to go back.

She drew her gun and crouched low to see if the rider would go on or notice the branch and stop to investigate. The galloping horse was suddenly upon her.

The rider, bent low over his horse's neck, didn't see the branch.

Simon Bullard, his face a mask of killing rage.

He was supposed to be gone, locked up. Ruthy knew something terrible had happened to Big John Conroy if Bullard was back and John wasn't.

Her stomach twisted to think of Bullard riding for town, furious. He probably knew Dare had been in on Big John's capture of him. That meant the gunman was riding straight for Dare and Luke, and they weren't expecting him.

Ruthy's first thought was to run for town and warn Luke and his Regulator friends.

She stopped.

She couldn't beat Bullard to Broken Wheel. And Luke might not be ready for Bullard, but he was ready for trouble. Luke and his friends had their job and she had hers. Luke had trusted her to take care of Glynna Greer and her children. Ruthy would shower prayers over Luke and leave him to handle Bullard.

Sick to think her brand-new husband might not survive this mess, Ruthy walked back to that blasted road. Casting the branch out of sight, she hurried on.

If Bullard was upsetting things at the ranch, then Greer might change his usual routine and head back for the house early. Ruthy rushed for her lookout, determined to do her part to make this day come out right.

Luke was so sick of waiting he wanted to smash something.

He heard the door shut on Dare's patient. He was listening close enough that he heard the front door lock. Racing downstairs, Luke was tempted to start kicking things, especially when he knew Ruthy was out on the trail, possibly in danger, getting ready to risk her neck saving the wife of the man who'd killed his pa.

He entered the kitchen just as Dare poured a cup of coffee and held it out to him.

"I have to hide all day while we wait for Greer?" Luke took a tin cup and clutched it until he'd likely have crushed it if the tin hadn't been tough enough. "I'm tired of it."

"I remember that about you, Luke. You always did like to face trouble straight on. Well, something tells me that today you'll get your chance." Dare got his own cup and took a sip when it still had to be almost boiling hot. Every move Dare made spoke of tension, worry for Ruthy and for Glynna Greer.

"We're going to get that woman out, Dare. We've set things in motion." He'd set Ruthy in motion while he hid. His wife, out on that trail, maybe overnight.

"Did I tell you I went out once, not so long ago, and treated Glynna for a sprained ankle?" Dare slammed his cup down on the counter.

"You said you were there before this last time. I don't recall you listing her injuries." Luke took a sip and wondered about Ruthy. What if Ruthy walked in on Greer somehow? "You reckon she was hurt by Greer that time too, don't you?"

Dare took a long drink, staring forward as if he were back tending Mrs. Greer. "She was so rude. Tried to throw me out. Said she wouldn't pay. Didn't want me touching her leg. I thought she was the snootiest thing I'd ever seen, and I was fuming by the time I got her ankle wrapped. I could tell by the way she moved she'd probably hurt her ribs, too. Now, thinking back, I know I saw an old bruise on her face. I should've dragged her out of there."

"And got shot by Greer's guards."

"I can't believe I didn't see it. I left her there to take another beating." Dare ran a hand through his hair. "I'm done, Luke."

"Done with what?"

"Done being a doctor." Dare turned furious eyes on Luke. "I figured I learned enough in Andersonville. I thought I was so much smarter than all the doctors who studied, spent time in school. I actually took *pride* in just learning from another doctor, then heading west to claim I was trained. No one questioned me. No one had any doubts. They came and they trusted their lives to me."

"You've done good for people, Dare. And I think most of doctorin' school is just working alongside another doctor. If you're bent on doing it right, go back East. Find a school that teaches medicine."

"Find a school that teaches a proud fool what a woman looks like and acts like when she's been knocked around? You think they have a school for that?"

"Well, if they don't, then you've got as much training as any doctor in such a thing. You could probably teach others about it."

"I've got no right calling myself a doctor. I'm a liar and a fraud. I'm ashamed of myself." Dare picked up his coffee and stared into the cup. "And I handled Lana Bullard all wrong."

"There's no right way to handle a madwoman. Maybe what you need is just to avoid women altogether. Glynna Greer will go back East. Lana Bullard will go on her way soon. And I'm not lettin' you touch Ruthy. So what you need to do is find a place with no women to treat, and as of tomorrow, that'll be Broken Wheel. You'll be fine here treating only men. It's women that are causing you trouble."

"Don't you want a doctor around for any babies you and Ruthy have?" Dare poured himself more coffee.

The thought of having a baby or two with his wife was so appealing, Luke forgot what they were talking about. Dare slapped him on the back. "Well, don't you?"

"Don't I what?"

Dare rolled his eyes. "Don't you think this town needs a real doctor to treat your wife and children?"

With a shrug, Luke said, "Sure, I reckon. If we can find one, he can come to Broken Wheel and set up a second doctor's office. And when that happens, you can quit. Until then, you need to face the fact that you're better'n nuthin'. And nuthin' is what Glynna Greer would've had without you, and nuthin' would be what Lana Bullard would've had without you. And I suppose some doctors are worse than nuthin', but not you. So just calm down and settle in. I want you here in Broken Wheel. I'm hoping Vince and Jonas stay, too. Maybe Big John'll give up being a Ranger and come be the lawman in town. We're gonna need a sheriff. I like having my friends nearby."

"I've made up my mind. I'm done. I'm going to—"

A horse charging toward Dare's door had them both moving fast. Luke ran out of the kitchen and up the stairs to hide. Again.

Dare hurried toward the door.

Someone twisted the locked doorknob violently, then the side of a fist slammed into the door until it threatened to smash open. "Get out here, Riker! I'm gonna see you dead."

Luke recognized Bullard's voice. What was Bullard doing in town? Where was Big John?

Luke jerked his six-gun from its holster as he turned back. He swung open the revolver with a sharp click, checked the load, snapped it shut, and headed down the stairs.

The time to hide was over.

Ruthy dragged herself up the last few feet of the red-striped cliff and rolled onto solid ground. Panting for a few seconds, she dragged up the supplies tied to the bottom of the rope. Then she went to check on the watchmen and the ranch.

Slipping along, crouched down and silent, she made her way to the line of scrub brush and saw both sentries in place.

A bang drew her attention to the ranch and she saw Greer rushing out of the house. He'd already been inside? This early? Had Glynna and the children gotten a chance to hide?

She was too far to hear what Greer was saying, but she heard his angry tone. Greer's horse stood saddled in the yard. His shouts didn't break his stride. He swung up on a dark red horse and wheeled it to head down the road that would take him to Broken Wheel, running flat-out.

Three men loafing around the ranch yard ran for the

corral. Greer yelled to his sentries as he galloped by. They answered but it was all just noise. Ruthy couldn't make out the words, though she didn't need to.

The guards vanished from their posts. They were abandoning the ranch. She didn't have to hide here for a single minute. Whirling, she raced down the faint trail Luke had shown her that led in a winding path toward the house.

She was halfway to the ranch when she heard more riders racing away. Dodger would either have the drop on the rest of them or they could be trusted. Either way they should all be out of sight and neither see nor hear her and Glynna leave.

Ruthy had time. If Greer was riding to Broken Wheel, he'd be gone for hours, yet she felt almost mad with urgency. Several steep spots slowed her down, but she pushed on as fast as she could.

She stopped when she reached a gap between her and the house. There was an outhouse and a chicken coop to slip behind. A buckboard was parked beside the chicken coop. It gave her one more place to hide. Ruthy suspected the buckboard had been left in just that place on purpose. With one careful look she saw no cowpokes visible around the ranch. She studied the lookout posts to make sure the men hadn't returned.

Determined, she darted from the trees to the buckboard. Crouching low, she hurried to the house and rushed inside. Luke had given her careful directions, and she went straight to the closet, opened the door, and then knocked on the small trapdoor to the cellar. She wouldn't have noticed it if Luke hadn't described it.

"Glynna? Glynna Greer, are you down there? Dr. Riker and Luke Stone sent me to get you out."

There was no response.

"Glynna, my name's Ruthy, Luke's wife. I'm here alone. Your husband has ridden off to town. He must think you've run off and he's going to Broken Wheel to bring you back. Please hurry. We need to get you and the children out of here."

Ruthy heard something stir under her feet. Slowly, as if shoved by shaking hands, something metallic scraping against wood slid beneath the trapdoor.

The door opened and a half-grown boy appeared as he inched the door upward. Blond hair, blue eyes, scared to death.

Ruthy caught the edge of the door and lifted. The boy blinked. The fear in his eyes broke Ruthy's heart.

"Come on out. I've got a way to take you to safety, and we'll make sure Flint Greer never touches any of you again." A mighty bold promise. Ruthy prayed fervently for God to help her keep it.

Dare said the children were Paul and Janet. Paul, his eyes suspicious, climbed out and slipped past Ruthy into the hall. He was taller than she was, still more boy than man physically, but mentally he was far too old. Without checking, she knew he was standing guard.

Next came a little girl who looked like she'd risk death before she'd so much as whisper. Ruthy knew that look. She'd worn it for a while with the Reinhardts.

"Come on out here, Janny." The boy spoke from behind Ruthy, and she heard something unsettling in the boy's voice. A deep anger, a willingness to fight and kill and die to protect his sister. A terrible thing to hear in a youngster.

Next came Glynna. Slow and steady and determined and exhausted. Her complexion pale, Glynna had golden hair and eyes to match. She was unusually pretty. If Ruthy ever had any time to spare, she might just sit down and be jealous.

"How long have you been down there?" Ruthy asked.

"Not long." The woman emerged from her self-imposed grave. She was an older version of her daughter. "Flint came in so early, we hadn't even thought to go down yet. We ran for the cellar and then listened while he hunted for us. Then he left."

Glynna stepped away and Ruthy let the trapdoor drop with a loud clap. Glynna started as if she'd heard a gunshot. Ruthy remembered that—the fear so close to the surface.

Leaving the closet with Glynna and the children right behind, Ruthy said, "We've got a place close to town for you all to hide until Greer's locked up tight." Or dead, but Ruthy didn't say that. These three all looked so fragile she couldn't add talk of killing to what they'd been through. "Let's go."

No sense waiting one minute longer. Ruthy felt her arm caught and she turned to face Glynna. Tears brimmed in the poor woman's eyes and suddenly she hurled herself into Ruthy's arms. Ruthy caught her and hung on tight.

The children came and grabbed hold, too. It reminded Ruthy of how it felt to be held by Luke. Oh, things were very different of course with a husband. But the contact was wonderful. It soaked into her skin and gave her strength.

She hung on for a long moment. Then Glynna let go, swiped tears away with her forearm, and her eyes changed from fear to resolve. "Let's get out of here."

Ruthy smiled and realized she had a tear or two of her own. She brushed at them, nodded. "Follow me."

She turned to lead the way out just as the kitchen door swung open.

CHAPTER 19

Bullard didn't have his gun drawn, so Dare swung his door open. What had happened to bring Bullard back and not Big John? The possibilities were limited and ugly.

"What's the problem, Simon?" Dare knew what the problem was. Bullard figured out that Dare had a hand in knocking him cold and sending him off to prison.

Concealing his side by standing close to the doorframe so his arm wouldn't show, Dare reached for his six-gun, in its holster, hanging on a hook by the front door. He slid the Colt out and tucked it into the waist of his pants.

He heard Luke behind him. Luke Stone was a good man to have at your back.

"You killed my son!" Bullard's hand flexed, only inches from his gun.

The accusation stopped Dare for a second. "What are you talking about? What son?"

"Lana told me everything, you yellow coyote."

"She told you I killed a defenseless baby?" Dare was so offended he couldn't think straight.

"Don't try and lie your way out of this, Riker."

"Simon, there was no baby born. You need to calm down and talk to me. You know she . . . she . . ." Was dropped on her head too many times as a child? Was a foam-at-the-mouth lunatic? Was crazy as a drunken she-weasel? ". . . was upset. But there was no baby born."

No baby ever to be born. But Dare didn't think Simon was quite ready to hear that.

"You think I'm gonna take your word over my wife's?" Simon looked to go for his gun, but then hesitated. The man had himself some doubts. Dare walked down the three steps on his front stoop and got close enough that Simon would have a hard time pulling his gun and shooting without Dare blocking his draw.

"I'm not saying your wife is lying, Simon. I'm saying she's wrong. Confused. She thought she was having a baby, but how many times has she done that before?" It was boiling in Dare to lash out. To pull his gun and fire. Big John was almost certainly dead or so badly hurt he couldn't get back to Broken Wheel. But near as Dare could see, Bullard had no notion of bringing that up. This was about doctoring.

"Let's go get a cup of coffee in the diner and talk this out." Dare turned a very confused Bullard around and started him walking back toward the one-block stretch of Broken Wheel businesses. The doctor's office was set back and near the woods that surrounded the town. They needed to move about a hundred feet to get to the raised board-walk that lined both sides of the closest thing Broken Wheel had to a main street. Dare wanted Bullard away from his house so Luke could have a chance to slip out. There were no horses or wagons in town besides Bullard's, standing ground-hitched by Dare's house. Duffy's Tavern and Tug Andrew's General Store were open. The door was ajar on Sledge Murphy's livery, which was down here on Dare's end of town but set back a ways. Dare heard a hammer ringing as Sledge banged it against an anvil.

He suspected Luke was so sick of hiding he'd take a chance on being seen in order to get to Vince with the news of Bullard showing up, and Big John's disappearance.

Bullard must've suspected his wife wasn't thinking right because he came along instead of drawing his gun.

Dare considered where to launch his attack. There'd be someone to notice them—Tug Andrew, the store's owner, was the type to watch out his window if anything moved— but Dare was tired of biding his time. Bullard was here right now. Greer might be coming any minute. They'd intended to take Simon out of the fight and now here he was back in town. This was Dare's chance to thin the herd, but he couldn't shoot Bullard in cold blood.

That's when Dare realized that on the way to the diner, they'd have to pass the jail. A jail with no one home and the cell sitting empty. Something mean curled inside of Dare. He didn't intend to let this brute hurt Big John and not regret it. He rested his hand on Simon's shoulder and then pulled it back when he realized he was getting ready to grab Bullard by the neck.

Dare stepped up onto the board-walk. "You really came in here thinking I killed a child? Haven't I taken good care of your wife?"

Simon nodded. "She's out of her head with grief, though, Doc. Something's wrong. You should come out and take a look at her."

"I should come and doctor a woman who's accused me of murder?" The jail was right ahead. It wasn't exactly fair, but nothing about this moment called to the straight shooter in Dare. Bullard turned to look across the street.

Dare pulled his gun and slammed it over Bullard's head. The man went down like a stunned ox.

∽

The jailhouse door swung open.

Luke, staying back, said, "Get that varmint in here. I want to know what he did to Big John."

"He ain't gonna talk for a while." Dare grabbed the back of Bullard's collar, dragged him inside, and kept going straight to the cell. Vince had the bars open, the key ready. Dare dropped Bullard on the floor none too gently.

"We've got to find Big John." Vince slammed and locked the cell.

"First we've got to make sure Ruthy is okay." Luke closed and locked the front door.

Thundering hooves came racing into town from the road to Luke's ranch.

Dare rushed to the window. "Both of you are wrong. First we've got to kill Flint Greer."

"How many are with him?" Vince asked.

"Six counting Greer."

"Then I suggest we don't run out into the street and face him head on." Vince stepped to Dare's side and looked at the oncoming mob. "This is the first place Greer will come to get the sheriff to back him. Unless we want to try and shoot it out from here, we need to fall back and come at their flank."

Vince thinking in military terms.

Dare knew how to take charge, too. "We leave Bullard locked up. If we take the key, it'll slow them down getting him out. It'd be better to tie him up, drag him out of town, and hide him, but we don't have time."

Jangling the keys, Vince said, "I got 'em." Vince was a natural leader, so Luke wasn't surprised when a few orders got tossed right back. "We need to get Jonas, then split those men up to even the odds. Six men. We can't just shoot an unconscious man, so we're going to have to hope Bullard stays unconscious while we fight the rest of 'em. Otherwise it's seven men, and Bullard is the toughest of them all. If he wakes up and they find a way to free him . . ."

"For what he did to Big John, we could justify dead or alive." Luke's eyes narrowed as he looked at Bullard.

"We maybe could to the law, if we lied," Vince said. "But we can't to ourselves or to God Almighty." Vince went on with his orders. "Luke, you take Greer. Dare, you—"

"No," Dare said, cutting him off. "I get Greer. I saw what he did to his wife. I owe him for that. I owe her justice."

"He stole my pa's land," Luke said with quiet rage. "He either killed Pa or had him killed. I owe him for that."

"If he hired him killed, who do you think did it?" Vince asked.

They all three looked at Bullard, lying motionless in the locked cell.

The riders began to slow and looked to be coming straight for the jail.

"Both of you capture Greer." Vince shoved Luke and Dare toward the back of the jail. "I'll take care of the other five myself. Quit arguing and let's get out of here."

Luke shoved the door open and almost smacked Jonas in the face. Vince came out last and closed and locked the sheriff's office.

"I'm gonna say this because it needs to be said." Jonas's eyes connected, one by one with each of them. "There may be killing done here today. But each of you are believers. I know, Luke, that you've got a burning need to avenge your father. Dare, I can see you almost breathing fire when you talk about Glynna Greer. Vince, you're ready for trouble at the drop of a hat and you don't mind dropping the hat yourself. But if you want God on your side, you'd better be on His. We take these men prisoner if possible and let the law handle them. If it's not possible and you take a life, well, we've all been through war and we've all killed. We know the burden of it. This day is about justice, not vengeance. Remember that."

Jonas casually clicked his revolver open, spun the wheel to make sure there wasn't an empty chamber, and snapped it shut. "Vince, we'll let these two get Greer together. We'll split the other five. I'll take two, you take three."

"Why don't you take three and I take two?" Vince asked in mock outrage.

"Cuz I'm a preacher. I try and keep my shooting to a minimum." Jonas shoved his gun into his holster with such ease it told its own story about how Jonas had lived before he became a parson. "And you'd best know that I intend to take all of mine prisoner. I'm not killing anyone." Jonas paused, then shrugged one shoulder. "Well, I might wing 'em. But I'm not shooting anyone dead."

"Let's go. We'll divide and conquer." Vince flashed a smile, and Luke knew his friend loved walking wild.

Wheeling away, Vince headed for his office, which would get him to the south side of town.

"I'll stay in that clump of cottonwoods." Dare jabbed his index finger at the woods right near the jail. There was about twenty feet of open space stretched between the back door of the jail and the trees on the edge of town. "I'll see who I can pick off."

"Let's slide around to the north and east, boy. Surround the town." Jonas clapped Luke on the shoulder. Jonas didn't smile. Not like Vince.

It cost Jonas to buy into the fight. He'd do it and figure it was right, but Jonas told the absolute truth that killing a man didn't sit easy on a conscience. Truth be told, as furious as he was, Luke wasn't happy about it. He'd left killing behind after the war and never wanted to have anything to do with it again. And now here he was. But it was justice for his pa and safety for a battered woman. Luke could do nothing but fight.

They reached the trees. Dare hunkered down. Luke and Jonas, using red boulders and scrub brush to conceal themselves, ran to the north, away from Vince's side of town.

They could get Greer and his men in a crossfire or get them spread out and take them one by one. Luke wished for Big John to help, but mostly he prayed his Ranger friend was still alive.

"Glynna Greer, you get out here!" Greer shouted it from on horseback. His anger, because of his wife, was a strange echo of Bullard's. Luke looked back and caught Dare's eye.

Low and quiet, Luke's voice still carried. "Ruthy's getting Glynna out right now. Our plan is working."

Dare jerked his chin in agreement and moved, dodging trees and boulders. He was soon out of sight.

The plan is working? Luke frowned.

Yep, things were going great.

Six against four. Seven if Bullard came around.

Women and children hiding in the wilderness, their lives hanging in the balance because Ruthy, even plucky as she was, couldn't get away to the next town with her little band.

Big John missing and maybe dead.

Oh, it was working great. They were one measly life-and-death gun battle away from things settling right down.

❧

The door to the kitchen opened, and the look on Dodger's face made Ruthy wonder for one heart-pounding moment if she'd trusted the wrong man.

"Let's go. Let's get you all out of here."

Ruthy started to breathe again. "With Greer gone, can you give us horses so we just ride straight for town?"

He shook his head. "Sorry, ma'am. I want you up that highland trail right now. Greer could turn around and come back. There's a long, narrow neck on that road and you can't get off it easy. I don't have enough men to protect you if we went that route. I don't know what'll happen in town, but if things go wrong for Luke, I want Greer to believe his wife snuck away and done a good job of it. I'll stay here and cover your tracks." Dodger paused and added, "Maybe I should come."

"No." Ruthy was just flat-out honored that a trail-savvy cowpoke like Dodger trusted her with this job. With a wash of fear, she knew that if Greer came back, it would almost certainly mean that Luke was dead. If that happened, Glynna needed to look as if she'd run off on her own.

Dodger looked torn apart with wanting to come along and protect them all. Finally he jerked his chin up and down. "Go on then. You said you had a place to hide the family near Broken Wheel, so get busy hiding them."

"I didn't expect to see you, Dodger. I thought you'd be holding any men loyal to Greer at gunpoint until we were gone."

"That was the plan. But all the bad seed rode off with

Greer." Dodger's eyes shifted to Glynna. "There ain't a man left on the place that will betray you, Mrs. Greer. We'll do whatever we can to help you all stay safe." He switched his gaze to Ruthy. "I know the spot you are going to use to hide. If you need help, I'll know it. Wait for me there and I'll help you all get to Fort Worth."

It sickened Ruthy to think what that meant, but she gave Dodger a firm nod. "Thank you." Ruthy looked back and saw Glynna, her eyes bright with determination. "If this day ends like I think it will—like I hope it will—this house'll never see Flint Greer or his ruffians again." Dodger held the door open. "Go. I'll quick look through the house and make sure you haven't left any sign of where you're going."

Ruthy thought of the trapdoor. She remembered the slap as it went shut. But had they closed the closet door? Had they moved anything that Greer would notice? She thought of the kitchen. Chairs tipped over and broken. The table on its side. A window broken. Pans thrown. Gouges in the walls. Destruction everywhere. She had a spark of anger at knowing this would soon be her home and she was going to have to clean up the mess.

Ruthy dashed out of the house with Glynna, Paul, and Janet on her heels.

She didn't bother winding around the chicken coop or the buckboard. If Greer or any of his henchmen were returning now, she'd hear hoofbeats. Hurrying was more important than sneaking. So moving quickly, they reached the base of her trail with no sign of Greer.

They started the climb. Ruthy looked back a time or two. The Greer family just kept coming. Paul first, Janet next, with Glynna close behind, favoring her arm but not slowing them down. A few times the trail got steep enough they were more climbing than walking, but without the sentries to be mindful of, they made good time.

They reached the highland, where Ruthy was supposed to lie in wait. Now she needed to lower two children and a badly shaken mother with a wounded arm and fragile ribs down a cliff.

She looked back at her companions. "This is going to be hard."

Glynna gave Ruthy a weary smile. "You've just described my whole life."

Ruthy had described her own life, too.

"I'll search every house in this town until I find you, wife!" Greer was working himself up into a lather. "Any man hiding her dies."

His shouts got louder, his threats uglier.

The folks in this town had stood by while Greer took Glynna back last time. What kind of men were they? Maybe Luke was up against more than six men. Maybe he was up against the whole town.

Broken Wheel seemed like a ghost town. No one stepped out into the street, curious to see what was going on. The banging from the blacksmith had stopped.

Greer wheeled his horse, his hands rough on the reins. The man sat on his horse like a king, expecting his subjects to obey. But he was a king with a stolen kingdom.

Luke intended to enjoy knocking that ill-gotten crown off Greer's head. Luke scanned the buildings, planning how to get closer to Greer to get this over with. He'd heard every word Jonas had said. He'd take Greer alive if he could.

Looking at the layout of Broken Wheel, Luke planned his next move. There was the row of businesses, five on each side of the packed-earth street, some of them empty. They had board-walks on each side of the street, and those were the only ones in town.

There were other buildings, maybe two dozen, most of them ramshackle and empty, and some homes scattered around, but no one had taken the time to make Broken Wheel orderly. Dare's house was near to hand, and Luke could've run in there and gotten a lot closer to the action. But he didn't want Dare's house shot up, so he thought it best to steer clear of it. The church was sitting off to the east on this end of town. It seemed wrong to hide out in God's house.

There was the livery that included a blacksmith between the church and the business row. Luke had heard someone pounding iron in there earlier, but there was only silence now.

The only visible activity anywhere was Greer and his five men. No one had come out in response to Greer's shouted questions about his wife. If the townsfolk were the pack of yellow cowards Luke suspected, they'd all dived under a table with plans to stay there.

Greer dismounted. He strode toward the jail. No doubt he expected to find Sheriff Porter inside and drag the man along to give any search the force of the law. The rest of his men were tying up their horses to a hitching post.

It was a quiet town on its best day and this was nowhere near the best. This was the kind of day where flying lead provided a chance for an innocent man to die.

Greer tried the jail. A new bout of rage came when Greer couldn't get the door open. Luke had locked it. No sense making a single thing easy.

The shouting drew all his men toward him. Luke moved far enough that the whole group was hidden by the livery. He ran into it from the woods.

Inside, he found the blacksmith sitting on the floor behind a heavy feed trough, his forge red hot and abandoned. The smithy, a man Luke had never met, saw Luke and raised both his hands.

"I'm not here to bother you." Luke had his gun drawn and figured he looked like all kinds of bother.

"Greer's a good customer."

"He killed my pa, and he's left his wife beaten and bleeding more than once. Is he a man you want to back in a fight?"

"Nope, customer or not, I've known Greer is trouble for a long time. I don't like the scars he puts on his horse. But I'm new in town. I ain't heard anything about him hurting his wife. And I don't know you, mister. I'm not likely to take your word on much."

Luke pointed to the back door. "If you don't want in, get out. Keep walking straight north for a while, then hole up in a spot where no flying lead will hit you."

"Sounds like good advice." The man hopped up and shot out the back door.

Luke studied the street through the mostly closed livery doors, which could be swung wide to drive a wagon through. He'd seen Greer a few times years ago. But this was the first time he'd laid eyes on him since coming home.

He'd never have recognized him. Wild beard, hair on the back of his hands and showing from the two open buttons on his sweat-stained broadcloth shirt. He'd needed a haircut for a year. When Luke saw him last, Greer had been tidy. A hard man but polished. Now he looked like an animal. Run to fat. Ham-sized fists, growling and shouting threats. Demanding to know where the sheriff was.

It was awful to think of him using those massive hands on his wife.

Picturing his father, Luke's hand went to his gun. He could do it. Greer was just a few yards away, and Luke was deadly with a pistol. He was even better with a rifle, but his six-gun would do. He could put a bullet in Greer and end this. Greer had his back to Luke and wouldn't even know. His men would probably ride off once their boss was dead. No one who made his living with a gun stuck around when there was no one to pay wages.

Luke could feel it. Feel the prodding from his gut.

Kill Greer. End this.

Another voice, more a whisper, came from his soul.

If you kill Greer like this, you become him.

He hadn't forgotten Jonas's words. *"If you want God on your side, you'd better be on His. This day is about justice, not vengeance."*

His gut spoke again.

Kill Greer. Stop this before anyone dies. One bullet. Think of Pa. Think of Big John. Picture him turning those massive fists on Glynna.

Luke heard a metallic crack and looked down to see he'd drawn his gun. He'd raised it. His finger settled rock steady on the trigger.

CHAPTER 20

"We need to send you down first, Glynna." Ruthy opened a loop in her rope.

"No, I want the children away from here." Glynna slid an arm around Paul and hugged him.

Ruthy saw Glynna's need to make the boy go, when the boy clearly wanted to take care of his ma.

"We need an adult up here and another down there. That's you and me, Glynna." Ruthy held up the heavy coils. "I need Paul's help to lower you. With your arm injured, we'll need to bear most of your weight. I don't know if I can do that alone." Ruthy looked at Paul. "But Paul and I, braced against a tree, along with you holding on to the rocks as much as possible to ease your weight, we can do it." She hoped.

Glynna didn't like it. Ruthy had a feeling the woman had gotten into the habit of sacrificing everything for her children. It might even explain how she'd ended up married to Greer.

Glynna nodded. "I can be down there and help the children get out of their ropes."

"You go over right here." Ruthy moved fast with getting a loop around the woman, then pointed to a spot that didn't look much better than anywhere else. But then she and Luke had climbed up and down with no rope at all.

Glynna sat on the ledge, turned over on her belly. With a suppressed wince of pain, she said, "I've found the first foothold."

"Wait before you go." Ruthy went to the nearest tree, not big but big enough, and circled it while holding the rope. "Paul, come and help me pay it out as your ma goes down. Janet, go watch your ma. Call out if you have any trouble, Glynna. Between us all, we can do it."

Glynna swallowed hard, moved her right shoulder gingerly, and flinched in pain. "All right. Let's get this done."

Vanishing over the edge, Ruthy felt most of Glynna's weight for just a second, and then the weight began to lessen.

"She's climbing down pretty fast." Janet watched over the cliff's edge. Ruthy wanted to go see, measure the progress. Instead, she held the rope tight, letting it out hand over hand, testing it constantly for a sudden jerk that might mean Glynna was struggling.

"I'm down." Glynna's voice came from the base of the cliff. "I'm free of the rope. Pull it back up."

"You're next, Janet." Ruthy dragged the rope up as fast as she could.

The little girl nodded as Ruthy secured the loop around her chest, tucked under her arms. Ruthy started lowering her, not waiting for the girl to find a handhold. After the little one was out of earshot, she looked over her shoulder at Paul, who was feeding out the rope as quickly as Ruthy was.

"You're going to mostly climb down. You can do it. I'm going to stand here bracing the rope just in case you slip and fall, but you can do this without help."

The boy's shoulders slumped. Ruthy worried the boy might be afraid of heights or some such thing.

"I couldn't protect my ma." Paul's voice was a near whisper. "I should have been able to, but I was too scared. I just stood by and let him hurt her."

"I had a family take me in when my parents died. They were heavy with the punishment, and I felt a fist or the back of a hand or a heavy boot whenever it suited them. I couldn't fight back. I was too small. I tried a few times and they seemed to like it; it gave 'em an excuse to hit me harder. Greer's a bully and a brute. Any man who puts his hands on a woman in anger is a coward. If he weren't, he wouldn't feel the need to show his strength against someone who can't best him."

"If he's such a coward, how come we couldn't scare him off?"

"The real trouble with a coward like Greer is, if you had been bigger and faced him and fought him, then he'd get sneaky." Ruthy thought of Luke back in town. Her husband was a man who faced trouble head on. "He'll shoot from cover or stab you in the back."

As she said it, Ruthy felt an almost frantic need to go to town, to back Luke somehow. She had a gun. She could keep watch, see if Greer was sneaking around, coming up from behind.

"I'm down." Janet's voice sounded from below. "Pull up the rope."

"Your turn, Paul."

The boy went to the ledge, looked over as hand over hand Ruthy recoiled the rope.

"What we're doing right now is sneaky." Paul studied the cliff, maybe looking for footholds.

"No it's not," Ruthy said. "It's smart. Luke and Dare—"

"The doctor? He's in on this?" Paul seemed interested, and Ruthy wondered what all had happened when Dare had treated Glynna. The rope was all the way up, and Ruthy looped it around Paul's chest.

"Yep, the doctor helped plan it. The two of them can handle that coyote of a stepfather of yours, and they've got other men fighting with them. We're carrying out our part of the plan exactly as we should. It's never cowardly to avoid a fistfight with a man who outweighs you by two hundred pounds."

Paul nodded as Ruthy tightened the rope. He looked at her, worried. "There's no one to lower you down."

"I've been up and down this cliff now a few times. I'm just going to climb. No rope."

A smile popped out on Paul's face. "Bet I can do it, too."

"I'll bet you can. I'll be holding the rope, but I don't expect to use it a single time."

With a nod Paul went over the ledge, scampering down the cliff with the confidence of a mountain goat.

He never put an ounce of weight on the rope, and Ruthy was smiling when she looked down at her friends. "Mind the rope." She dropped it, then turned and climbed down herself.

Now all she had to do was get them to the hiding place near town, then get her gun and go fight for her husband.

Honestly, with all the work she had to do today, she probably should've made a list.

❦

Luke jerked his finger away. He'd almost done it. Shot Greer in cold blood.

"If you want God on your side, you'd better be on His."

Greer lifted one foot and slammed it into the jailhouse door. Luke could go charging out. Brace Greer, demand a shootout. Face-to-face wasn't murder. The chance would slip away when Greer got inside.

Kicking again, Greer splintered the door. He rushed inside. Luke heaved a sigh of relief. He hadn't killed, and he hadn't died. Waiting had been right.

From inside, Greer shouted, "Get in here!"

Every one of his men hurried inside. Luke lowered his gun. He saw Vince poke his head out the door of his law office. Luke stepped into sight briefly so Vince would know where he was.

"Bullard!" The cell door rattled. Greer yelled as he fought the door to release his hired gun.

Garbled yelling went on inside. All Luke could make out was when Greer shouted, "You three men find my wife. You two bust the window out of this cell."

Five men burst out of the sheriff's office. Two of them went to their horses and led them around the back of the jail. The other three fanned out, one to the general store, one toward the livery, and one down the board-walk toward Vince. Luke watched the hired gun head straight for him. He might not get Greer, but he could get someone.

Then Luke heard another crash—the back door of the jail being kicked open.

⌘

Greer kicked the front door open to the sound of shattering wood.

Dare listened from his spot behind the jail as the idiots tried to break Bullard out of jail. Their efforts, from what he could tell, were mainly directed toward banging on the cell door and swearing.

He knew they were getting desperate when two of them led mounts to the back of the jail.

Greer kicked open the back door as his men came around and met him. "Tie ropes to the window, then yank it out with the horses."

"Will do, boss."

Dare recognized one of the men. He'd been at Greer's house the second time Dare'd come out. The coyote had stood guard after Greer threatened to shoot Dare for tending his unconscious wife.

Six men in all. Two of them back here, stringing ropes from their horses' saddles to the cell's window. The buildings blocked his view of any other movement, except for one man angling toward the livery. Dare had seen Luke slip in there. If the two others were wandering, Dare hoped Vince and Jonas got them out of the fight.

Greer stomped his way back into the sheriff's office, impatient with watching his men secure the ropes. A motion to Dare's right drew his attention to Vince, who was walking bold as brass toward the two men. It struck Dare that he didn't really need to hide—except for the very real possibility that Greer would focus his rage on the doctor who'd been out to his ranch. But honestly, *Luke* needed to hide. Dare belonged in this town. He could walk its streets. He straightened and strode toward the two men. They were distracted, working on the ropes, knotting them to the bars so they didn't see him coming.

Vince picked up speed so they'd reach the men at the same time. Dare wondered if hitting a man over the head from behind would make Jonas proud. Dare took the one on the left, the one he recognized. The polecat who'd stood guard to keep Dare from protecting a beaten woman. With one wicked stroke from his gun butt, he knocked the man out cold.

Vince's man went down at the same instant.

"Get 'em down to my place, quick." Vince, in charge whether it was his fight or not, grabbed his man by the feet and dragged him away.

Dare's victim wasn't a big man, so he tossed him over his shoulder and rounded the horses that stood calmly with their backsides toward the jail.

They made quick work of rushing to Vince's place. "We'll tie 'em up and gag 'em, and then lock them in here for now. There's a man out front who might wander close enough to grab."

"Luke's got one heading for the livery, where he's hiding." Dare flipped the man off his shoulder and used the man's own handkerchief to gag him. "There's one more I couldn't see."

"He went into the general store."

"Is that where Jonas went?"

"I haven't seen hide nor hair of Jonas. I'll handle these men. You take the horses to the woods and hide them. Greer might think his men ran off."

"Go help Jonas if you can find him." Dare started to head out. "Hate to make a preacher resort to violence."

Vince let a smile spread over his face. "Always thinking of others, my friend."

⁂

"We've got to hurry. I need to hide you and then get to town. We'll move fast for as long as we can." Ruthy didn't bother bringing her heavy pack. She took Janet's little hand and set a pace just short of running.

"Where we going to hide?" Glynna's voice shook. Ruthy could tell the woman didn't believe she was safe from Greer yet. Smart woman.

"We've found a place not far from Broken Wheel that gives you good cover."

"You shouldn't go back to town. Not until we're sure it's over." Glynna had her right arm clutched against her stomach, yet she kept up without a word of complaint.

"I suppose I shouldn't." Ruthy couldn't explain the pressing need she had to get to town. Luke wouldn't like it, but Ruthy felt as if God himself was telling her she needed to get into the fight.

The men weren't expecting Bullard. And Bullard's presence proved Big John had met a grim fate. Which meant Luke and his friends would be killing mad at the exact moment they needed most to keep cool heads.

There weren't any lookouts to fret over, so Ruthy pushed fast, not worrying about keeping to cover. When they reached the spot to cross the trail, she said, "Hold up."

She listened but heard no riders on the road. She raced on, knowing that Luke's life might depend on her getting there to help him. She couldn't shake the mental image of Bullard shooting Luke in the back, or men holding Luke while Greer worked him over with his fists.

Moving faster as the image overwhelmed her caution, they followed the faint game trail. Ruthy regretted she hadn't taken the chance of following the road to Broken Wheel; they could've reached the hiding place for Glynna and her children much faster. But she remembered her promise to do exactly as Luke had said.

Her going to town wasn't doing as he'd said—pure opposite in fact. She figured that if she was going to disobey him so thoroughly in that, she'd as soon mind him in other ways.

They were an hour pushing for town through rocks and woods, twisting and turning on this blasted, poky trail that snaked around the red mesas and rugged washes. At last they came to the spot Luke had picked—an overhang fronted with a heavy stand of trees. It was almost like a cave, with room inside for all three Greers.

"In here," Ruthy said. They were now close enough to town for her to walk the distance in a few minutes' time.

"We stowed some food and water for you." Ruthy pointed to the supplies stacked in a back corner. "A rider can pass by right in front of this place and not know you're inside here, so long as you're quiet." Ruthy drew a pistol and two boxes of cartridges from the supplies. "Here. I'm leaving you a gun."

Ruthy gave Glynna a hard look. Mrs. Greer didn't seem all that tough to Ruthy, but then the woman had been through a hard spell. Besides that, they'd just met. Who could tell what the woman was made of?

Glynna took hold of the gun and cartridges held out for her. "I should come with you. The children could stay here and hide."

"Nope. If this goes bad, the children will need you. No one'd miss me much, or Luke, come to that. We'd miss each other of course. But you've got young'uns who need you, Glynna. You need to protect yourself for their sake."

Glynna nodded and looked at the gun. "You're right. I don't like hiding while you face danger on my behalf, but you're right. Thank you, Mrs. Stone. Ruthy. Thank you for helping us. No one else in this town would risk my husband's wrath. God bless you for taking the chance."

"Remember, Dodger will come for you if I don't. Whatever happens to the rest of us, you and your children are going to be fine. I've gotta keep moving." Ruthy tucked her own gun and bullets in a smaller bag, said goodbye, and sprinted toward town.

Dare rushed out of Vince's office by the back door and took a long chance. He pulled his knife and slashed the ropes tied to the jail window and led the horses away at a trot, aiming for slabs of red rock high enough to hide a horse. He needed to get behind them.

Just as Dare rounded the slabs, Greer bellowed, "What's taking so long?" The back door of the jail banged open.

Dare froze behind the rocks. Had Greer seen him? Had the horses been out of sight? If they weren't, maybe Greer'd come chasing after Dare, giving him a chance to face him man to man. He had to hurry if he wanted to take care of Greer. Luke wanted that honor bad.

If Greer thought his men had run off, he'd look to the trail north, away from Luke's ranch. And if Greer went after his men, they could get this fight out of Broken Wheel and away from unlucky townsfolk who might find themselves in the way of a stray bullet. Although everyone seemed to be laying mighty low.

"Where'd you men get to?" Greer was purely roaring now, and that meant Dare had gotten away. He lashed the horses to a mesquite. He should hide them better, but there was no cover good enough without walking a long stretch.

"Boss, come in here," a voice called from inside the jail. "Cal's back and we're almost ready."

Dare hurried back to see what they'd try next to get Bullard out, wishing he could get his hands on another man or two, or maybe even grab Greer.

The back of the jail was clear. Dare couldn't tell what was going on in there and he wanted to know. He left the cover of the trees and made a dash for the jail.

He was just a few paces past a clump of cottonwoods when an explosion ripped the jail apart.

The back door blasted straight at him. It slammed flat into Dare and sent him hurling backward.

⁂

An explosion sent Ruthy diving for the ground.

Landing flat on her belly, she looked up and saw smoke coming from less than a hundred yards ahead. Leaping to her feet, she felt God pushing her, urging her on at top speed. She stumbled to a stop when she saw two horses tied in the woods, wearing Greer's brand. Were his men searching the woods even now?

Ruthy dropped behind a tall clump of red stem grass and listened hard. Why were those horses here?

Caution told her to be careful, to wait it out. To go back to Glynna and protect her.

But she couldn't, not with Luke in such danger. She knew she could be making excuses for herself, but she felt as if the very hand of God was urging her to her feet, telling her to get to Broken Wheel fast.

Jumping up, her hand tight on her pistol, she ran on toward town.

She closed the gap with each stride, and she caught

her first glimpse of the buildings just as she tripped over a body.

⁓

Luke eased back from the crack in the livery door as one of Greer's men came slowly into the barn, his gun drawn. Just as the man's foot appeared and Luke reared back to strike, Greer and another of his men slammed open the jail door and drew the attention of the man approaching Luke. The man turned to head back to his boss. Frustrated, Luke saw Greer and his cowpoke leap off the board-walk and drop to their bellies in the dirt.

The jailhouse exploded.

Luke staggered back. Splintered wood hit the side of the livery, and a shout of pain told Luke it'd reached the man who'd been coming in.

The man fell to the ground but jumped up immediately. Not hurt bad enough to take him out of the fight.

Greer, sheltered from the blast, looked over and yelled, "Jesse Ray, get over here. We've blasted Bullard out."

Luke wondered how well Bullard had fared, considering shrapnel from the explosion had reached across the street.

Jesse Ray rushed to where Greer and his other cowpoke stood. A fire curled up the sides of the jailhouse door. Greer kicked at the flaming wood, shoving it out into the dirt, where it could burn harmlessly.

The three men went inside. Luke heard someone ask, "Where are the rest of the men, boss?"

"Shut up and help us get Bullard." Every word Greer spoke seemed like a threat. Luke noticed his cowpoke shut right up.

Luke hadn't seen three of Greer's men in a while, but he'd been paying attention to the one coming toward him.

Poking his head around the door so he could be more visible, Luke saw Vince come out of his office and head down the board-walk, fast but not running. If Greer saw him, Vince would sound convincing, saying he'd come because of the explosion.

Dare oughta do that too and be bold. But there was no sign of him. And where was Jonas? Where were the three unaccounted-for men who rode in with Greer? Had Jonas and Dare both been taken out of the fight? Were they lying somewhere dead all because Luke wanted revenge? Was Big John dead, too?

It made him sick to think of it. If his friends died because of him, he'd regret it for the rest of his life.

With the image of his friends lying somewhere in the dirt, breathing their last, suddenly Luke got real tired of playing this waiting game. If it was only Vince and him left and Vince was charging straight for trouble, then Luke would face that trouble with his friend.

Luke stepped out of the livery and started for the jail. Vince saw him and shook his head.

It occurred to Luke that he had no idea what'd been going on. Exposing himself had been rash, and Luke knew better than that. Wars were won by patient men. And Luke had once upon a time been the most patient of them all.

He reached the board-walk just as there was movement in the doorway of the jail. Vince waved him away frantically and leapt between two buildings. Luke dived sideways, landing on his belly just as heavy footsteps told him Greer had stepped out. Dragging himself along in the dirt, Luke slid under the board-walk. There were big enough cracks that Luke could see Greer and, right behind him, Simon Bullard. Bullard had his gun drawn, was bleeding and covered in dirt and wood splinters, but standing tall with fury etched on his face.

"If you don't bring out my wife right now," Greer roared at the town, "I'm gonna burn Broken Wheel to the ground."

 ∽∾

Someone shook Dare's shoulder, and he flickered his eyes open to see Ruthy. Horrified, Dare whispered, "What are you doing here?"

"Press this against your forehead."

He felt pressure ease on his head and knew she'd been holding it there for a while. He took the fussy little hand-kerchief out of her hand and returned it to his head. Unless he was mistaken, this was his own blood.

"You're bleeding from about ten spots, but it all looks minor." She sounded impatient. Dare was foggy so it might be he was forgetting something important. "You've got a goose egg on your forehead; I think that's the worst of the damage."

Dare looked around. The pain in his head almost knocked him out again. His vision went gray, but the jiggling on his shoulder kept him from sinking all the way into the dark.

"Get up." Ruthy—who was turning out to be a nag— tugged on his arm. Since he outweighed her by about a hundred pounds, her chances of getting him to his feet were slim.

"You remember where we planned to hide the Greer family?" She gestured toward the south with a gun. Tough woman. Loaded for bear.

"Yep, I'm the one who showed it to Luke." It hurt to talk. And his vision was blurred. Not good. Luke needed help.

"Dare, pay attention."

"There are three of you." She might be kinder if she knew that.

"I'm the one in the middle. The Greers are hidden there. Go defend them against trouble. If Greer is still standing when this ends, get them out of here. You're out of this fight. I doubt you're dying, but you're too wobbly to be of help."

Dare staggered to his feet, determined to show her she was wrong. Then his knees buckled and he ended up sprawled flat on his back again.

"Can you even get to the hideout?" She sounded annoyed.

Dare decided to have a talk with Luke. Warn him that his wife lacked compassion.

"I can just drag you into the underbrush and cover your body with leaves. You can nap while we clear these vermin out of Broken Wheel. I'm sure Glynna can defend herself."

It might be best for Luke not to have children with this merciless woman. "You're talking like this to get me to help, goad me into trying harder, right?" He hoped.

"Maybe." Ruthy glared at him. "You're slowing me down."

"I hope I'm right, otherwise you've got a mean streak, Ruthy Stone. I worry for my brother-in-arms."

"Quit worrying and head for that hideout. It's not that far. Crawl it if you have to."

"Mean streak for a fact." But the taunting was getting his fighting spirit up and he rolled onto his hands and knees.

Crawling like a mewling baby to the nearest tree, he pulled himself to his feet and leaned for far too long.

"Can you make it, Dare?"

He heard the kindness. "You're slipping, sweetheart. You're being so nice I'm likely to just fall straight back down to the ground and fetch myself a little nap."

Ruthy patted him on the back. "In your shape, you're just someone else Luke has to protect. You're more trouble than help. Get out of here."

Dare closed his eyes until the world stopped spinning . . . mostly. Then he straightened, held himself upright with no help from the tree whatsoever. "I'll go. If my head clears, I'll come back. But you're right. As things stand now, I can't hit what I'm aiming at. I'd have to shoot everyone three times to make sure I got the right man. I'm going to go find that woman and make *her* bandage *me* up for a change."

"Good idea. And hold this handkerchief on your forehead. I know head wounds bleed a lot, but you want to keep most of your blood inside your body where it'll do you some good. A doctor oughta know that."

"Mean streak." Dare looked at the feisty little redhead who never quit working. She was going to make a great rancher's wife. "It suits you."

"I'm going now." Ruthy patted him again. "I'll check back later, and if I find you in a heap on the ground, I'll bury you with leaves until I've got some spare time."

"We've got two men out of the fight, locked in Vince's office. There were six; we cut them down to four. And the jail just blew up."

"That was the explosion?"

"Yep. I reckon Greer found gunpowder or maybe even

nitroglycerin at the general store and used it to bust Bullard out of jail."

"You had Bullard locked in jail?" She sounded relieved . . . and impressed.

"For a little while. If Greer sprung Bullard, he's got five men left. Last I knew, Luke, Vince, and Jonas were all fine. Be careful. Luke'll feel lower'n dirt if he accidentally shoots you."

"My man knows better than to shoot blind."

"You've only known him a few days and you've never seen him shoot a gun."

"You have though, right?" Ruthy asked.

"Yep, and he never shoots blind. You'll be fine."

"Go on now. Make yourself useful. Glynna was scared to death when I left her." Ruthy looked up and down Dare's body and grimaced. "And seeing you isn't likely to make her feel any better."

CHAPTER 21

With Bullard loose, the fight got a whole lot worse.

Luke saw Vince appear at the end of the board-walk, under it with him. He wanted to crawl the length of the walk and talk things over, but Vince gave him a casual salute, flashed that reckless smile, turned, and slid out of sight.

Divide and conquer. That was the plan.

Luke hadn't done his share of conquering by a long shot.

Peering out from under the board-walk, Luke saw one of Greer's cowhands rush the livery. Braver now with Bullard glaring at him. Luke should've stayed at his post.

Bullard had his gun drawn. The man was a mess, his clothes in tatters, blood trickling down his cheeks and his neck. But considering he'd just been blown up, he was in real good shape.

Of all the rotten luck.

Bullard's edgy alertness rubbed off on the other men so that everyone was paying attention now. Greer was sharper, too. Another of his men ran up to Vince's law office and hammered on the door. The third man, Jesse Ray, who had almost come into the livery earlier, stayed by Greer.

Bullard said, "Go check the buildings on the northwest. And I want to know if the doctor's in town. If he is, drag him out here." Bullard had it in for Dare and there was no mistaking it.

Jesse Ray turned and headed back in Luke's direction. The lousy polecat walked straight to Dare's house and kicked the door in.

Luke was useless under here. Then he had an idea. He moved forward until he reached the jail. The building was battered enough, Luke could work his way into the crawl space beneath it, then climb up through a hole in the floor. The jail was destroyed. The cell's door hung from one hinge. The back wall was half gone. Luke went to the back. Risking exposure, Luke raced across the open space and got himself back into the woods. Where was Dare? He was supposed to be covering this part of town. Well, Luke wasn't where he was supposed to be, either.

Luke went to the spot he and Rosie had picked for a hiding place every night as they waited for the sun to set so they could get in and out of Dare's without giving themselves away.

Where Luke was, Bullard and Greer couldn't see him. But Jesse Ray could if he looked out a window. Blast it.

He saw movement inside. Jesse Ray was shoving things around in Dare's office. Smashing things for no reason except because he was a low-down varmint. Jesse Ray headed for the storeroom that Luke and Rosie had hidden in the first time they'd come to Dare's house. He opened the door, his back to Luke.

Tired of not being in the action, Luke ran toward the house. Quietly he swung Dare's back door open and edged himself inside. It was a solid house, not a lot of creaking, and Luke had spent the last few days sneaking around so he knew where the loose floorboards were. He approached the open door to Dare's office just as Jesse Ray turned away from the storeroom and saw him. Jesse Ray went for his gun.

Luke beat him to the draw. "Don't move."

The man froze. He'd looked young through the window, but up close he had deep lines on his face. This was a man who'd ridden some hard trails.

"Get your hands up." Luke cocked the gun just to underline the threat.

Greer had probably hired his men for toughness, but Jesse Ray must not've been as tough as Greer thought, because he obeyed without hesitating.

He had more men to catch, so Luke hurried to get this one out of the fight. "Turn around."

Given enough time, Jesse Ray might find his backbone, so Luke strode toward him and relieved him of two six-guns. Luke found a hideout knife and tossed it across the room after the revolvers. Prepared for just this problem—capturing a man and not knowing what to do with him—Luke pulled at the rope wrapped around his waist.

Jesse Ray struck like a rattler. With three lightning moves he rammed his elbow into Luke's gut. His arm came down hard on Luke's gun hand and knocked the weapon to the floor. Then he plowed a fist into Luke's mouth.

Luke staggered back. Diving for his gun, Jesse Ray stretched out flat. Luke leapt on him and they tumbled to the floor. The gun was only inches away, and Jesse Ray, on his belly, heaved himself toward it. Luke clawed at Jesse Ray's hand, knocking the gun out of reach.

Luke outweighed him, but the varmint was wiry. It was like wrestling a slippery snake. Jesse Ray threw his head back and slammed it into Luke's jaw so hard his ears rang.

Then the snake rolled onto his back and slugged Luke in the belly.

A slippery snake with a hard head and iron fists.

Jesse Ray kicked his legs up and threw Luke over his head. Luke went tumbling, sprawled out flat on his back, whirled and dove in again. He tackled Jesse Ray, knocking him back from the Colt.

Luke put every ounce of power he had into a left cross. Jesse Ray reeled but was right back, punching with both fists.

Luke landed two blows hard enough that Jesse Ray fell back against Dare's desk. Charging, he rammed his shoulder into Luke's belly and got him in a clinch. Too close to punch, Luke took both of them to the floor. The snake landed two brutal blows. Luke blocked the next just as Jesse Ray caught Luke's throat with one crushing hand.

His breath cut off, Luke jerked sideways. But the man held on, letting Luke's motion roll them until Jesse Ray was on top.

The one strangling hand became a vise. To throw Jesse Ray off, Luke wrenched himself sideways and saw his gun within grabbing distance. He reached for it and brought it around hard against Jesse Ray's skull, knocking him aside. Luke staggered to his feet, brought the gun around to shoot. Jesse Ray was on him before he could fire. He dragged Luke back to the floor. Both hands gripped Luke's neck. Luke raised the gun. Jesse Ray let go with one hand and caught Luke's wrist and pushed the gun downward. Luke gained the advantage and the gun inched back up. Jesse Ray's grip cut off Luke's air supply completely. His strength faded. He tried to throw the man off, but he didn't have the breath in his lungs to make his body obey.

The edges of Luke's vision began to go dark. One hand wrestled with the gun, and one tried to tear Jesse Ray's choking hand loose.

Luke was going to lose this fight. And all he could think of was Rosie. His sweet Rosie. Like an echo that came from his heart, he sent up a prayer, wishing he could've seen her one more time.

A dull thud barely penetrated Luke's ebbing consciousness.

Jesse Ray's hand convulsed on Luke's throat, then went slack. Luke got his first breath of air in too long a time.

Jesse Ray slumped sideways and then toppled to the floor, which allowed Luke to see . . . Rosie, pistol in hand. Luke was pretty sure she'd just applied the weapon, gun butt first, to Jesse Ray's skull. Their eyes met, and she looked a little sheepish, in a bloodthirsty kind of way. She lowered her raised foot, which she'd just used to kick Jesse Ray off Luke's body.

He got to see Rosie. God had granted Luke his dying wish.

Then air got to his brain. "What the devil are you doing here?"

❧

"Get down." Glynna barely made a sound as she hissed the warning.

The children hit the ground flat.

She saw Paul pick up a rock, and although he stayed back, she saw the furious determination on his face.

His inability to protect her from Flint had almost destroyed her son. Glynna dropped to her knees and hunted for a spot in the tightly woven trees that would allow her to keep watch. As long as she was kneeling anyway, she prayed as she poked her nose between two slender trees and came face-to-face with . . .

"What are you doing here?" Glynna leapt to her feet and rushed out of the shielded overhang, gun in hand.

Dare Riker. She watched him fall to his knees, his head hanging low.

"I've . . . I've come to . . . to protect you . . ." Then he collapsed to the ground.

Glynna ran to him. Glancing back at Paul and Janet as they emerged from cover, she said, "Quick! Help me drag him into the shelter."

He wasn't all the way unconscious, so he helped a bit, and they had him inside their hideout within moments.

"What happened?" Glynna dropped to her knees at his side. "Is Ruthy all right? Has Luke regained possession of the ranch? Is my husband—?"

"Hold up." The doctor grabbed her wrist so hard it hurt. "Can we wait on the questions? I'll tell you everything. Soon. I need water."

"Oh yes. Of course. I'm sorry." Glynna was tired of telling people she was sorry, especially since she wasn't all that sorry honestly—unless she counted being sorry about nearly everyone she'd met in the last few years. In fact, with the exception of her children, she was sorry for most everyone she'd ever met, including her pathetic spineless rat of a first husband.

Well, she liked Ruthy. But if Glynna's life wasn't messed up beyond repair, she would've never met Ruthy. All in all, she'd trade her spunky new friend for a little peace and quiet.

"Get the canteen, Paul. Let's see how bad his injuries

are." He had some cuts, but his main injury seemed to be an ugly lump on his forehead. "We'll get him bandaged up and then we'll get some answers."

Dare let go of her wrist and slumped flat onto his back, as if grabbing her had used up the last remaining bit of his strength. "Thank you."

Glynna opened the canteen lid, slid her arm under Dare's shoulders, and lifted him. He drank deeply, rested, then drank more.

Every swallow was a vibration that Glynna could feel. It felt good to hold a man. She thought of the men she'd held in the past and how they'd betrayed her, and that helped her to ignore Dare's weight and strength and his blasted vibrations.

"Enough." He turned away from the canteen.

Glynna stopped tipping instantly, which only proved how closely she'd been watching him. She lowered his head, glad to be done with cradling him in her arms.

His eyes closed and his muscles went slack. He still might not be unconscious, but Glynna had the unsettling feeling that he'd like to be.

The welt on his head looked like a terrible blow that accounted for his addled state.

She tore off a strip of her petticoat, soaked it in water, and rested it on the ugly goose egg. Dare blinked. His eyes focused on her.

"Here's more water." Glynna slid her arm under his shoulders again and lifted. This time he used his elbows to prop himself up. She needed to stay close to support him; she had no choice, although it was disturbing.

When he'd finished drinking, she eased him back to the ground. Then she remembered how kindly he'd tended her and she was glad for a chance to return the favor. "Your only serious injury is that lump on your head. Did you get hit by someone or—?"

"An explosion." His eyes narrowed as if he were thinking hard. "I . . . I must've been hit by flying debris. Not sure. Ruthy found me. I don't know how long I'd been lying there. She got me on my feet, reminded me of where you were hiding and aimed me here."

The doctor reached up and touched the cloth on his forehead and flinched. "That's a real lump. Ruthy said I needed to get out of the fight, that I was useless. Reckon she was right considering I've slept a good chunk of the day away."

"I wonder how things are going back in town." Glynna didn't want to wish her husband would die. That was all wrong.

She caught herself doing just that on occasion, but she shut down the thoughts as soon as they came.

"I've got to get back. They need me." Dare surged up until he was sitting. He wavered, then caught himself by bracing both hands on the ground. "More water, please."

Glynna wanted him to go back. She wanted every man possible in the fight. But unless Dare got a lot steadier, he was worse than useless. He'd make his friends step back from the fight to protect him.

Yet with him in good fighting shape, they would have a much better chance to win and that would set her free of her husband.

Except of course their marriage vows bound them for life.

❧

"What I'm doing here is I came to save you. And yes, you're very welcome." Rosie's eyes narrowed as she flipped the gun so it was in her hand as a firearm, not a club.

Luke saw the evidence of her talent with a pistol in the easy way she slid the gun around.

She reached in her pocket and came up empty-handed. "Blast it! I gave my handkerchief to Dare." Looking around, she went for a stack of rags that'd been thrown to the floor.

A lot of this mess had happened when Jesse Ray was searching the house, with more being added during the fight.

"You're bleeding." Rosie got a rag and gently dabbed at his face. She sounded gruff, all business, but her hand shook as she cleaned him up. "There's a cut on your head that could p-probably use some threads. If only Dare were here."

"There's no time now," Luke said.

"And your lip is split and you've got a nosebleed." Her eyes were a little damp, like maybe she was going to cry.

Luke didn't like it because he needed to yell at her for being here in the middle of a fight when he'd done everything he could think of to make sure she was well away from it. Now, quick before he dragged her into his arms, was the time to scare her into going back to the hideout. "You saved my life. I thank you for that. But you endangered yours."

Luke wasn't yelling. He was finding it pretty hard not to. "Let's get you headed for where you were *supposed* to hide with Glynna." It occurred to him that she'd done her job. Done it well. Gotten Glynna hidden. Rosie was doing better than he was.

"Dare's with her now. He's protecting her." Rosie quickly explained the condition Dare had been in. "He said he and Vince got two of Greer's men under control. Now you and I"—Rosie arched a brow as if challenging him to deny her help—"have taken care of a third one. That leaves how many?"

"We've got four men to face: Greer, Bullard, and two gunslicks."

Rosie swallowed hard. "Where did Big John get to?"

Luke shook his head. "We'll set out hunting for him as soon as we finish with Greer. For now, I saw a man go into the livery. Let's see if we can't do some dividing and conquering. So far we've managed to do it quietly, without firing a shot. I'm hoping we can end this thing without bloodshed."

Rosie touched another rag to his lip and drew it away, crimson. "Too late."

"Okay, without too much bloodshed anyway."

"Unless you count Dare having a building explode onto him."

"I do count that. I wonder if Glynna can patch him up and get him back into the fight. He's a tough man. I'll get this varmint hidden. Let's get over to the livery and try to get the man that went in there. That'll cut Greer's men down by one more." Luke turned Jesse Ray onto his belly. He bound the unconscious man hand and foot, gagged him, and dragged him into the storeroom.

"Let's go." Rosie rushed out of the room. Luke chased after her. He decided then to tell her this wasn't her fight, making it clear he wasn't going to let her get any more involved.

But he felt the pain in his throat and thought of the ugly

bruises that would be there tomorrow, and wondered if she wasn't a better man than he was.

They circled until they were behind the livery. He turned to Rosie. "Let me go in alone, please."

He sounded like he was begging when he should have been issuing orders. The more he got to know his wife, the more begging seemed like the better choice.

"I'll stay here. I don't want to be in the way if there's going to be gunfire. But I'll be listening. If I decide you need help, I'll come in."

Luke kissed her. This was the strangest fight of his life. No kissing in war, not even a speck of it.

He turned to watch the back of the livery and the large window of the hayloft. He edged closer, ready to break from cover and race across the open space.

When no one showed himself, he sprinted, keeping low until he got to the barn. Pressing his back to the wall beside the door, he leaned in, an inch at a time, and saw no sign of movement. Had the man gone back to Greer?

He drew a steadying breath and leaned in again. Seeing a mound of hay close to the door, he darted in and ducked behind it.

Listening, he thought he made out a rustling sound over-head. How was he supposed to get up there and get the drop on this ruffian? No one could miss the sound of a man climbing a wooden ladder, and this one looked none too sturdy. It was bound to creak loudly.

He had to wait for the man to come down. Crouched there, each second seemed to take a minute. He'd left Rosie outside, hiding, but the little woman didn't seem to have a lick of sense. By having to take care of everything for those no-account Reinhardts for so long, she'd just plain gotten the bit in her teeth and was used to doing everything and thinking herself capable of any task—which she probably was. But that didn't mean Luke wanted her to accompany him to a gunfight.

The noise changed overhead, and Luke braced himself as footsteps moved with catlike silence, barely audible, and only that because Luke was listening with every ounce of concentration.

The quiet steps reached the ladder. He saw a man's boot appear on the top rung, then another. Luke felt like a coiled rattler waiting to strike as the man's back appeared from overhead, then his shoulders, then . . . bright red hair.

"Jonas?"

The kindly pastor whipped his Colt out, dropped the last six feet of his climb down, and aimed the muzzle straight at Luke's chest. They made eye contact as Jonas landed, and immediately he relaxed and lowered his gun.

"Good to see you, Luke. I got one up there and another in the general store. So who's left?"

"I'm left." Bullard stepped through the big front door of the livery, two guns drawn and pointed at Luke and Jonas. "Greer's left too."

Luke had a moment of hope that Greer would step in behind Bullard, giving Vince a chance to get the drop on them. Instead, Bullard stood there alone. No idea where Greer had gotten to.

"I got 'em, Greer!" Bullard's triumph gleamed in his eyes.

Gunfire erupted across the street. Right about where Luke thought Vince would be.

Luke braced himself to draw the second Bullard reacted to the gunfire, only he never did. His guns never wavered.

"You're Luke Stone. I've never seen you, but I'd recognize you anywhere. You're the image of your pa. Did you come home to try and steal back his ranch?"

"I can't *steal back* something I own. I've got proof that'll hold up before a judge, and I've made a will so that if I die, Greer loses the ranch anyway."

"Whoever comes to get it will have as much trouble taking it back as you did. Your pa picked a likely site for his house. It was good thinking."

"Greer killed my pa, and I don't aim to let him get away with it." With a flash of insight, Luke added, "I always figured Greer was too yellow to have shot Pa, and it's said he had a solid alibi. He had you do it, didn't he?"

The cold smile on Bullard's face was as good as a confession.

"Are all my men gone? Did you manage to kill every one of those drifters Greer hired? I told him there was a difference between a backstabbing snake and a hard man with a gun who'd face danger. I reckon I was right. Maybe Greer will ask me to do his hiring from now on."

As if he'd been summoned, Flint Greer stepped into the barn beside Bullard. "I caught that lawyer trying to come up behind me and shot him."

Vince? Vince couldn't be dead. He was the sharpest of them all. Luke wanted to run at Greer, tear his heart out with his bare hands. Right in front of Luke stood the man who'd killed his father and the man who'd hired it done. They'd killed Big John and Vince and hurt Dare bad enough he'd had to leave the fight.

"Just so you know, Greer, I've got legal documents in the hands of others proving I still own the ranch. You can't have a legal deed because I have it. Pa knew trouble was coming, so he sent me the deed with papers signing it over to me. Even if you kill me, you're going to be run off. I've left this land in my will to some mighty hard men who'll come to claim it with guns blazing."

That might've been true when he'd willed it to his sister and, by extension, the Kincaids. Ruthy was another story, though. Still, he saw no reason to give Greer any hope.

"You stole it when this land was in chaos because of the war. But the law's coming to Texas and you can't stand against the whole state."

"That don't scare me none." Greer leveled his six-shooter right at Luke's heart. "I own the law in Broken Wheel."

"Where's the doc?" Bullard looked from Luke to Jonas. "He's the one knocked me cold. He must be in on this with you."

"I'll bet he's behind my wife disappearing." Greer took a step forward so he was just a bit ahead of Bullard. The man liked to remind everyone he was in charge. "That means wherever he is, I'll find her. I'll never stop hunting. He'll die for taking her away from me, and I'll drag her home and teach her a lesson she'll never forget."

Greer turned his attention to Jonas. "The preacher too? How'd you convince the preacher to buy into this gunfight? What are you all to each other anyway?"

"We're Regulators," Jonas said. "We were in Andersonville Prison together and we came away with a bond closer than brothers. You hurt one of us, you hurt all of us, and there are more Regulators. Not just those of us in town. And they'll all come riding when they hear Big John and

Vince were killed. But I'm praying we can end this without any more shooting."

Thinking of Vince, Luke knew they were past that point. Greer and Bullard couldn't ride away and leave witnesses to this day's dirty work. Even knowing it was hopeless, Luke let Jonas have his say. Maybe he'd find the right words to bring all this to an end.

"You're both murderers," Jonas went on. "Greer, you're a brute to hit your wife and a marked man for shooting Vince. Vince Yates has friends. You can't kill him and expect to get away with it. Bullard, you killed Luke's father, and where's Big John Conroy—the Texas Ranger who arrested you?"

Bullard smiled. "Was he a friend of yours, too? He's dead. Any man who crosses me ends up dead. And now you're going to end up just that way, too."

"Which one do you want?" Greer laughed.

Bullard raised his gun. "I killed the father, so now I'll take the son."

"That leaves the preacher for me," Greer said.

The sudden crack of a revolver froze them in their tracks.

"Drop your guns and get your hands where I can see them. Now!" Dare Riker, bandaged and bloody, stepped into the livery behind Greer and Bullard.

Luke braced himself, knowing neither of these men would go down easy. He saw Greer begin to stretch his hand out as if to drop his gun, but then he launched himself sideways. For a second, without Greer in the way, Dare was aiming dead center at Luke's chest.

Dare wheeled around and fired. A line of bullets lit up the smoking forge on the north side of the livery as Greer clawed his way behind it. Sparks exploded into the air.

Bullard dived to the north, firing. Jonas staggered, dropped, and crawled behind a feed trough.

Luke jumped behind a heavy post and returned fire. Horses on that side of the livery reared and whinnied. Bullard pulled a door open and a horse charged out. Luke couldn't get a shot at Bullard in all the chaos.

Bullard leapt to his feet, still firing. With a running dive he crashed through a window, the glass spraying around him.

Luke rushed out the back door. He wanted Bullard, the man who'd killed his father. Jonas was down, hit. That left Dare to handle Greer.

He rounded the livery. Bullard was waiting for him and fired two shots. But both missed their target because Luke was moving fast. Then Bullard's gun clicked on an empty chamber.

Luke fired, and Bullard's gun was shot out of his hand. With a shout of pain and fury, Bullard fell, but as he landed he came up with another pistol.

A gun roared before Luke could fire again. He glanced down at his chest, expecting to find himself bleeding, dying. There was nothing.

He looked back to see Bullard falling forward. He sprawled flat on his face. Dust kicked up when he landed, and beyond the dust stood Big John Conroy—his gun smoking, a grim look in his eyes, his arm in a sling.

Gunfire from inside the livery said there wasn't even time to be glad Big John was alive.

Big John ran for the front door as Luke raced for the back, reloading at the same time.

Luke rushed in just as Greer slugged Dare in the face. Dare staggered back, and Greer lunged, sending Dare reeling toward the red-hot forge. Both men were unarmed.

A pistol lay on the side of the forge, either Dare's or Greer's. The gun was close enough to the fire that the wooden gun butt smoldered.

Greer reached crushing hands for Dare's neck to give him one last shove into the fire. The sick glow of pleasure in causing pain twisted Greer's face into something devilish. Dare's hands flew back and landed on the gun.

Luke raised his Colt just as Big John leveled his weapon. With a cry of pain from the burning weapon, Dare swung his gun around and pulled the trigger. Luke and Big John both fired.

Three explosions of gunfire blasted within a second of each other.

All of them hit Greer dead center. He was knocked backward under the blows of flying lead.

Dare then dropped the gun and clutched his hand. Turning to the water bath beside the forge, he thrust his hand in to cool it.

Greer looked down at three gunshot wounds, all close enough together on his chest that one hand could cover them.

"No!" Disbelief blazed from Greer's eyes. "I'm the biggest rancher in these parts. I'm too strong to tangle with. Nobody . . . nobody crosses me." A few seconds later he fell to his knees, and then onto his back in the dirt.

Luke went over to where Greer lay sprawled out. "Texas is a state that tangles with everyone, Greer. You've used your so-called strength against women and children. That makes you a coward and a weakling."

Shaking his head as if his own death was impossible for him to believe, Greer said, "Your pa wasn't a woman or a child and I bested him."

"No, shooting my pa was hired out to Bullard. Just more proof you're yellow."

"This can't . . . be happening. I'm in charge . . ." Greer said, his voice growing more quiet and garbled.

Jonas slipped past Luke and knelt at Greer's side. "What you are is a dead man. If you've got one ounce of strength left in your body, you'd best spend it making your peace with God."

Jonas was right, yet Luke knew with shame he never would've been able to say the words, offer this last chance to Greer.

The air was thick with the smell of burning sulfur, the same thing it was said hell was made of. Greer didn't answer. One last choking protest was the last sound he made before he died.

Dare stood soaking his hand on the far side of the forge. Smoke curled from the muzzle of Big John's six-gun, which reminded Luke to holster his.

Big John said, "Where's Vince?"

They all froze. "Bullard said he killed him." Luke moved first.

They ran out and saw Vince lying on the board-walk, facedown, a pool of blood around his body. Rosie was kneeling beside him.

Luke sprinted toward his old friend. No one could lose that amount of blood and survive. As he reached Vince, Rosie said, "I think he's going to be fine."

Luke thought she'd taken leave of her senses.

Dare, only a step behind Luke, dropped to Vince's side. Gently, with Luke's and Rosie's help, Dare rolled Vince over.

"It looks like it just creased him," Rosie said.

Dare shuddered so violently Luke caught his shoulder, afraid he'd collapse. Even kneeling seemed too much for Dare right now.

"What happened to you?" Luke thought he looked like he'd been through—

"He's been through an explosion," Rosie said.

"I'd forgotten about the explosion." Luke wished he could forget the whole day.

Fumbling at Vince's neck for a pulse with his left hand while cradling his burnt right hand to his stomach, Dare was silent for too long until finally he sagged with relief. "He's got a pulse. I think you're right, Ruthy. His heart is steady. He's knocked out from the blow of the bullet and he's lost a lot of blood, but he'll probably be all right."

Big John came up beside them. "Bullard and Greer are both dead. Are there more?"

Jonas came walking across the street, his sleeve red with blood. "I left one in the livery's hayloft and one in the back of the general store under a pile of flour sacks, both of 'em tied up. Unconscious, but not dead."

Vince was unconscious. Dare was burned and bandaged. Big John was battered and looked unsteady on his feet. And Luke was beat up from his fight with Jesse Ray. Rosie alone seemed to be in perfect condition. And that was as it should be.

Big John looked at Jonas. "You got two by yourself? I ain't surprised, preacher man."

"Glad to see you, John." Jonas gave John a tired smile. "Bullard said he killed you."

"He had himself a go at it." John tugged at the sling on his arm. "Is that all of 'em?"

"I left one in the storeroom in Dare's office. Alive."

Luke wondered if he had the strength to pick Vince up and carry him to Dare's for doctoring. Luke was probably in the best shape of any of them—not counting Rosie, but she couldn't carry this big lug two feet. Luke didn't say that out loud, though. No sense giving her something to prove.

"Vince and I tied two of them up and stashed them in his office." Dare ripped a chunk off his shirt to press against the ugly cut on Vince's head.

No one added any more names.

"That the lot of them, then?" Big John looked gray and none too steady, as if he was staying upright only through iron will.

"I saw six come to town. They broke Bullard out of jail, so seven in all." Luke hadn't figured on doing so much arithmetic during a shootout. "All accounted for."

"We need to send someone to get Glynna from the hideout." Rosie's eyes slid from one man to another. "You know what? I think I'll go."

She looked to Luke, as if she was asking permission. He had the sinking feeling that this was about as close to *obey* as he was ever going to get from his wife.

"That's a good idea, sweetheart. You go get them and bring them to Dare's house. That's where we're heading."

As soon as Luke found the energy to haul Vince over there.

Rosie took two steps and froze when more men rode into town. Luke jumped up to catch Rosie. He decided she hadn't oughta go out alone.

Big John hailed the newcomers and walked toward them in such a friendly way, Luke's worry subsided. Then he saw a Ranger star on every chest. He heard Big John give rapid orders. The Rangers split up in the direction of the concealed captives, while others came toward Vince.

A moment later, Dodger rode in from the ranch. He surveyed the situation and dismounted. He had men at his back, all of them armed, coming to find justice for Luke.

"I'm going to help Rosie fetch Mrs. Greer," Luke said. The smell of gun smoke still hung in the air. This was a hard land. Even a tough Texas wife might run into something she couldn't handle.

Jonas smiled. "Go."

Luke looked at his friends, battle weary, wounded, more blood on their hands than they'd had before he'd come to town, and they'd already had too much. "Thank you all."

Big John didn't hear him. Vince of course didn't hear him. Dare was focusing all his energy on tending Vince. That left Jonas.

"'There is a friend who sticks closer than a brother.'" Jonas gave Luke a casual salute. "You'd have done the same for any of us. Go take a walk with your wife."

Luke took Rosie's hand in his. He didn't think he could have stopped himself from going with her even if his friends had asked him to, but he was sure glad they hadn't. As he reached the corner of the building, he paused and looked back.

Two Rangers picked Vince up with a decent amount of gentleness, considering they were a rough-looking bunch.

Jonas came to Dare's side and helped him to his feet. Big John caught Dare's shoulder to steady him. The three of them followed Vince toward Dare's house.

"There is a friend who sticks closer than a brother."

Luke picked up his pace because his strong, energetic little wife was dragging him along, in a hurry to get every chore done that presented itself.

CHAPTER 22

Ruthy considered herself a woman of great strength and boundless energy. A woman who wasn't afraid of hard work. A woman who never rested while there was a job to be done. But she was just purely tired to the bone and ready for this day to end.

She opened the door to Dare's house and almost stepped back out. It was full of strangers, all of them wearing badges.

She held the door for Glynna and her children. Luke was at Ruthy's back and slipped a strong hand onto her waist. She relished his support.

As soon as they stepped in, the Rangers doffed their hats and began shuffling out. Ruthy knew she should offer them a meal, try to find a place for them all to sleep, mend their ragged shirts. But she was just too tired.

In all honesty they looked more than capable of caring for themselves.

The men looked at Glynna with admiration as they passed. Ruthy understood, for Glynna was a singularly pretty woman. Their eyes shifted to Ruthy, and she earned flattering looks, too.

Considering the wretched state of her appearance, their

regard served to remind her there weren't many women around these parts.

When the Rangers were all gone, the house was still plenty full. Dare had washed up and changed to clean clothes. An ugly bruise had formed on his forehead, but otherwise he looked pretty decent. Dare stood talking with Vince, who lay flat on Dare's examining table, his head heavily bandaged. Able to respond now, Vince spoke in a voice too quiet for Ruthy to make out, but at least he was conscious.

Jonas knelt before the fireplace, adding logs. His right sleeve was cut off, and strips of white cloth dressed his wounded upper arm.

Big John came out of the kitchen, wearing a sling. These men had been through a hard day for a fact.

"I've got some stew simmering," John said. "Come and get it."

Luke said, "I'm going upstairs to put on a clean shirt." He headed up, his tread heavy on the stairs. Ruthy wanted to follow him, but then decided to give the man a moment of quiet. She could help serve dinner.

In the hallway, Big John turned his attention to Glynna. "You're Mrs. Greer, is that right, ma'am?"

Glynna nodded.

"Have you been told that your husband is dead?"

Nodding, Glynna asked in a shaky voice, "Who shot him?"

The way she spoke, so faint, Ruthy wasn't sure what to expect. Luke had already given Glynna the news, and Glynna's response had been grim silence. She had no use for her husband, but that didn't make burying him easy. Still, Luke hadn't told her any details, including who'd fired the killing shots.

"I did, Mrs. Greer." Dare came out of his office and stood facing Glynna. He wasn't going to make this easier on himself. "I didn't plan to. I hoped to take him alive, but—"

A cry tore out of Glynna's throat, and she threw herself into Dare's arms, weeping. Dare staggered back under the impact. His hands lifted as if someone had pulled a gun. His eyes wide with surprise, he looked at Ruthy, then at the children, then at Big John.

"I was about to tell you I killed him, Mrs. Greer."

Glynna ignored him, and Big John frowned as if he thought he had a hug or two coming.

"Luke shot him, too." Big John must've decided Glynna should know the full truth.

"Thank you." Glynna managed to get the words out between sobs. Dare lifted his hands a bit higher, then shrugged one shoulder and wrapped his arms around Glynna and held her as she wept.

Ruthy said, "Come and eat, children. Let your ma have a minute to"—throw herself into a man's arms two hours after her husband died?—"compose herself."

Janet looked inclined to hide in the folds of Glynna's skirt. Paul gave Dare a look of such loathing, Ruthy was afraid the young man might shove himself between Glynna and Dare. Ruthy couldn't blame the youngster. They'd just gotten rid of one man; it was not time yet for another, no matter how much better. But Glynna's tears had nothing to do with any man except her husband, and she needed to pass through this emotional storm.

"Give her some time, Paul." Ruthy reached for him. He ducked from letting her touch him, but rested a hand on his little sister's back with too much maturity for one so young. Ruthy felt a connection to the kid, probably because she'd had to grow up too young, too.

When they'd been climbing down that cliff, Ruthy had thought she and Paul had reached something of an understanding. He'd worked with her willingly. Now all she saw was sullen anger. The half-grown boy gave a long, burning look at his sobbing mother, then turned and guided Janet into the kitchen.

Luke came back downstairs. He'd washed and put on a clean shirt. Ruthy thought he'd have a black eye tomorrow. He had bruises forming on his neck, and his bottom lip was swollen, but for all that he looked wonderful.

Watching the children go into the kitchen, Luke said, "You come in too, Ruthy. You haven't eaten all day."

There'd been a quick breakfast before dawn. The shaky way she felt might be cured by a good meal.

There were more chairs in the kitchen. Usually Dare had four, which was plenty, since Dare and Vince never sat down.

Now there were six, scrounged from her room upstairs. Six chairs. Nine battered people.

Bending over a massive pot, Big John scooped stew onto a plate, dropped a biscuit on, and turned to hand it to Paul. John stopped, took a long look at the skinny kid reaching for the plate, and added another scoop of stew and a second biscuit. Paul grabbed the stew and a fork and went to a corner of the kitchen, dropping to the floor.

Janet took her food and sat beside her brother. Ruthy decided if they needed another chair, she'd go sit in the corner, too. But she suspected they had enough. Vince wasn't coming to dinner.

Ruthy got served next. She took the plate and sat down.

Only after she picked up her fork did she realize how tired she was, sitting while someone waited on her. She popped to her feet and swiped the ladle from Big John.

"Sit down and eat. You look worn clean out." She returned her plate to him.

"I look like a man who got stabbed and left for dead," Big John said. It was a mark of how bad he felt that he minded her and went to the table to wolf down his meal.

The next serving was Luke's. "You look a lot better all cleaned up," she said.

"Yep, a fistfight does nuthin' but harm a man's appearance." Luke took the food and sat across from Big John.

Ruthy looked at the children in the corner behind Luke, eating in silence, then looked at the food supply. Big John had made a vat of stew. "If either of you wants more, there's plenty."

Jonas led the way into the room. Glynna was next, her eyes rimmed in red but her shoulders straight and square in a way Ruthy hadn't seen before. Dare was a step behind.

Giving food to each of them, Ruthy saw even restless Dare drop into a seat. All his energy had been drained. Glynna sat next to Big John, facing her children. Jonas sank into the chair at the head of the table. The table was none too wide, but they managed to squeeze two chairs in. There was one chair left, the one around the corner from Luke.

"Go ahead and sit, Ruthy." Dare gestured to the chair beside him. "Vince is going to stay flat on his back until morning. Doctor's orders. He's already eaten to the extent he's able."

Ruthy turned, expecting to see Vince come in, smile, and lean on that door, standing guard as he always did. It didn't happen.

Vince was ailing.

Dare had a building blown up in his face.

Jonas was shot.

Big John stabbed.

All for Luke Stone, and since she was now Mrs. Stone, it was all for her, too. "Would anyone like more to eat?"

She might've felt better if she'd made the stew herself. One more way to say thank you. When no one spoke up, she dished herself up a plate and took a seat.

"What happened to you, John?" Ruthy asked.

"Bullard was fast and mean and he bested me. My horse came and stood guard over me. Leastways that's where my horse was when I woke up. By guarding me he kept Bullard away from my guns, so my stallion saved my life. Bullard grabbed the horse I had him draped over and rode off. He probably thought he'd killed me, and he came almighty close. He headed for the fray here and never looked back. I was a long time getting to my feet, mounting up, and riding for help."

"Not so long," Luke said. "You got here in time. Just exactly in time."

Big John nodded. "We managed to reconstruct enough of the jail to keep Greer's men confined until we leave tomorrow. I recognize two of them. I wouldn't be surprised if there was a wanted poster on all of 'em, and that reward money will be given to whichever of you caught 'em. Greer and Bullard confessed in front of three witnesses to killing your pa, so no judge will bat an eye over them being shot."

Dare and Luke both flinched. Big John looked solemn, but he'd had more time to get tough over this harsh part of his job.

They'd all three had a hand in killing Greer. Big John

could cover his feelings, but Luke and Dare were hurting. Since she had no skill at healing wounds to the heart, Ruthy said, "Would you like more stew?"

For a time the only sound was the scrape of forks on tin plates. There were some second helpings but no one asked Ruthy for them; they just got up and served themselves.

"Mrs. Greer, that ranch is mine." Luke spoke hesitantly, looking to Ruthy as if asking for help. "I know it's your home, too. If you want—"

"You and the children can stay out there for as long as you need to," Ruthy interjected.

Luke nodded and gave her a grateful look.

"No, we're done with that house." Glynna laid her fork down with a sharp click. "I never want to set foot in it again."

"I understand that you want to get away from a place that holds such bad memories, ma'am." Luke took another bite of stew.

It was thick with vegetables and meat, swimming in savory gravy that smelled wonderful. Ruthy probably should ask Big John for the recipe.

Meeting Glynna's eyes, Ruthy said, "But you need a place to stay. And the evil wasn't from the house or the land; it was from your husband. He's gone now. Why don't you come out and stay with us just until you're at full strength. Once you're healed, we can figure out a new place for you."

"No, thank you. I've got a few dollars—we'll stay at the boardinghouse, and I'll look for work."

"Can't think what work there'd be for a lady in Broken Wheel," Dare said. "I hope the town will grow again now with Greer gone, but it'll be a while."

"This is Indian territory. It'll never get too big," Luke said.

"One thing this town could use," Jonas said, standing to put his plate in the sink and pour himself another cup of coffee.

"What's that?" Glynna sat up, interested.

"The man who ran the diner up and left town after the fighting today. He said he was done with this town for good. Can you run a diner, ma'am?"

Glynna's children both gasped quietly. Ruthy turned to see why.

"I could do that." Glynna's hopeful tone caught Ruthy's attention and distracted her from the young ones.

Sitting forward, Glynna asked, "Would I have to spend a lot of money? I have a bit." Then she hesitated and looked at Luke. "No, I don't. It's all yours. Every cent my husband had was ill-gotten."

"There's the building," Dare said, looking energized by the conversation. "If the owner abandoned it without selling, I'd say it's yours for the taking. I'll bet the bachelors in this town—which includes every man except Luke— would be glad to see a woman turn her hand to cooking. You could make a great living at it. In the meantime, you can stay here at my house."

"My ma isn't taking up with another man." Paul stood and took his plate to the dry sink and threw it and his fork in with a sharp clatter.

That stopped all of their talking for a while. Finally, Dare said, "I can see that wouldn't be right. I'll stay in Vince's rooms above his law office."

"You need to stay and watch over Vince," Jonas said. "Vince has one bedroom. My house by the church has two. No bed in one of them, but I can build a bedstead by tomorrow night. For now, you folks take my house. Paul, you can sleep on a bedroll on the floor tonight. I'll stay at Vince's. By the time Vince is better, we'll have had time to sort this all out."

"There might be a couple of bedrooms above the diner," Dare said. "If you're going to run it, you can live there."

Glynna looked between Paul and Janet. Her lips quivered. Ruthy could see she needed to cry again. She was still bruised. Favoring her arm and making slow moves to protect her ribs. "I'm so sorry I married Flint. Just so sorry, children. I won't take up with another man. You have my word on it."

"Never?" Paul asked.

Glynna opened her mouth, hesitated, then said, "Never without your blessing. You have my solemn promise."

Janet got up and came to Paul's side. Her quiet was almost as much of an accusation as Paul's anger.

Nodding, Paul looked from his little sister to his ma to Dare. "Never without our blessing. Agreed."

For no real reason she could understand, Ruthy thought that was a bad bargain. But the boy's grim expression eased. Maybe it was best to give him power over this decision, for now anyway.

The sun had set, though there was still a dusky light. Luke said, "I'd like to ride out to my house and stay there tonight, Ruthy. Have you got the energy for one more long ride?"

"Yes, I'd like to go home." Ruthy had seen the house and, though it had been badly battered by Greer's temper tantrum, it was a lovely home. She looked forward to starting her life there.

Luke slid his warm, strong hand up to rest on the back of Ruthy's neck. "Good."

They all sat silently for a time, until finally Ruthy stirred herself to clear the table. She scooped water out of the wells on Dare's stove. Glynna came to work beside her, and they had the dishes washed in no time. Big John must have washed up after the Rangers, because there weren't any dirty plates left from earlier.

"Let me walk you over to the church's parsonage, Glynna." Jonas motioned for the children to come along, too. The four of them left.

"I've got a room for you upstairs, Big John. Let's get you to bed." Dare lifted himself out of his chair with such careful movements, it reminded Ruthy of his almost being blown apart.

"Do you need us to stay?" Ruthy asked. "Luke and I can take a turn sitting up with Vince."

"Nope, there's nothing here tonight that rest won't heal. You go on home. Get started ranching, boy." Dare slapped Luke on the back and managed a weary smile.

Luke walked into his house. His home. A wave of such pleasure washed over him, it brought the burn of tears to his eyes.

He held them back, of course. No sense shaming himself in front of his wife. He looked around—away from her—until he had himself under control. By the front door, cast blue in the moonlight, he spotted a lantern hanging from a hook. Right where it had always been. He lit it and recognized most of the furniture in the rooms to the right and left of the stairway.

It brought back such powerful memories of Ma and Pa. Of Callie when she'd been a sprite. The years melted away and Luke felt like a boy again. A boy, just like Dare and Vince and the rest of them always called him.

He almost expected his pa to come charging in, scolding everybody. Ma had been the calm one, who poured oil on troubled waters. Once she was gone, there was little peace.

In the flickering light he saw that his ma's nice womanly touches were all gone, yet he couldn't blame that on Greer. Most of them had worn out and been thrown away before Luke had gone to war. Callie had no sense of being womanly, wanting to ride the range with him and Pa every minute. The three of them had lived a spartan life. He hoped Ruthy would go to dragging in fancy fixings. He'd enjoy every moment of that.

"You're home, Luke." Ruthy wrapped her arms around his waist. "You did it. You reclaimed your ranch and got justice for your father."

He pulled her into his arms as they stood, side by side, looking at the house. So many memories washed over him, he couldn't move for a while. Ruthy seemed to realize that and let him soak in the pleasure and pain of being home.

Dare had told of finding Glynna unconscious at the base of the steps. It was no wonder she hadn't wanted to return.

"At a terrible price," he said, "but yes, we did it."

"Dodger must've cleared things out a bit. Greer had the place ripped apart this morning."

"Things seem fine now. Let me give you a tour." He plucked the lantern off its hook and led the way. The moon was bright, and he could see well enough he could've almost left the lantern behind, but he liked the warmth of it.

Walking into the kitchen, Ruthy stepped ahead of him

and pointed at a boarded-up window. "Greer busted the glass. The table was tipped over. The chairs were broken. Pans thrown all over."

Luke could see the chairs had been repaired. Not pretty work but sturdy. Good enough to suit him. If Ruthy wanted something nicer, he'd see to it. "It looks like Dodger restored order after you left."

"Yes, and then he couldn't stay here."

"I reckon he couldn't stand sitting it out, not even if it meant putting Glynna in danger. But she'd have been in danger anyway. Greer wouldn't have quit looking for her. I should have asked for his help. I just didn't want anyone else getting hurt. But Dodger's a man who cares about right and wrong. I remember that about him."

A rap at the back door almost sent Luke grabbing for his gun. He realized then how on edge he still was.

"That you, Luke?" Dodger rapped again.

Luke let more of the day's tension go. He swung the door open and saw his hired man, coming to the door to talk business, just like the foreman had always done for his pa.

"It's me." Luke smiled. "Thanks for everything you did today. Come on in."

Dodger stepped into the doorway, pulling his hat off to hold it in front of him. "Good to have a Stone back in this house, boy. And I'm pleased to see you've brought your wife along."

Ruthy came up beside Luke. "I'll get some coffee on."

Shaking his head, Dodger said, "Reckon not tonight. I just saw the light and thought it best to see what was what. I'll come by in the morning to talk ranching. Tonight I'll let you young folks keep to yourself. It's a courtin' moon."

Dodger replaced his hat, spun around, and left, striding

toward the bunkhouse. High above him, the full moon gleamed.

Luke swung the door shut and turned to face his very own wife. He wasn't real used to the notion of having one yet, but he found he liked the idea well enough. "Dodger says it's a courtin' moon."

"What do you think he meant by that?"

Luke leaned down and kissed her, hoping she'd take the hint.

After a minute, she pulled away. "Well, I should get to work. I need to get this house cleaned up so it's presentable when Dodger comes by in the morning. Get a batch of bread rising."

Maybe she thought a courtin' moon had something to do with it being light enough to work by.

Deciding he hadn't made things clear, he kissed her again and did a better job of it this time. It wasn't long before she was clinging to him as if she were afraid of oncoming floodwaters.

Finally she pulled back just a few inches and smiled. Her red corkscrew curls caught the lantern light and shimmered and danced as she tossed her head and wrinkled her little freckled nose. "I think I figured out what a courtin' moon is."

"Then you probably also figured out that the next step of this tour is upstairs." Luke slid his arm around her waist and swept her away.

Mary Connealy writes romantic comedy with cowboys. She is the author of the acclaimed KINCAID BRIDES, LASSOED IN TEXAS, MONTANA MARRIAGES, and SOPHIE'S DAUGHTERS series. Mary has been nominated for a Christy Award, was a finalist for a RITA Award, and is a two-time winner of the Carol Award. She lives on a ranch in eastern Nebraska with her very own romantic cowboy hero, Ivan. They have four grown daughters—Joslyn, married to Matt; Wendy; Shelly, married to Aaron; and Katy—and two spectacular grandchildren, Elle and Isaac. Readers can learn more about Mary and her upcoming books at:

maryconnealy.com
mconnealy.blogspot.com
seekerville.blogspot.com
petticoatsandpistols.com

An excerpt from
TROUBLE IN TEXAS, Book 2

Fired Up

Mary Connealy

Available September 2013

BETHANYHOUSE
a division of Baker Publishing Group
Minneapolis, Minnesota

CHAPTER 1

NOVEMBER 10, 1868

A breeze fluttered Glynna Greer's skirt. The nearest horse reared, sending the buckboard rolling backward. The other horse in the team whinnied and shifted nervously.

"Whoa there." Jonas Cahill jumped for the rolling wagon and scrambled up, pulling on the brake.

"Mama!" Janet cried out and grabbed at the wooden seat. Terror flashed in Janny's golden hazel eyes, which were a match for Glynna's.

Glynna had sworn she'd never let her children feel another moment of fear. A stupid oath to take as it turned out.

Janny and Paul were tucked into the bit of empty space right behind the driver's seat in the back of the small buckboard. Glynna took one step to go to them and protect them.

"Stay back." Dare Riker caught Glynna by the arm and dragged her to a halt. "Let Jonas calm the team first."

Dr. Riker's strong hand and raspy voice struck a chord in her. She pushed the sensation away as the near horse tossed its head and snorted, fighting the bit.

"We shouldn't have used that thoroughbred filly to

307

pull." Luke Stone hurried down his front porch steps, where he'd stood beside his wife of one month, Ruthy, and headed for the horses. "I've been breaking her to the harness and I thought she was doing well." He turned to Vince. "Your horse is as steady as they come. Switch my mare for your gelding."

"No, wait." Glynna was so eager to get out of there, it wasn't rational. "There's no need for that."

It had taken her weeks to come out and get her meager possessions. In the end, it was pure necessity that drove her to Luke and Ruthy's ranch—Glynna's former home. No one knew what was hers. They'd have hauled everything in to her, but Glynna didn't want anything that was once her dead and unlamented husband's.

Luke and Ruthy didn't want it either. Glynna hadn't thought to gather so much. But the Stones started loading until it had added up to a buckboard stacked high with crates. They'd given it to her over her protests, and she had to admit the very sparse rooms she lived in with her children could use a lot of these things. Avoiding detestable memories was a luxury she couldn't afford.

Jonas, Broken Wheel's parson, quieted the horses. Dare, with his shaggy blond hair, and Vince Yates, tidy and dark, each had a horse, and they were ready to ride. These men had risked their lives to save her from her husband and they were still helping her, surrounding her with support when they barely knew her.

"My skirts spooked the mare." She glanced from the horse to her young'uns. She had to sit up on the high buck-board seat beside Parson Cahill, as there wasn't room for her in the wagon box. "Are you sure she won't run away?"

"An animal's a living critter." Luke shrugged. "No one

can predict for sure what they'll do, but I'd have thought the horse was okay. I admit I've never trained it with a woman wearin' a skirt. Never thought of it."

"We can begin work on it right away." Ruthy, Glynna's best friend—well, her only friend if she didn't count the men—stood in the doorway to the house, frowning at the fractious horse. There was no situation that Ruthy didn't try to solve by working. Although Glynna had thought Ruthy was moving a bit slower today, and she was more pale than usual. Glynna had a good idea why a new bride might be feeling a bit puny.

"Changing the horse you've got hitched up will take a while. I'd just as soon get going." Glynna caught her skirts as the wind gusted. "Can we give the mare another chance?"

Dare rubbed one hand thoughtfully over his mustache, then strode to the horse's head and held her reins. He moved so his body blocked the horse's vision of Glynna and her skirts. "Alright, give it a try. Move easy."

Glynna gathered her skirts securely against her body and stepped toward the wagon. The horse wasn't fooled, however. It tugged on the reins, trying to watch Glynna. Its eyes were white all around, wide with fear.

Retreating until the horse calmed, she crossed her arms, disgusted with the delay of hooking up another horse.

"Can you ride?" Vince asked.

Glynna looked back at the handsome lawyer. "Yes, I've been riding all my life."

"Instead of switching the teams, you take my horse. I'll go with the buckboard." Then he added a warning: "You'll have to ride astride."

The chance to leave without delay made her almost giddy. She gazed at Dare. She shouldn't look to him, she knew it, but how often had she caught herself doing just that? "I'd enjoy riding. It's been a long time."

In fact, it had been a very long time since she'd had any kind of enjoyment.

She walked up to Vince's big red gelding and swung up on its back, relishing the feel of a horse under her. She adjusted her skirts. They were wide enough for modesty, also wide enough to scare a skittish horse, apparently.

Looking at her children, they watched her with dead-earnest expressions. They always watched her. They were forever braced for trouble.

She was too, so she couldn't blame them.

Nodding at them as Vince climbed up beside Jonas on the buckboard, Glynna turned to wave at Ruthy. "Thank you. It was a lovely day."

"Come out again anytime. I'm planning a big Thanks-giving dinner. I want you here for that."

"We'll see." Glynna truly did love Ruthy Stone. But that house . . . there wasn't an inch of it that didn't have terrible memories for her.

And now, as the heavily laden buckboard drew away, she was bringing some of those memories to her new home above her diner in Broken Wheel.

The buckboard was stacked so high she couldn't see the children anymore once they sat down. They were sur-rounded by boxes and furniture and other leftovers from their miserable life with the late Flint Greer.

Her tension eased as they rode away. Dare guided his horse to her side, smiling. "You ride that horse like you were born in a saddle, Mrs. Greer."

A twist of humiliation surprised her. "Can we not attach the name Greer to me ever again? Call me Glynna, please."

"It ain't exactly proper, but I don't mind burying that sidewinder's name along with him." Dare's smile was gone. Glynna was sorry she'd had a part in wiping it away. Dr. Dare Riker had killed Flint in a gun battle. The doctor wanted to heal, not kill, but Flint had given him no choice.

The buckboard creaked along. The weather had turned cool; even Texas had to let go of summer at some point. Vivid yellow cottonwood leaves still clung to the trees lining the road to town. A few fell and fluttered around them, dancing on the breeze.

The bluffs rose on the side of the road. The edges were striped red, strange pretty layers of stone in this rugged part of north Texas some called Palo Duro Canyon. Juniper, cottonwoods, and mesquite were strewn here and there among the big blue stem grass and star thistles. Some places the trees were tall and thick, other places they clung to patches of dirt over stone that didn't look deep enough to support roots.

Glynna stared at the highlands, remembering the guards Flint had posted to keep Luke Stone out, and her in. The bluffs were studded with boulders of all sizes. Looking ahead at the trail, she saw many had rolled down and been tossed about. Soon the bluffs grew closer. A stretch not far ahead was almost a tunnel where the canyon walls nearly formed an arch over the road. It was a tight passage that ran about a hundred feet.

"Luke said he's going to start an avalanche deliberately one of these days. A rock comes down now and then. He'd like to wipe them out at a time of his choosing."

"He'll end up blocking the whole road if he does that." Glynna watched the buckboard enter the narrow gap and realized she was mentally pushing it. She didn't like her children in there.

"If he does, Luke'll just clear the rubble and that's all. Not much backup in that boy."

Laughing, Glynna took a break from her constant worry, a weakness she was working on with God's help. "Boy? Luke Stone has to be your age."

"He's some younger." Dare was smiling again. "The youngest of all of us."

Glynna was glad she'd teased him. It helped to put thoughts of Flint behind them.

A sharp *crack* drew her attention forward and she realized the buckboard was almost through the passage. She and Dare had just entered it.

The crack, though . . . What had caused—?

"Ride!" Dare slapped her horse on the rump. "Avalanche!"

Her horse leaped forward as a rock struck the ground behind her. A low rumble pulled her eyes up to the bluff on the left side of the trail. Rocks rolled, crashing into others, knocking them loose. They bounced off the far side of the canyon, starting an avalanche on that side, as well.

Her horse made a wild surge forward, going from walking to a gallop in a single step. Glynna lost her grip on the reins and fell backward.

Dare caught her wrist and jerked her forward with a hard hand. "Stay with me!"

Clawing at the pommel, she leaned low over her charging horse's neck to make a smaller target. Thundering rocks sped up. One the size of Flint's fist hammered Glynna's shoulder.

She lost her grip and went down between the racing horses. Crushing, iron-shod hooves thundered around her, then were gone as her borrowed horse rushed onward.

She scrambled to her feet. A powerful grip sank into the front of her calico dress and she was airborne. Dare yanked her up in front of him. He'd spun his horse around and come back for her. Now he wheeled his horse to chase down the buckboard.

Small stones pelted Glynna's face, and then a boulder whizzed past her eyes, barely missing Dare's horse running flat-out.

More stones poured onto the wagon. Jonas slapped the reins and shouted. Vince threw himself back, twisting his body, doing whatever he could to shelter the children.

Vince's horse, the horse that had thrown her, sprinted past the wagon and cleared the narrow stretch. A heavy rain of dust and gravel cut off the world outside the deadly corridor.

"Hang on!" Dare yelled to be heard over the onslaught. Overhead, the rumble shifted to an earsplitting roar. He looked up as he spurred his horse on.

One minute they were galloping, the next Dare threw them off the horse and rolled with her toward the sheer rise of the bluff. Dare's weight knocked the wind out of her as he landed on top, shielding her. "Keep your head down!" he shouted.

A boulder pounded into the ground only feet in front of her. Dare's horse reared and staggered backward, saving the horse from being crushed. As the boulder slammed past, the horse leaped forward and disappeared into pouring stone and grit that followed the boulder.

If they hadn't been hard against the bluff, it would have crushed them both.

The boulder, huge as it was, bounced. How could something so massive bounce? It hit the far side of the tunnel and ricocheted.

"Get up. Move!" Dare dragged her to her feet, but she didn't need to be dragged. She saw the great chunk of granite careening toward them. They got by it as it crashed into the spot they'd just left.

Staggering forward, the raining pebbles cut into her face and neck. The dust choked and blinded them until it was nearly impossible to see the next boulder coming.

Dare picked up speed to a full sprint. He stumbled in the debris, went down, and she went with him. Instantly they were back up, moving again. Surely they had only a few more yards to go.

Then a jagged rock struck Dare in the back and knocked him to his knees. A few seconds later, a cascade of smaller stones knocked him sideways.

Glynna snagged a handful of Dare's shirt and yanked him to his feet. She shouldn't have been able to lift him, but desperation gave her the needed strength.

His knees wobbled. His head slumped forward, yet he wasn't unconscious, just stunned. She wrapped an arm around his waist and pushed on into the raining rocks.

Out of the tumult Vince and Jonas appeared. Jonas caught her. Vince got his arm around Dare. They stumbled on together.

The blinding debris finally thinned, and she could see again. The roar was behind them. Somehow they'd made it through.

Dare pitched forward. Vince had a firm grip or Dare would've fallen on his face. Jonas had been hanging on to her, but he left and caught Dare to keep him from further injury.

The intensity of Vince and Jonas as they carried their friend brought tears to her eyes while she rushed behind them. They'd run *into* a landslide. They'd risked death to save their friend.

Glynna hadn't known men like that existed.

Her children shouted as they clambered down from the buckboard and hurled themselves at her.

"He's hurt. A big rock hit his back." Glynna stumbled and might have fallen, except her children ran into her, holding her up just by being there.

Jonas and Vince knelt at Dare's side. Glynna saw the blood.

Too much blood.

His shirt had a huge tear right by his left shoulder blade. Jonas grabbed the frayed shirt and ripped it right off Dare's back.

"Ma, your face is torn up." Paul, his voice tight with fear, pulled out a handkerchief and handed it to her.

A crash shook the earth. Glynna looked back at the canyon pass. An immense red rock slab, taller than a horse, fell and crashed into smaller rocks, bounced and rolled straight for them, standing up on its side like a massive wheel.

"Run!" Glynna caught her children, saw Vince and Jonas drag Dare to his feet, one of them on each side, and they ran. How far would that slab of rock go?

Glynna heard an almost explosive thud and looked back. The boulder had picked up speed. The horses—those on the buckboard and the ones they'd ridden—were just ahead, and they'd be killed, too. The buckboard team, rearing and snorting, strained at the buckboard. But the brake was set.

"Glynna, get the children behind those trees!" Vince shouted with all the force of a commanding officer. "Jonas, get that team out of here!"

One glance told her he'd thrown Dare over his shoulder

315

and was charging for the trees, running at her side. Jonas sprinted for the horses. He shouted at the saddle horses Glynna and Dare had ridden, and they bolted away.

Jonas threw himself onto the wagon seat, jerked the brake loose. With a slap of leather to the horses' backs, they broke into a run.

Glynna veered for the side of the canyon, hard on Vince's heels. Her children needed no urging; they were outpacing her now, pulling her along.

As they reached the trees, Glynna glanced back to see the boulder coming straight for them.

They reached the shelter of a clump of undersized juniper trees and dashed behind it just as the huge rock hit. The slender trees bent, and for a few terrible moments they seemed about to snap and crush all of them in the process.

Janet flung herself against Glynna's legs. Her brother Paul grabbed her too, coming from the other side.

The trees held. At last the boulder stopped its rolling, then tipped over to land flat on its side with a thud that shook the earth.

Vince ran out of the trees, still carrying Dare. He took a fierce look around at the avalanche and its aftermath. The pass was choked with dirt and gravel, and rocks still tumbled down with a grating racket. But the worst seemed to be over. Some of the tension left Vince's shoulders.

"You think it's done?"

Glynna emerged from behind the trees, the children still clinging to her. She inhaled silted air and coughed, then said, "I thought it was done before."

"Yeah, me too." Vince, his face coated in dirt, flashed his glowing white smile. "But this time I'm sure."

His actions said he wasn't being careless. He walked well away from the pass before he crouched and eased Dare off his shoulder to lay him down on a grassy stretch alongside the canyon road. Blood flowed from several scrapes on Dare's face, and two big knots were rising on his forehead. Yet the ugliest wound was on his back.

Jonas left the buckboard again, shaking his head. "How much control you got over that horse of yours, Vince? We need the water in your canteen."

Vince saw puffs of dust in the air where his horse had galloped away. He paused from examining Dare, lifted his fingers to his mouth and a deafening whistle blasted.

Dare flinched and his eyes flickered open, then quickly closed again.

Glynna wanted to go to his side with an urgency that surprised her. Her children held her back. She realized then that blood was dripping onto her dress and that she still clung to Paul's kerchief.

Dabbing at the raw scratches on her cheek, she watched Vince and Jonas tend to Dare.

"Wh-what's going on?" Dare slurred his words and tried to roll over.

Vince's horse came trotting around the corner toward them. Glynna noticed its flank was bleeding. Then, far behind, she saw a second horse—Dare's—coming much more slowly, acting skittish, and who could blame it?

A gasp of pain coming from Dare got her full attention. His shirt had been ripped away and so had a flap of skin on his back.

Kneeling beside Dare, Vince said, "He's losing a lot of blood."

Vince pressed a kerchief to the open wound. Dirt stuck to

it everywhere. Vince grabbed the remnants of Dare's shirt, folded it roughly and pressed it against the vicious gash.

Dare groaned in pain and pulled both arms up so he wasn't quite flat on the ground anymore. He propped himself on his bent arms, enough to lift his head.

Pounding footsteps from behind turned their heads. Luke Stone appeared at the other end of the canyon's narrow neck, barely visible through the grit and dust still lingering in the air. "I heard the avalanche," he called.

"Can you get through?" Vince yelled back.

"I think so, yeah."

"Luke, make sure there aren't any more rocks falling before you step in that gap."

Luke paused and studied the hillside.

"Have you got water?"

"Nope. I just heard the crash and ran to see what happened. Do you need me right now?"

"No, go fetch some water first." Vince twisted to look at his horse walking toward him, slow and nervous. "We've got a little water on our horses, but we might be a while rounding them up."

"Hang on!" Luke took off running for the water as if his friend's life depended on it.

Another decent man.

Glynna turned back to Dare and his wound. Vince did too. Quickly they went to work, doing all they could to stop the shocking flow of blood.

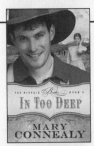